D1399835

THE COPYCAT

THE COPYCAT

Wendy McLeod MacKnight

GREENWILLOW BOOKS

An Imprint of HarperCollins*Publishers*

This book is a work of fiction. References to real people, events, establishments, organizations, or locales are intended only to provide a sense of authenticity, and are used to advance the fictional narrative. All other characters, and all incidents and dialogue, are drawn from the author's imagination and are not to be construed as real.

The Copycat
Text copyright © 2020 by Wendy McLeod MacKnight

All rights reserved. No part of this book may be used or reproduced in any manner whatsoever without written permission except in the case of brief quotations embodied in critical articles and reviews. Printed in the United States of America. For information address HarperCollins Children's Books, a division of HarperCollins Publishers, 195 Broadway, New York, NY 10007.

www.harpercollinschildrens.com

The text of this book is set in 12-point Calluna.
Book design by Paul Zakris

Library of Congress Cataloging-in-Publication Data

Names: MacKnight, Wendy McLeod, author.
Title: The copycat / Wendy McLeod MacKnight.
Description: First edition. | New York : Greenwillow Books,
an Imprint of HarperCollins Publishers, [2020] |
Audience: Ages 8–12 | Audience: Grades 4–6 |
Summary: After several moves, twelve-year-old Ali and her quirky family finally find a home in Saint John, but Ali's ability to blend in at school hits a snag when she discovers she is more different than she thought.
Identifiers: LCCN 2019030860 | ISBN 9780062668332 (hardcover)
Subjects: CYAC: Middle school—Fiction. |
Schools—Fiction. | Shapeshifting—Fiction.
Classification: LCC PZ7.1.M2587 Co 2020 | DDC [Fic]—dc23
LC record available at https://lccn.loc.gov/2019030860
20 21 22 23 24 PC/LSCH 10 9 8 7 6 5 4 3 2 1
First Edition

GREENWILLOW BOOKS

To my grandparents Hooey (a Sloan without an "e"!)
and Kenny Ryder, brilliant, remarkable
originals who made Saint John magical!
To Lauren, a wonderful friend and mentor whom I adore.
To my family and friends: I would happily spend
the rest of my life copying each and every one of you!

The fog comes
On little cat feet.

It sits looking
over harbor and city
on silent haunches
and then moves on.

—Carl Sandburg

ONE

Ali Sloane knew her father was about to launch into his first-day-at-a-new-school lecture when he literally transformed into her. As in, features rearranging themselves, bones and muscles contracting, hair lengthening, and plaid work shirt and jeans morphing into a purple hoodie and black leggings. He didn't stop until Ali was staring at a mirror image of herself. It would be impressive if it weren't her father and her face.

"Remember: be yourself, Ali-Cat, and everything will be fine."

They stood in her great-grandmother Gigi's living room and waited for Ali's mom and Gigi to come downstairs for the obligatory first-day-of-school photograph.

"Seriously? Says the man who just turned into his twelve-year-old daughter?"

Digger, which was what everybody called her father, including Ali, shrugged.

Ali sighed. She didn't like it when he turned into her; it made her uncomfortable. This morning's transformation was his long-standing trick to get her complete attention. But she wasn't three years old anymore, she was twelve, and all he had to do was ask. Besides, it was the same speech he delivered every time she started a new school.

"I don't know why you tell me to be myself. You know I can't be anything but myself." She turned her attention to her knapsack, double-checking that everything on the seventh-grade supplies list was accounted for, along with her library book.

Digger refused to be put off. "I just worry when every report card says you're too concerned about getting along with people, to the detriment of yourself and your schoolwork."

Ali snorted. If Digger had had to change schools

as often as Ali—this was new school number ten—he would understand why she tried so hard to fit in. She yanked on the knapsack's zipper and it caught on the canvas. After trying to fix it herself for a full minute, she gave up and passed it to Digger. "Can we please not have this conversation again?"

ALI'S LIST OF TOWNS (SO FAR)

Kindergarten: Campbellton
Grade One: Bathurst
Grade Two: Miramichi
Grade Three: Milltown
Grade Four: Lawrence Station, Harvey Station
Grade Five: McAdam, Woodstock
Grade Six: Sussex
Grade Seven: Saint John

It was odd to watch another version of herself unstick the zipper. A blink later and he was himself again, all sympathetic eyes. "I know it's hard, Ali-Cat."

They were interrupted by Gigi, who hobbled into the room resplendent in a fuzzy pink bathrobe, a fresh coat of red lipstick, and leopard-print mules. "Ginger will be right down. She wants to take the picture outside. And Ali's right, Digger; leave her be. Are you worried about her being herself or that she'll turn into a Copycat? Because if it's the latter, you know Copycats begin to change soon after birth."

Despite being almost one hundred years old, Gigi's ears missed nothing.

Thrilled to have an ally, Ali added, "How many times did you test my abilities when I was little?"

"Too many to count," said Digger.

"See? I'm not a Copycat, just a regular old person like Mom. Stop worrying."

"Don't change the subject, Ali-Cat. You know that's not what I was talking about. I know it's hard to change schools, but the best way to make new friends is to be yourself."

Like Digger had a clue about friends. He had only one friend: Ali's mom, who was hurrying down the stairs toward them, applying her lipstick as she went.

"You're supposed to be outside, people! We need to hurry; I just got a text from my supervisor. They need me as soon as I can get there." She'd started work at a local nursing home the week before and, to make a good impression, went in early and stayed late.

Two minutes later, Ali and her parents stood on the

front porch and watched Gigi struggle to adjust the camera lens.

"Stupid fog," Gigi muttered. "It makes you look like ghosts."

Ali, too nervous to sleep, had watched the fog roll in from the bay at five a.m., a thick line of chalky mist as unstoppable as the waves that broke on the shore. Within half an hour it had swallowed both the city and the sun, and the temperature had dropped twenty degrees.

When Ali had moved in, Gigi had given her a dusty old book about the fog by some long-dead Sloane relative. A quick skim revealed it to be the most boring book ever. Even worse, it smelled funny, and there were stains on the cover. The only interesting thing about it was that Digger and his cousin Teddy had written funny notes to each other in it when they were Ali's age, probably because they thought it was as boring as she did. Besides, if she wanted to learn about fog, she could borrow her mom's cell phone and search the latest scientific information.

"Hurry, Gigi," Ali's mom said. "I'm half frozen!" She was dressed in the nurse's-aide scrubs Ali loved best, the ones covered in cheery daisies.

"I'm hurrying," Gigi said, but she stopped to tighten the belt of her robe instead. "You three need to squeeze together. All I can see of Digger is his ear."

Digger muttered something and moved closer.

"I need smiles!" Gigi ordered.

"For heaven's sake, Digger, smile," Ali's mom directed through a toothy grin and chattering teeth. "Ali and I have to go."

In response, Digger sprouted a tail and wagged it against Ali and her mother, who giggled. Satisfied that he'd lightened everyone's mood, he smiled for the camera. Ali didn't need to look to know that his smile was awkward. Digger loathed having his picture taken.

"Perfect!" Gigi cried, and snapped three pictures in a row.

"I'll never get used to this fog," Ali's mom grumbled. She broke away and hurried toward their rusty car.

"The weatherman says it's sunny and twenty degrees warmer fifteen minutes outside of the city, can you believe it?" She had said the same thing every foggy day since they'd moved to Saint John two weeks ago. Which, because Ali liked to keep track of things, was nine days out of fourteen.

Talking about the fog was the number-one pastime of Saint Johners: how thick it was, when it would burn off, how it compared to yesterday's fog, if there would be fog tomorrow, bay fog versus inland fog. Everyone except Ali agreed that the city would be perfect if there was less fog. For her, Saint John equaled fog, but it also equaled Gigi, her own bedroom, and maybe, if she was lucky, staying put. Fog was something to celebrate, not moan about. Of course, it wasn't always convenient. Today's fog was damp and frigid and plastered Ali's hair against her head.

Ali took a deep breath to calm the familiar queasy lurch in her stomach. "Have a nice day, Gigi," she said as she wrapped her arms around her great-grandmother's bony frame. She inhaled Gigi's comforting scent of lavender talcum powder and Ivory soap.

"You'll be fine, Alison. We Sloanes are strong. Don't you forget that."

Digger waited beside the front passenger door. "Everything will go well, Ali-Cat." Like he could possibly know that. When he went around to kiss Ali's mother goodbye, it was impossible to miss the uneasy smiles they exchanged. If the past was the best predictor of the future, Ali would be anything but fine.

It was a twenty-minute walk from Gigi's house to Princess Elizabeth School, but Ali's mom insisted on driving her. "At least I can start you off on the right foot the first day," she said, as if that made up for the fact that she could never attend school functions because of her shift work. "Try not to be nervous. Digger went to Princess Elizabeth School and liked it a lot."

It was hard to imagine Ali's homebody father at school. He spent his days poking around the house or working on his art, only leaving on the rare occasions he found work. Last week he'd gone down to the port to draw caricatures of the cruise-ship tourists. He was supposed to be there all day, but came home at lunchtime because conversations with strangers, and staying in his human form all day, was just too hard. School must have been torturous. She could relate to that.

Ali's mom leaned over the steering wheel as the car crept along. Now and then she eyed the dashboard clock and bit her lip. The fog lights haloed other vehicles and pedestrians in their eerie glow. Ali stared out the window at the nothingness, startled when a boy emerged from the mist. He swung his knapsack as he walked, as if he didn't have a care in the world. If Ali was a Copycat like Digger was, she'd copy someone like him. He looked so happy.

Her mom must have sensed her mood. "It'll be okay. We're here to stay."

Ali wanted to believe that, but didn't. "Digger gave me 'the talk' this morning." Then she did her uncanny impression of her father, right down to his deep baritone and furrowed brow. "Be yourself, Ali-Cat."

"Oh, dear. He just wants things to go well for you today."

Unlike the last few schools. Ali was glad her mother didn't try to rehash her failures; she did that enough herself. Like how she'd skipped school last year because her friends had dared her to, and got detention for a week. Or when she cut her hair in fifth grade so she'd look like her new friend, Caitlen, who was so furious she'd refused to speak to Ali for the rest of the school year. When she was younger it had been easier to change schools, but now it was a nightmare. Her attempts to fit in always failed. Would this time be different? Ali doubted it.

To stop her mom from worrying, she asked, "What advice would Maya have for me?"

Maya was Maya Angelou, a famous dead author and poet who was very much alive to Ali's mom. Maya's number-one fan, she believed there was no problem Maya's wisdom couldn't fix. The opportunity to dole out Maya advice always put her in a good mood, so Ali wasn't surprised when her mother's shoulders relaxed.

"She once said, 'If you can't change it, change the way you think about it.' Maya would tell you to march into that school like you own it, like you're doing them a favor by going there."

Ali grunted, but her mom was on a roll. "Maya also said, 'You may not control all the events that happen to you, but you can decide not to be reduced by them.'"

There was no chance to ask what that meant. Princess Elizabeth School appeared out of the thick haze like a fairy-tale castle. And just like in a fairy tale, Ali knew that the world inside its brick walls promised potential happiness or wicked treachery. Ali's mom eased into the drop-off lane and gave Ali a quick peck on the cheek. "I'll send you happy thoughts all day."

Ali nodded. But the truth was, she didn't want happy thoughts. She wanted a friend.

Two

Ali survived her morning classes and only got lost once, but the mornings were always easy when she started a new school. It was the cafeteria at lunchtime that was the real beast, with kids rushing to claim a table and shouting at one another in excitement after summer break. Ali stood in the doorway, one foot in and one foot out, a silent sentinel. And she did the same thing she did at every new school: she wondered if there were any Copycats.

Gigi and Digger believed that around one percent of the population had Copycat abilities. One time she and Digger had passed a stranger on the street in Campbellton, and he and the man had high-fived.

When she'd asked Digger who the man was, he'd said they could both tell the other was a Copycat. When she'd pressed him on *how* he could tell, he'd said, "Because both of our features shifted slightly, like there was a magnetic pull that wanted us to change into the other. It happens so fast and is so subtle that someone who isn't a Copycat doesn't notice. But we do." The other man appeared to be a Constant to Ali, the term Copycats used to refer to people who couldn't change. Now, standing in the doorway to the cafeteria, Ali did a quick calculation. More than a hundred kids meant that at least one could be a Copycat.

Despite her years of experience as a new student, Ali had never gotten used to the blur of unfamiliar faces and the dreadful realization that they were all strangers. She took a deep breath, straightened her spine, and forced herself to step into the cafeteria. Everything would be fine if she followed her rules.

Ali liked rules. In third grade, she'd discovered there were scientific laws for things like gravity, time, and the orbit of planets, which helped people understand the world around them and create order from chaos. Ali decided she needed her own laws to make sense of things she couldn't control, like Digger's Copycat powers and her family's constant moving. Laws sounded too fancy, so Ali called them rules, and copied each one into a tattered green notebook in her spidery cursive handwriting. Gigi said cursive writing was a dying art, but that Ali should master it, because someday she might have to write a thank-you note to a king or queen. Over time, there were so many rules she was forced to put them into categories, like New School Rules or Digger Rules, which pleased her because the laws of nature were categorized, too.

The most important new school rule was: *Sit at a table closest to the teachers when you don't know anyone.* That way no one could try any monkey business. She'd learned that at Milltown Elementary School in grade three, when a boy covered in freckles named Carl stole her lunch. Which wasn't a big deal because that was the year her family was on welfare, and all Carl got was half a peanut-butter sandwich on stale rye bread. He never bothered her again. Ali scanned the cafeteria, spotted the teachers' table, and dodged her way through the crowd until she reached the table next to it. She was pleased when her homeroom teacher, Ms. Ryder, smiled and waved.

The next thing was to snag a seat in the center of the table between two groups of kids. This was a trick learned at Port Elgin Regional School in grade four, when she'd realized that sitting at the end of a table by yourself was a recipe for unwanted attention. And not just of the bullying kind, but of the look-it's-a-new-kid-let's-be-her-friend kind, which led to: *Get the lay of the land before you make friends.* It had taken her months in Port Elgin to extricate herself from a group of girls who talked about nothing except their favorite TV

> ALI'S NEW SCHOOL RULES
> 1. Sit at a table closest to the teachers when you don't know anyone.
> 2. Sit between groups of kids.
> 3. First day outfit: T-shirt, jeans, and sneakers.
> 4. Get the lay of the land before you make friends.
> 5. Always carry a book.
> 6. Try not to tell people that you don't own a television or a computer.
> 7. Always act like the popular kids. They're popular for a reason.
> 8. Join a club to meet people. Ideally, a swim team, except there never is one.
> 9. FIT IN!

shows, something Ali couldn't do because her family didn't own a TV.

The spot she found today was perfect: to her right were two kids—a boy and a girl—who smiled at her when she sat down, then resumed their heated debate about interstellar travel. They seemed familiar, which meant they were probably in one of her morning classes. To her left, three girls whispered and painted their fingernails. They didn't glance up when Ali sat down next to them. She'd chosen well.

Eating lunch alone wasn't horrible, thanks to a rule she'd created in fourth grade at Lawrence Station School: *Always carry a book.* You were never alone when you had a book. She pulled *The Golden Compass* out of her knapsack. She and Gigi had started a book club two years ago because Gigi thought it would give them something to talk about during their weekly phone calls. So far, they'd read the Anne of Green Gables books and the first two Harry Potters. The book club kept going after Ali moved in, and the latest book was *The Golden*

Compass. Ali was anxious to read whenever she got the chance. Gigi was the faster reader and had a tendency to share spoilers. Lyra's adventures didn't erase Ali's cafeteria loneliness, but they did make it bearable.

"Emily Arai!" someone squealed.

Ali glanced up and saw a bunch of girls chasing a boy with a basketball. She didn't need to know who they were to know they were popular. She recognized the girl named Emily from homeroom, because when Ms. Ryder had read her name, Ali had thought it was pretty. Plus, like every popular kid Ali had ever known, Emily had a hidden spotlight that shone on her at all times, so you couldn't help but notice her.

The five of them did another loop around the cafeteria, only this time the boy skidded to a stop next to interstellar boy and girl. The girls smashed into him, and uproarious laughter ensued.

Basketball boy pointed at interstellar boy. "We could use you on the team this year."

The girls disentangled themselves and nodded to interstellar boy. Ali knew she shouldn't stare at popular kids, so she began to read again, allowing herself a quick grin when interstellar girl muttered, "As if."

Interstellar boy laughed. "You know I hate sports, Tom. Now if you want to play Dungeons and Dragons . . ."

"But you're like the tallest guy in grade seven," Tom whined. "We could use you."

"Sorry." Interstellar boy did sound apologetic.

Tom didn't seem to want to take no for an answer. "It's not because you don't want to leave your girlfriend, is it?"

The girls exploded into shocked giggles. Ali glanced up in time to see interstellar boy glare at them and at Tom, which Tom took as his cue to leave. "Whatever. You know where we are." He ran off, the girls in hot pursuit. Ali returned to her book, happy she wasn't part of the drama.

"Man, I hate that." But interstellar boy didn't sound mad. He sounded tired.

Ali understood his weary tone. One of the most

important new school rules was: *Always act like the popular kids.* Whatever the popular kids did, Ali did. It was important not to make yourself a target, and if Ali knew anything after attending nine other schools, popular kids were never a target. Did interstellar boy not realize how much easier school would be if he just went along with what the popular kids wanted?

"They're just being stupid," said interstellar girl.

Interstellar boy was ready to change the topic. "Hey—I saw Alfie Sloane this morning."

A stunned Ali let the book slip from her fingers. Was it true? Was Alfie Sloane here, in this building? Because if he was, everything was about to change.

Chapter One
HOW FOG IS FORMED

There are many myths about the origins of fog. I prefer one of the Inuit myths myself. A man being chased by a bear swims across the river. When the bear arrives, he demands to know how the man has forged the river.

"I drank the river," the man replies.

Anxious to catch his quarry, the bear drinks and drinks until he bursts and a fine mist of water fills the air, creating fog.

—PERCIVAL T. SLOANE,
   A History of Fog in the Bay of Fundy *(1932)*

This is not true.
—Edward Andrew Sloane
   (Teddy), age eleven, adventurer

Bears are not this dumb.
-Digger, age eleven, pirate

Your real name is NOT Digger.
You need to use your real name!

Avast, you son of an urchin-pocked coxswain!

Whatever, Richard.

THREE

Ali had been positive she didn't know anyone at Princess Elizabeth School, but now she knew that wasn't true. Alfie was here. But how? Her mind swirled with questions: did Gigi know? Where did he live? It occurred to her that he might be living with his grandfather, who lived only a few blocks from Gigi. Not that she'd ever met Gigi's son, Andrew Sloane. Or any other Sloanes, for that matter. All because of the Sloane Family Feud.

"Alfie Sloane?" asked interstellar girl.

"You know, the kid I told you about, the one I met in science camp last week. He's the best. We like all the same stuff."

"Oh. Right" was the glum response.

Interstellar boy didn't seem to notice how unenthusiastic his friend was. "Guess what?"

"What?"

"He said he'd join debate club. We need at least four kids to have a team. Ms. Ryder told me this morning that so far, I'm the only one who's signed up."

"I might join."

"I thought you weren't interested."

"A person can change their mind. You always say how great it is, and my mom just joined Toastmasters International to become a better public speaker, so I thought I'd give it a try." Ali could hear the defensiveness in the girl's voice.

"Okay. You'll like Alfie; he's a riot. He's in eighth grade and has lived in London for like his whole life. Cool, huh?"

"My mom and dad went to London once."

Interstellar boy ignored the comment and stood up. "I think we should go look for him, make sure he's not off by himself somewhere." The thoughtfulness of the comment made Ali wistful; she wished someone cared enough to check on her, too.

The girl didn't respond but must have agreed, because paper crinkled, lunch bags zipped closed, and chair legs scraped. Then they were gone. And even though she didn't know them, their absence tugged at her.

Alfie Sloane was somewhere in this school right now. Thrilled, Ali let that fact sink in. She'd wanted to meet Alfie her whole life. What was he like? She'd only seen one picture of him, taken in front of the London Eye when he was five years old. He'd looked like her, but she knew a lot could change between the time a person was five and twelve. Interstellar boy had described him as funny. Like Digger on the front porch this morning, wagging his tail to make her and her mom laugh. She was surprised Alfie was a grade ahead of her; they were born in the autumn of the same year. Maybe he was super smart and had skipped a grade.

The biggest question was this: was Alfie a Copycat? Ali wasn't sure if she wanted him to be one or not. In some ways, it would be nice if he was a boring old

Constant like her. But if he *was* a Copycat, he'd be able to change into anything, just like Digger, which would be kind of cool. No, that wasn't the biggest question. The biggest question was: would Alfie want to meet her? Did the Sloane Family Feud extend down to their generation? And if it did, why?

She pulled out her notebook and drafted a new category: Ali's Rules for the Sloane Family Feud. She jotted down three points. A quick review told her they were a to-do list, not rules, so she drew a line through the heading and gave it a new title: Ali's Plan to End the Sloane Family Feud. Satisfied, she closed the notebook, packed up her things, and headed for the exit. She'd follow interstellar boy and girl and find Alfie.

When she reached the cafeteria door, she paused. Was she ready to meet Alfie? Nope, at least not out of the blue like this. But how could she meet him in a natural way? Then she smiled. She'd use new school rule number eight: *Join a club to meet people.* She was about to learn how to debate.

> ALI'S PLAN TO END THE SLOANE FAMILY FEUD
> 1. Find out what started it.
> 2. Meet Alfie Sloane.
> 3. To be continued.

FOUR

Ali might not be ready to meet Alfie yet, but she did want to *see* him. She scanned every face she passed in the hallway for the rest of the day. But she was out of luck: no one looked like they could be her cousin. Based on the photograph, she imagined Alfie as a mirror image of herself—short, with dark frizzy hair and pale gray eyes like Digger's that reminded you of tarnished silver. She was pleased to see interstellar boy and girl in her science class; it was like they connected her to Alfie. Had they found him at lunch? Based on the grumpy expression on interstellar girl's face and the happy one on interstellar boy's, she guessed yes. When the dismissal bell rang, she bolted, anxious to get home and tell Gigi and Digger about Alfie.

Unlike previous days, the fog hadn't burned off. Some of it floated past her like wispy magic carpets, while fatter tufts settled into the trees. Its frigid tendrils wrapped her in a foggy coat, but she was too excited about her news to mind the cold. Half a block ahead, she spied the same boy she'd seen on the way to school. He still swung his knapsack and, like her, was surrounded by the creeping mist.

Digger was asleep when she arrived, stretched out on the Oriental carpet in front of the fireplace in the parlor. Except he wasn't Digger; he was Digger's favorite thing to change into: a black collie-Labrador retriever mix. Ali knew she was the only kid to arrive home from school to find her father's tail wagging from a happy dream. She didn't mind that he spent so much time as a dog. In fact, sometimes she preferred Digger the dog to the real Digger, because he was always cheerful when he was a dog.

She gave him a gentle nudge with her foot and he started, his dog eyes wild until he realized it was

Ali. The wolfish grin he flashed her was cute, but she needed to share her momentous news with human Digger. She dropped into a comfy wingback chair and waited for him to change back.

"Good day?" he asked when he was capable of human speech.

Ali pointed to his furry left ear. "You missed a spot."

"Whoops!" Then he was all Digger, though he continued to lounge on the carpet. Digger wasn't much for furniture. "How was school?"

Ali gave him a sassy smile. "I was myself all day long, which was super easy, because I didn't talk to anyone."

Digger chuckled. "You win. I won't bug you about being yourself anymore. Maybe the fog is getting to me. It makes me squirrelly and anxious for some reason."

"As in, you want to chase a squirrel?"

He grinned. "Maybe."

"Gigi will kill you if you start chasing her squirrels." Her Alfie news was so stupendous she wasn't sure how to share it, so instead she asked, "How was your day?"

Her question was met with a dramatic sigh. "I spent half my day doing laundry. Gigi spilled every mug of hot chocolate I gave her. The spilled drinks and constant bird and squirrel visits are driving me round the bend. I didn't get to my art at all today."

Ali thought of her mother working twelve-hour shifts at the nursing home. She hoped Digger was smart enough not to complain to her. Time to change the subject and share her news. "Guess who goes to my school?"

"Who?"

"Alfie Sloane."

Digger sat up. "They came back," he said, more to himself than to Ali. "Did you meet him?"

"Not yet. Someone said he's joining the debate team, so I am too."

Digger cocked his head. "You hate public speaking. You were going to join the swim team at the aquatic center."

It was a valid point, but Ali brushed it aside. "Nope. Debate team. It's the easiest way for me to meet Alfie."

"Huh," said Digger, which bugged Ali because he always said "huh" when he didn't agree with something but didn't want to be confrontational. The idea of public speaking already worried her; she didn't need him to make it worse.

"It'll be fun." She tried to sound cheery, but it came out flat, liked she'd said, "It'll be like sucking on a lemon" instead.

"I bet he looks like you. People used to think his father and I were twins." According to Ali's mom, Digger and Teddy were like brothers, not cousins, which was one of the reasons Ali was so desperate to meet Alfie. She just knew that if they met, they'd be friends for life too.

"Teddy."

Teddy's name made Digger wince. Ali didn't know much about the rest of the Sloane family, but she knew Teddy had died three months before Alfie was born and four months before she was. His death was the reason the Sloanes didn't speak. Alfie's mom had moved back home to England right after the funeral, where she gave birth to Alfie, and Ali's parents had left Saint John. In fact, Ali knew so little about the Other Sloanes—the name she used to refer to the Sloanes she'd never met—that they'd become characters from a fairy tale in her mind, a family separated by an ancient curse or a wicked spell.

Digger stood up. "I've got to get supper ready." He patted her on the head like she was a puppy and disappeared into the kitchen.

Ali wasn't surprised by Digger's escape; when he didn't want to talk about something, he disappeared. The thing about Digger was that he was always home, and yet his mind was often somewhere else. Still, she'd seen his excitement when she'd mentioned Alfie. Her plan to end the Sloane Family Feud would work. Digger didn't know it yet, but she was going to fix everything.

> ALI'S DIGGER RULES
> 1. Don't tell anyone that Digger is a Copycat.
> 2. Don't mention Teddy Sloane.
> 3. Don't force Digger to talk when he doesn't want to.
> 4. Don't complain. It won't change things.

FIVE

Gigi's great joy was feeding the neighborhood's critters. When she stopped in to share her news, Ali wasn't shocked to find a chubby red squirrel nose-deep in a pile of sunflower seeds on Gigi's outstretched palm. Digger wasn't a fan of the practice, probably because it was hard for him to control the urge to chase them. He called them rats with bushy tails. Ali worried that they'd bring strange germs inside with them. But it was Gigi's house, and the family lived with her rent-free. She could do what she liked. To placate Digger and Ali, Gigi kept her bedroom door closed. So far, no pesky creature had tried to move in, but why would they when there was so much food in Gigi's room?

Gigi's room was magical, so different from the cruddy apartments Ali had grown up in, with their secondhand couches, torn upholstery, wobbly chairs, and mattresses of questionable origin. There were no scratched tabletops here; Gigi's tables were covered with colorful scarves collected during her travels to Istanbul and Morocco. Oriental rugs overlapped on the floor, and the Oz-green walls were covered with paintings and photographs from the places Gigi had visited. One wall was a shrine to Gigi's favorite old-time movie star, Walter Pidgeon, who was born in Saint John and was one of the biggest movie stars of the 1940s.

"He was even nominated for Academy Awards," she'd said with pride.

Walter's face appeared in no fewer than ten frames. He'd autographed them all the same way: *To Gigi, with much love, Walter.* Gigi had been in her twenties in the 1940s. Ali wondered if they'd ever met.

Gigi deposited the seeds and squirrel on the windowsill and waved her over. Despite Gigi's flannel nightgown and the fact that she was cocooned within several layers of thick wool blankets and seated on a chintz-covered chair, she exuded the aura of a queen in her throne room: regal and elegant. A mug of hot chocolate still steamed on the small table next to her. A copy of *The Golden Compass* lay open on her lap. Ali made a mental note not to mention it, to avoid further spoilers.

Since the squirrel was still on the windowsill, Ali hopped onto Gigi's bed so there was at least ten feet between herself and its germs. Though Ali had only lived with Gigi for two weeks, she already knew that some days were better for her great-grandmother than others. Today was a better day; her hair and makeup were done. Sure, the part was crooked, the rhinestone hair clips that held back her bangs were lopsided, and the blush was a little too pink, but at least she'd tried.

Gigi leaned forward and peered at Ali over the top of her turquoise glasses. "So?"

> ALI'S ANIMAL RULES
> 1. It would be nice if the dog in your house wasn't your father.
> 2. Wild animals belong OUTDOORS.

"It went okay. Guess what? Alfie Sloane goes to Princess Elizabeth School!"

Gigi clapped her hands. "I thought he might!"

"Why didn't you tell me he was in Saint John?" Ali demanded. She received a shrug.

"I'm old. I forgot." Gigi said that a lot, but Ali didn't buy it. Gigi knew everything. "Isn't it amazing that you've both moved to Saint John at the same time?" Gigi continued. "It's like it was meant to be. Did you meet him?"

"Not yet, but I will soon. He's joining the debate club, so I am too."

"I'm not surprised. Did you know I was a debater at university?"

Ali shook her head. She knew very little about Gigi's life. Until two weeks ago, she'd never set foot in Saint John. Gigi had come to visit Ali's family three times a year until the apartments became too ratty for even her adventurous spirit. After that she stayed in hotels and took them out to eat in fancy restaurants.

"Once I meet Alfie, I'll bring him home to meet you."

"You're a sweet girl, Alison. Wouldn't it be nice if he came to my hundredth birthday celebration?"

Gigi's birthday was only weeks away. As far as Ali knew, there were no plans for a party, but she didn't tell Gigi that.

"Do you think he's a Copycat like you and Digger, or a Constant, like me?"

"It's hard to say. He may not even know about his abilities. His grandfather never liked being a Copycat, and his mother has no powers."

"But even if he didn't know about them, wouldn't they come out by themselves? You're either a Copycat or you aren't."

Gigi took a sip of hot chocolate and shook her head. "It's not that simple. For a Copycat to have full use of their powers, they need to be trained. If they aren't taught properly, their skills wither on the vine, or they make reckless mistakes. Alfie's grandfather, Andrew, hated being a Copycat. He rejected all attempts to help him, nor would he allow us to teach his children, Teddy and Karen, either. On the other hand, your grandfather Richard reveled in what he could do. He and I coached Digger. I think there are many Copycats in the world who don't have a clue about who they really are. Not surprisingly, many of them are gifted mimics and wonderful actors."

"I can mimic people, but I'm not a Copycat."

"There are exceptions to every rule. Alfie might be one but not know that he is. We won't be able to tell until we meet him. Don't tell him about Copycats before then, just in case."

"I won't." It felt strange that she hadn't met Alfie yet and there was already a secret between them. "Was that what caused the Sloanes to fight?"

Gigi shook her head. "No. Andrew and Richard had different beliefs, but they loved each other. And then—"

"Teddy died."

Gigi nodded.

"Will you tell me what happened? Digger won't talk about it."

"Well, that makes two of us." Gigi saw the

disappointment on Ali's face and tried to soften the blow. "It's hard to talk about." She began to cough, a dry painful sound that went on too long and made Ali's heart pound. Ali passed Gigi the cup of hot chocolate and watched her sip it between the spasmy rasps. Five long minutes later, the cough subsided, but Gigi was spent. Seconds later, her soft snores bubbled up and floated around the room.

As Ali watched her great-grandmother sleep, she had a wonderful idea. She *would* throw a hundredth birthday party for Gigi. A big one. She would invite everyone, including Alfie. She would have cake and a piñata. Soon Ali was napping too, dreaming of balloons.

SIX

The fog worsened overnight. Ali and her parents ate their breakfast in silence, as if the gloomy haze outside had seeped into the kitchen and made them glum, too. The only sound came from the radio on the counter.

"Folks, take your time this morning," the radio announcer said. "Visibility is down to thirty feet in some places. It's so foggy, a herd of seals has come ashore on Tin Can Beach."

"Where's Tin Can Beach?" Ali asked Digger.

"Out where the south end of the city juts into the bay, just down from the port and Market Square. The fog must be terrible if the seals went there." A mosquito flew past his head. He swatted at it and missed.

Ali's mother pretended not to notice as Digger turned into a bat to chase the mosquito. "Are you sure you want to join the debate team, Ali? You've always wanted to join a swim team, and now that we're finally someplace that has one, I hate to see you cast that aside."

Ali exhaled. Her mother had said the same thing last night when she'd told her about Alfie. "Mom, it's a good way to get to know him. Besides, Digger called about me trying out for the Fundy Tide swim team last week. It costs a lot of money if I make it. Debate is free."

Digger the bat dive-bombed the kitchen sink but missed the mosquito. Ali giggled, but her mother wasn't done with swim team. "We can find the money, sweetie."

"Mom, I've made up my mind."

Her mother nodded, took a sip of coffee, and watched Digger chase the mosquito out of the kitchen.

"It makes me dizzy when he does that."

Ali laughed. "Me too." There was a thud in the distance, which meant Digger had hit a wall again. At least he hadn't broken another lamp. "Do you like your new job?"

"I do, but it's hard work." Her mother stretched her arms overhead. "I hope Digger finds a part-time job so I don't have to work so many hours. . . ."

Ali smirked. Digger never found work, at least not for very long.

Her mother grinned. "You're right. I'm just glad that he and Gigi are spending time together. It's good for both of them. Family is important." She reached for Ali's hand. "You know, I get how much you want to meet Alfie, but promise you'll think about swim team. I don't want you to give up your dreams." She kissed Ali on the cheek and went off to search for the bat before she left for work.

Ali was putting her cereal bowl in the dishwasher when a triumphant Digger returned, this time as himself. "Your mother's right about swim team."

> ALI'S ANIMAL RULES
> (AMENDED)
> 1. It would be nice if the dog in your house wasn't your father.
> 2. Wild animals belong OUTDOORS.
> 3. Eating insects is GROSS DON'T DO IT!

"I know, but I want to be Alfie's friend. Debate team is something we can do together." She pointed to a black smudge on Digger's bottom lip. "You didn't eat that mosquito, did you? Because that would be gross."

Digger grinned.

"You are impossible!"

"Impossible or amazing?"

"Both."

The whole way to school, Ali practiced what she'd say to Alfie when she met him. There was the cool approach: "Oh, hey, Alfie, it's me, Ali, your long-lost cousin." The enthusiastic approach: "I'm your cousin Ali and I've waited my whole life to meet you!" Neither sounded quite right.

It wasn't just the introduction that worried her. There was the sticky problem of how to raise the subject of the Sloane Family Feud and her plan to somehow reunite the family.

She needn't have worried. There was no sign of Alfie or interstellar boy and girl in the cafeteria at lunch, and no opportunity to ask them about debate team during class. It was the same thing the next day. Ali was sure they were eating lunch with Alfie in some wonderful secret place while she was stuck eating her peanut-butter sandwich by herself in the crowded cafeteria. Even worse, she didn't know when debate team started. What if she'd missed it? She vowed to ask interstellar boy and girl before science class that afternoon.

It was awkward to position herself outside the classroom door like she was standing guard, but Ali pretended not to care when her classmates gawked at her on their way inside.

"Two minutes, Ali," said Mr. Corby, the science teacher, as he entered the classroom.

Another minute passed, and still they didn't come. Had something happened to them? She was about to give up and go inside when they came around the corner, deep in conversation. They'd almost passed her before she got up the courage to speak.

"Excuse me," she whispered. Her voice was so low it was a surprise when interstellar girl stopped. She was almost as tall as interstellar boy, which meant she towered over Ali, though her freckled pink skin was a stark contrast to her friend's dark skin.

"Yeah?"

"Do you know when the first debate team meeting is?"

She was rewarded with a smile. "Are you going to join?"

Ali nodded. Interstellar boy and girl traded delighted grins.

"The first meeting is Monday after school in Ms. Ryder's classroom," said interstellar boy.

"Thanks," she managed as she followed them inside.

Four more days until she met Alfie. Ninety-six hours until she could put her plan in action. Five thousand, seven hundred and sixty minutes until the beginning of the end of the Sloane Family Feud.

Chapter Two
THE BAY OF FUNDY

The Bay of Fundy has the highest tides in the world. Twice a day, the tides roar up the bay, bringing with them billions of cubic feet of water. In some places, the high tide is fifty-three feet higher than low tide. Those who ignore the coming of the tide do so at their own peril, for there are many sad tales of individuals from away who discover that the massive boulder upon which they stood to watch the tide is soon under water.

—PERCIVAL T. SLOANE,
   A History of Fog in the Bay of Fundy *(1932)*

SEVEN

All thoughts about Alfie evaporated as soon as science class started. Mr. Corby clapped his hands to bring the class to order. Once everyone was quiet, he unfurled a small banner that read TEAM ANIMALIA. He held it above his head for several seconds, then shouted: "My kingdom for a classification!"

A startled Ali thumped back against her chair. From the sound of the nervous laughter behind her, she wasn't the only one taken aback by Mr. Corby's outburst.

"Just wanted to see if everyone was awake," joked the teacher. "I like to start new topics off with a bang and a little Shakespeare."

Someone giggled.

"The first thing we'll study this term is the classification system for organisms." He pointed to the back of the class. "Your ability to giggle, Miss Arai, is thanks to being classified Animalia, or as it's more commonly called, Animal."

"I knew it!" a boy shouted.

Mr. Corby held up a hand. "Careful, Mr. Power—you're Team Animalia too. In fact, as far as I know, everyone here is Team Animalia." He leaned over and pressed a button on his laptop, and a list, titled "The Five Kingdoms of Organisms," filled the SMART Board. Ali wrote them down in her notebook: monera, protists, fungi, plants, and animals. "And I've got fantastic news: your first project of the year is going to be a team project."

Everyone, including Ali, groaned. Team projects were the worst. And if you were the new kid, they were worse than the worst; they were torture. How many times had she been the last person picked? Enough that her stomach was now tied up in knots.

"Don't worry—I'm choosing your partners." Mr. Corby seemed delighted by the students' obvious dismay. "In a couple of days, you and your partner will have time to brainstorm an idea for a small project about the classification of organisms. If you have trouble, I can help."

He began to read pairs of names. Ali slunk down in her chair and waited.

"Ali Sloane and Emily Arai."

"No!" a girl Ali recognized as a friend of Emily's gasped. "Nothing personal," the girl added.

Ali wasn't surprised. Popular kids always preferred to work with other popular kids. Still, it smarted to be singled out.

"Mr. Corby!" the same girl called out again.

"Yes, Taylor?"

"Me and Emily want to work together."

Someone snickered. Interstellar girl caught Ali's eye and shook her head. In spite of how embarrassed she was, Ali grinned. She could tell interstellar girl was thinking the same thing she was: popular kids didn't think the rules applied to them.

"I've assigned you to work with Jason Hunt," said Mr. Corby. He sounded unimpressed.

"But Mr. Corby—"

"Discussion closed, Taylor. You've stated your desire, and I've stated my intention."

"I tried," Taylor whispered, loud enough for everyone to hear.

"I know," Emily responded with equal drama.

The rest of the pairs were assigned, and Mr. Corby began to teach. Ali was so engrossed by the topic that she started when the bell rang. As she gathered her things, Emily Arai appeared.

Emily smiled, revealing perfect white teeth. "I hope you didn't take that personally,"

Ali smiled. "No, I get it." If you wanted to make friends, you had to get along.

Emily leaned in, her shiny dark hair billowing around her face like she was in some kind of shampoo commercial, and whispered, "Taylor always wants us to be partners, but I don't mind being yours. Which school are you from?"

"I just moved to Saint John."

The news seemed to please Emily. "That's so cool. Have you met many people yet?"

Before Ali could respond, there was a loud rap. Taylor stood in the doorway, her face pinched. When Emily waved, she pointed to her watch.

> **ALI'S RULES FOR TEACHERS**
> 1. Do not make kids do team projects. It's cruel.
> 2. Don't let popular kids sit together. It makes them too powerful.
> 3. Don't look sympathetic even if you know the kid is a loser. It only makes them feel worse.

Emily gave Ali a what-can-you-do? shrug. "I gotta go. Start thinking of ideas." Ali watched her hurry away and sighed.

Mr. Corby must have heard her. "Sorry about that Emily-Taylor thing. Something tells me they'll benefit from working with others."

Ali wasn't sure that was true, but nodded. "It's no big deal."

"You have the right attitude. Are you joining any clubs?"

"Debate team."

"Impressive. Good luck. And if it's not for you, remember: we've got a fun science club headed by a competent teacher."

Ali giggled. "Thanks, I'll keep that in mind."

As she hurried to her next class, Alfie popped back into her head. Why couldn't he have joined something easy, like science club? Then she'd meet him *and* have fun.

EIGHT

When she was younger, Ali had tried hopelessly to change into something or someone else. It was embarrassing to be a Sloane without powers, even if Digger and Gigi said it was no big deal. It was a big deal to Ali, because the fact that there were Copycats meant magic existed, which meant that dragons, fairies, and wizards could be real, too. Even better, if *she* was magical, she'd find a way to make money so the power wasn't disconnected and the refrigerator was full.

But standing outside Ms. Ryder's classroom, Ali was truly relieved for the first time not to be a Copycat, because if Andrew Sloane was against the family's powers, it meant Alfie probably wasn't one, either. They could be boring Sloanes together. The thought made her smile.

Ms. Ryder was at her desk when Ali arrived for debate team Monday after school. She smiled when she saw her. "What a nice surprise!" She handed her two pieces of paper and motioned for her to take a seat in the front row. "Take these forms home. One of them is an information sheet about the basics of debating, and the other is a permission slip for your parents to sign."

Ali took the papers and sat down. Her stomach roiled like a ship on a storm-tossed sea. She was about to meet her cousin *and* talk in front of a group of strangers. What had she gotten herself into?

The next person through the door was interstellar boy. Tall, kind of cute, and funny. He seemed self-confident and mature, like if the school caught fire, he'd be the one to lead everyone to safety. "Hey, Ms. R.," he said as he slid into the empty seat next to Ali.

Ms. Ryder grinned. "Hello, Murray. I'm expecting

big things from you this year now that you've got a year of debate under your belt."

Interstellar girl was next. She grabbed the seat on the other side of Murray.

"I wondered how long until Murray talked you into coming, Cassie," said Ms. Ryder.

Two other kids arrived: Ashok, who paused to size up the front row before taking a seat behind Ali, and Carolyn, a blond-haired, blue-eyed girl whose pierced nose both thrilled and repulsed Ali. She was too chicken to even have her ears pierced.

"My grade eights," Ms. Ryder said. She eyed the clock above the Smart Board. "It's three thirty-seven. I think anybody who planned to come would be here by now. Let's get started."

Both Ali's and Murray's shoulders drooped. Since Alfie was the sole reason she'd come to debate team, Ali wondered how silly she'd look if she bailed now. Ms. Ryder went to the door and had it three-quarters of the way closed when a sneaker appeared in the opening.

"Sorry I'm late! Still trying to find my way around this school."

In stepped Alfie Sloane.

Three things hit Ali. The first: of course it was Alfie Sloane; he could be her brother, they looked so much alike. The second: he was the same boy she'd seen on the way to and from school. How had she missed the resemblance? The third: she was *not* ready to meet him. As he scanned the room for an empty seat, she dropped her head, relieved when he sat beside Cassie.

"Six team members!" Ms. Ryder crowed. "That's two more than last year!"

"Um, thanks to me," Murray reminded her. Ms. Ryder saluted Murray, who saluted back.

"Before we learn the basics of debate, let's introduce ourselves. Don't tell me your life story, just why you're here. I'll start. You know I'm Ms. Ryder, but you don't know that when I was a high school senior, I represented New Brunswick at the senior national debate championships. We came fifth. It was exciting; if we'd won, we'd have gone to the Worlds."

"Nice," said Murray.

Ms. Ryder smiled. "I know, right? Now at this age, the most you can hope for is to participate in the middle school debate competition later this fall, but that will give you a small taste of what debate competitions are like." She pointed to Carolyn. "You first."

It was almost impossible to pay attention as Carolyn explained that she wanted to be a teacher someday and Ashok said he just loved to debate. Ali had a bit more interest in Cassie and Murray—Cassie said she'd read that debates were like mental gymnastics, and Murray talked about how he needed to learn to debate because he wanted to run the country when he grew up—but they were like the coming attractions when all you wanted to see was the movie.

"You're next, Alfie," said Ms. Ryder.

Ali couldn't see Alfie's face unless she leaned forward, and no way was she doing *that*. She kept her eyes fixed on the Smart Board, where a diagram explained the parts of a sentence.

"Alfie Sloane. I've lived in England my whole life.

My mom brought me to Saint John so I could get to know the place where my dad grew up. The preparatory school I attended in London had a debate team, and I quite liked it. Murray talked me into joining."

The English accent and his use of the word "quite" made Alfie sound extra smart to Ali. But what surprised her the most was how confident he was. If he was nervous speaking in front of everybody, he didn't show it. They might look alike, but they were not alike at all.

Ms. Ryder smiled. "Thanks, Alfie. I can't wait to hear more about what debate is like in Great Britain. Last but not least, Ali."

Something hard lodged itself in Ali's stomach. She'd been so anxious to hear Alfie speak she'd forgotten she'd have to as well. If Alfie was smooth, Ali was scratchy. "A-Ali Sloane," she stuttered. "I've never debated before. I want to be a lawyer someday, so it might help."

It all come out in one fell swoop. Where had the lawyer comment come from? The idea had never occurred to her before. But everyone else's introductions were so impressive; she'd realized she needed to say something interesting too.

The teacher smiled. "I'm not surprised. Your great-grandmother was a real pioneer here in Saint John." As if she realized that the other students might not understand, Ms. Ryder added, "Ali's great-grandmother was one of the first female lawyers in the city."

Cassie's hand rocketed upward. When Ms. Ryder nodded for her to speak, she turned to Ali first and then pivoted to Alfie. "So, are you guys related or what?"

"Cousins," said Ali, forcing herself to look in Cassie's and Alfie's direction.

"Really?"

She waited for Alfie to respond. Several terrible seconds passed, and then he said, "Yes." Ali's face burned. Why had she thought this would be the best way to meet him?

Ms. Ryder glanced from Ali to Alfie, as if she

expected them to say something more. When they didn't, she said, "I think that's enough introductions for now," and pushed a button so that the grammar lesson was replaced by the same debate information she'd passed out earlier. "Many of you are old pros at debate, but some of you are new, so we'll take a couple of minutes to review the basics."

Ali reached into her knapsack and grabbed a notebook and pen.

"You don't need to write this down, Ali," Ms. Ryder said.

Ali flushed. "I like to write things down. It helps me remember."

Murray pointed at his own pen and paper. "Me too. Plus, it's been scientifically proven that when a person writes something down, they remember it better."

Ali glanced over at the fancy penmanship in Murray's notebook, all loops and curls, and did her best to imitate it.

Ms. Ryder chuckled. "I stand corrected."

For the next ten minutes, they discussed debate

styles, and how one team put forth a proposition while the opposing team tried to tear it apart. Ali took notes, but none of it sank in. All she could think about was Alfie sitting three chairs away. Was he surprised that she was at Princess Elizabeth School? Did he want to be friends too?

Cassie's jiggly right leg and frantic arm-waving brought Ali back to the meeting. "Are we going to talk about rebuttals and refutations?"

"Someone's been reading ahead,"

> ALI'S RULES FOR WHAT
> NOT TO DO WHEN YOU
> WANT TO MEET SOMEBODY
> 1. Don't join a club you have
>   no interest in joining.
> 2. Don't catch them off guard.
> 3. Don't say stuff just to say
>   something. A lawyer?
>   Not in a million years.

said Murray, which made everyone laugh.

Ms. Ryder smiled. "We'll get to that next time, when we practice debating. If any of you are as enthusiastic as Cassie, you can read about them on the sheet I gave you." She pushed another button, and a video filled the screen. For the next ten minutes, they watched eight kids from Boston debate the pros and cons of exams. Ali watched the teams go back and forth and knew she would never have the courage to debate anyone.

Her fear must have been visible, because Murray leaned over and whispered, "Scary, huh? But I bet you'll be great." Murray was nice, but he was wrong. She would *not* be great.

When the meeting ended, Ali dawdled until Alfie left the classroom. Heart thumping, she followed him out the door, ignoring Cassie's attempt to chat with her. It was time to really meet her cousin.

NINE

Alfie didn't seem surprised when Ali caught up to him at the end of the school driveway.

"Can I walk with you?" she asked. Could he hear the quiver in her voice?

Alfie nodded. "Uh-huh."

They walked in silence for the first block. The moment was so significant to Ali that she half expected a brass band to step out of the fog and lead them down the street. The late afternoon sky was a hazy gold. It seemed brighter today, as if the sun wanted to banish the fog and celebrate the fact that Ali and Alfie had finally met.

Ali knew that she needed to use different tactics

to get to know Alfie than what she used in Ali's Rules for Making Friends. She had to be herself, act natural. But it was hard; she'd never done that before. She knew she shouldn't dive right in about their family troubles, so she decided to start with the favorite conversation of all Saint Johners: the weather.

> ALI'S RULES FOR
> MAKING FRIENDS*
> 1. Be friendly.
> 2. Do what the other person wants you to do.
> 3. Agree with them.
> 4. Don't a) talk too much; b) be a know-it-all; or c) give up.
> *note: Alfie Sloane is different. Try to be yourself.

"Lots of fog, huh?"

"Yup. We get a lot of fog in London, too, but nothing like this."

They continued on, quiet once more.

Ali tried another topic. "I was nervous about the debate team."

Alfie glanced over. "How come?"

It was time to tell the truth. "I don't really like public speaking. I joined the debate team to meet you." She held her breath, fearful of his reaction.

"Huh," said Alfie. It sounded like a surprised "huh," which Ali took as a hopeful sign, though the fact that he wasn't swinging his knapsack was a worry.

They turned onto Douglas Avenue, and she paused. She loved her new street, which ran the length of a narrow peninsula separating the Saint John River and the Bay of Fundy. The peninsula's existence created the city's famous Reversing Falls, thanks to the twice daily twenty-eight-foot ocean tides that rushed into the bay and forced the river to flow backward. A reluctant Digger had taken Ali to see the falls the previous week, even though he'd said there wasn't much to see. She'd stood on the observation deck and watched the water churn, thinking about a scientific law she'd studied in sixth grade—Newton's second law of motion—which explained what happens to a mass when it's acted on by an external force. The massive bay and its tides might push the river back twice daily, but the force of the river was unyielding. Thanks to force, something small could stand a chance against something much larger.

Gigi's Victorian house came into view. Did Alfie know this was where she lived? As they got closer, she pointed up at the turret. "That's our great-grandmother's room. Notice the open window?"

"Uh-huh." Alfie studied the window like it was a problem to be solved.

"She always leaves her window open to feed the birds and squirrels. My dad hates it when she does, because he worries the house will be taken over by animals."

Alfie chuckled.

"Want to come in?"

Ali imagined taking Alfie inside. She'd introduce him to Digger, then take him upstairs to meet Gigi. It made her shiver with excitement about how thrilled they'd be. She was already on the first step when Alfie shook his head and began to walk away. Stunned, she gaped at his departing back, then ran to catch up with him.

"You don't want to come in?"

Alfie shook his head. Ali swallowed her disappointment. She hadn't even told him about Gigi's party yet.

"Can we talk for a few minutes?" She pointed

toward Riverview Memorial Park in the distance. Maybe he'd be willing to talk someplace else. He didn't say no, so they kept going. They passed the old New Brunswick Museum, with its imposing pillars and dark stone, and arrived at the park on the other side, cutting across the leaf-strewn grass until they reached the statue of a Boer War soldier. They took a seat beneath the sad-looking man, who clutched his bayonet as if he expected to be called into battle at any moment.

Alfie checked his watch. "I have to be home in ten minutes."

Ten minutes wasn't much time if you had a lifetime of questions you wanted answered.

"Did you know that my parents and I were living here?"

"My mom told me last week."

Phew. That meant seeing Ali at debate team hadn't been a total shock.

"Our families don't speak," she said, dipping a toe in the Sloane Family Feud waters.

"It's so stupid."

The knot in Ali's chest unraveled a bit. "I think so too. I was worried you wouldn't want to be friends with me." In the distance, seagulls called to one another as they fished for their supper. Their screeches sounded like *please, please, please* to Ali.

"We can be friends," said Alfie after a torturous minute, as if he'd reviewed all of the possible alternatives and chosen this one.

Thrilled, and braver now, Ali turned to look at him. "I'm throwing a birthday party for Gigi. She's turning one hundred."

"Gigi?"

Duh—of course he didn't know her nickname! Ali giggled. "It's what I call our great-grandmother. She wanted me to call her Gertie, but I couldn't pronounce it very well, so Digger said to call her G. G., for 'great-grandmother,' which is what he and your dad used to call her. I thought he was saying 'Gigi.' The name stuck."

"Gigi? I quite like it," said Alfie.

"You've never met her."

"Nope." Ali sensed years of regret in that simple word.

"But now that you know me, you can meet her, and you can come to her birthday party."

Alfie shook his head. "Impossible."

"No, it's not. If you come to the party, then the rest of your family will too, and the Sloanes will be reunited! It'll be the best gift ever for Gigi!"

Alfie made a half-choking, half-grunting sound. "Never going to happen."

"Why not? We've just met, and the world hasn't ended. If all the Sloanes come to the party, I'm sure they'll make up."

"My grandfather will never go."

Then it hit her: maybe she didn't need all of the Other Sloanes to come to Gigi's party. Maybe one would be enough. "Will you come, at least?"

"No."

Ali's excitement fizzled like a spent sparkler. "I don't even know why they're fighting."

"It's about my dad. My grandfather blames your father and Gigi for his death. My mom and my aunt don't, but it doesn't matter, because Granddad does."

"But one person can't boss everyone around!" Ali protested.

Alfie stood up. "I love my grandfather. So even though I'm dying to meet Gigi and your dad, I can't go against him. My mom says family has to stick together, even if you don't agree. If they won't go to the party, I can't go either."

"But we're your family too! We're blood. We even look alike!"

Alfie grinned. "When I walked into the classroom, I recognized you straightaway."

"Can't you at least ask them to come?" Ali didn't try and hide her distress. "Maybe if he knows you want to come, your grandfather will change his mind."

"Look . . . I'll try, but don't get your hopes up. Do you want to eat lunch together tomorrow? Murray and Cassie and I have eaten in Mr. Corby's classroom the past couple of days because they were working on a project, but we're eating in the cafeteria tomorrow."

That was one mystery solved.

"Okay." Surely the rule about not making friends too soon didn't apply to cousins.

Alfie swung his knapsack as he walked away. When he reached the sidewalk, he turned. "I'm glad you came to debate team!"

Chapter Three

DEADLY WHIRLPOOLS AND FOG: A DISASTER IN THE MAKING

The second-largest whirlpool in the world, the Old Sow, is found near Deer Island, where the Passamaquoddy Bay meets the Bay of Fundy. Harold Lord of Lord's Cove, Deer Island, recalls accidentally going through the Old Sow on his small schooner, the *Island Girl*, in 1897, whilst returning home in the fog. "There was a great sucking sound, and the water roiled and boiled around me. Were it not for the wits of my first mate, Lionel Lord, and his ability to maintain a course around the funnel, the *Island Girl* and its three passengers would have been lost.

—Percival T. Sloane,
  A History of Fog in the Bay of Fundy *(1932)*

TEN

Digger was in the kitchen making apple pies when Ali arrived home. She wasn't surprised that he didn't glance up when she came in. Whenever Digger baked, it meant he was stressed.

"What's up?" she asked.

He didn't respond right away. The only sound was the dull rumble of the rolling pin as he worked to flatten the pie dough. A couple of minutes passed, and then he flashed her a strained smile. "Gigi's cough got worse this morning. I called the doctor, and he had me bring her in. He's worried it might turn into pneumonia, so she's confined to bed."

Ali started to get up, but Digger held up a floury

hand. "She's asleep. You can see her when she wakes up. She needs to rest."

Ali sat down and ran her fingers through her hair, a nervous habit her mother loathed because it resulted in Ali's hair going everywhere. Gigi being sick frightened Ali. Gigi was so old; sometimes she reminded Ali of the stuffed birds and mammals mounted in display cases at the New Brunswick Museum: fragile and liable to fall apart if handled too much. It wasn't fair. She had so much more to learn about Gigi and her remarkable life. Even worse, if something happened to Gigi, Alfie would never get to know her at all.

Time to share some happy news. "I met Alfie today."

Digger's eyes lit up. He put down the rolling pin and leaned against the counter.

"What's he like?"

"You'd like him so much, Digger. He's funny and smart."

"Is he tall?"

"Nope—short like me. Well, not quite as short as

me. And he's a grade ahead of me even though he's only a month older."

"Huh."

"We look alike."

Digger beamed. "Didn't I say that? Just like me and Teddy." The smile vanished. "It's awful that I don't know Teddy's son." He began to scoop pie filling into the pan with renewed vigor.

> ALI'S RULES FOR
> WHEN DIGGER BAKES
> 1. Encourage him to
>   use sugar.
> 2. If he's making something
>   elaborate, like a seven-layer
>   cake or cream puffs, don't
>   ask him what's wrong. You
>   DON'T want to know.
> 3. Don't offer to help.
> 4. Try to lighten his mood.
> 5. Eat whatever he bakes,
>   even if it's horrible, even if
>   it means picking raisins
>   out of your cookie.

Ali sighed. "I wish the Other Sloanes didn't hate us."

Digger paused. "They don't hate us, Ali-Cat."

"They act like they hate us."

"It's complicated." Complicated was the word grown-ups used when they didn't want to tell you something. "Do you think Alfie is a Copycat?"

"Nope. He wasn't all twitchy like you are sometimes. Of course, I can't tell if people are Copycats like you can. Gigi told me not to say anything. He might not know about Copycats."

"I don't act twitchy!" Digger protested. Then: "Do I act twitchy?"

Ali raised her eyebrows. "When you're dying to change but you can't."

"Huh." He laughed and morphed into a raccoon with floury paws.

"You know Mom doesn't like wild animals in the kitchen," Ali reminded him.

Digger changed back. "Technically, I'm not a wild animal."

"Tell it to the judge," said Ali's mother, who appeared in the doorway. Her hair, slicked back into a tight bun that morning, had mostly escaped its elastic and hung around her face in frizzy tendrils. After quick kisses for Ali and Digger, she collapsed onto a chair and popped a piece of pie dough into her mouth. "Any change in Gigi?"

"Not since we talked earlier this afternoon. Ali was just informing me that I sometimes act twitchy. Do you think I act twitchy?"

Ali's mother chuckled. "Only when you're awake."

Digger made a face and turned his attention back to his pie. After fluting the crust with the precision of a pastry chef, he popped it in the oven and wiped his hands on his apron. "Ali met Alfie today."

That made Ali's mother sit up straight. Eyes wide, she turned to Ali. "You did?"

"He's so great, Mom! We're going to be friends!"

Her mother's eyes watered. "I think about him and Colleen a lot. His mom and I were such good friends. She was the one person I could talk to about what it was like to live with a Copycat. We wrote for a while after they moved away, but eventually the letters stopped."

"How come?" asked Ali.

"She needed to get on with her life. You can't live in the past. It's not healthy."

Ali sensed the comment wasn't directed at her. "You should call her, go for coffee."

"Maybe. Did you meet Alfie?" she asked Digger, who shook his head.

"I tried to invite him in," said Ali. "But I think he

was nervous because of the Sloane Family Feud." She turned to Digger. "You should pop out and say hello when he and I walk home together tomorrow."

"I'm not going to do that, Ali-Cat."

"How come? He said he wants to meet you!"

Her father shook his head. "Someday you'll understand that just because you *can* do something doesn't mean you should."

"That doesn't make any sense!"

"A lot of things in this life don't make any sense. You'd better get used to that." An instant later he changed into Digger the dog and fled the kitchen.

Ali harrumphed. "Why won't he talk about the Sloane Family Feud?"

Her mother leaned across and smoothed Ali's fog-frizzy hair. "It was a dark time when Teddy died. I know Digger is happy that you met Alfie, but it also reminds him of how much he still misses Teddy."

"But Teddy's been gone for years."

Her mother stood up. "I'm going to take a quick shower before supper. I know this is confusing, honey.

The truth is, grief doesn't stick to a timetable. Your dad's doing the best he can. Someday he'll move on. Until then, we just have to support him. The Sloanes are a complicated family." She kissed Ali on the forehead and left.

That word again: complicated. But why were the Sloanes complicated? Was it because they were Copycats? Because of Teddy's death? It was clear it wouldn't be enough to have the Other Sloanes come to Gigi's birthday party; she had to find a way to help her dad let go of the past.

ELEVEN

It wasn't hard to find Alfie and the others in the cafeteria the next day; he was wearing the world's most hideous Hawaiian shirt, a pea-green monstrosity splattered with chocolate flowers and orange parrots. It was so ugly it hurt Ali's eyes. She slid into the empty chair beside Cassie, so mesmerized she didn't say hello.

Cassie nudged her. "I see you're hypnotized by Alfie's shirt."

"Not me," said Murray, who sat beside Alfie on the other side of the table. "It makes me want to throw up."

Alfie grinned.

"I dared him to wear it," Murray continued. "We went to the movies last night and he told me he owned the ugliest shirt in the universe. I didn't believe him, so I made a bet with him. As you can see, I lost. It *is* the ugliest shirt ever."

Even though Cassie was still smiling, she'd stiffened when Murray said he'd gone to a movie with Alfie.

"My precious," said Alfie, running his hand across the shiny fabric.

"What did you bet?" Ali asked him.

"Whoever lost had to bring the winner lunch for a whole week."

Ali's mouth formed an O. "You must have been sure you'd win."

Alfie pointed at his chest. "Hello—have you seen this shirt? It was a no-brainer. I've given Murray a list of my favorite foods: quesadillas, meatball sandwiches, and nachos." He patted his nonexistent belly. "Next week is going to be sooo good."

Murray slurped his water. "It's worth it. You should

have seen everybody pointing at him when he walked into the cafeteria. I think a girl fainted."

Alfie stroked a sleeve. "Whatever. I quite like this shirt—my dad wore it in the nineties."

"He should have left it there," Cassie said. Her face turned a deeper pink. "I'm s-sorry," she stammered, "I forgot your dad is dead."

"It's okay. I bet he's looking down right now, saying, 'Way to go, son.'"

Cassie turned to Ali. "It's weird that you guys are cousins but you never met before."

"We both just moved here," Alfie pointed out. "There was this little thing called the Atlantic Ocean separating us."

"Well, yeah, but didn't you ever have family reunions? We Andersons have one every summer at my grandma's house."

"Nope," said Alfie.

Cassie pressed on. "So how exactly are you related?"

"Our grandfathers were brothers, and we share the same great-grandmother," said Ali.

"That makes you guys second cousins," Murray pronounced.

"You're like a robot," Alfie told him. "How do you even know that?"

Murray grinned. "You say the sweetest things, Alfie." He puckered his lips, then pretended to be hurt when Alfie shoved him away. "Enough with the family tree stuff, Cassie."

Cassie flinched.

Murray leaned across the table so that his nose almost touched Ali's. "Just so you know, this is a sports-free table. Cassie and I may be tall and I may be black, but we are not sports people, and we will not discuss hockey or basketball. Ever. On the other hand, feel free to talk about video games, Harry Potter, and science fiction."

Ali giggled. "Except for swimming, I don't know anything about sports."

Murray grinned. "You and I are going to get along just fine. If you love Harry Potter, we'll be best friends."

Given his obvious intensity about the things he loved, Ali decided it was best not to tell Murray she'd read only the first two Harry Potter books. As soon as she finished *The Golden Compass*, she'd borrow the third Harry Potter from the library. She unpacked today's lunch—strawberry yogurt, a banana, and three chocolate chip cookies—thrilled that Digger had agreed to

> ALI'S FOOD RULES
> 1. Vegetables are not your friends.
> 2. Raisins are an unwelcome surprise.
> 3. Mushy bananas are GROSS!
> 4. Always cut toast on the diagonal.
> 5. The cinnamon and sugar should not be mixed in advance when you make cinnamon toast.
> 6. If you've never eaten it before, do NOT agree to try it.

let her make her own lunches. Otherwise, she'd be eating last night's dinner, a couscous salad so full of finely chopped vegetables it was impossible to eat around them. Meals like that were the reason she'd created Ali's Food Rules. The one problem was that she'd have to grow up before she could live by them.

Cassie leaned across the table to Murray. "Want to watch *Doctor Who* after school?"

A look—maybe guilt—crossed Murray's face. "I'm hanging with Alfie after school."

"Maybe we could all—" Cassie began, but she was cut off by the warning bell. Afternoon classes were about to begin.

Murray and Alfie jumped up and gathered their things.

"See you, Ali!" Alfie called over his shoulder as he followed Murray out of the cafeteria.

"See you!" She turned to Cassie, who hadn't moved since the bell rang. "You okay?"

Cassie shook herself and smiled. "Sure. Just thinking about school. Hey . . . you don't want to come over to my house after school and watch *Doctor Who*, do you?"

Ali, who'd never seen an episode of *Doctor Who* before, shook her head. "I can't." The twinge of guilt at blowing Cassie off made her uncomfortable, but she'd already broken her new school rule about not making friends too soon for Alfie. She couldn't break it for Cassie too.

Cassie bit her lip and began to pack up her lunch. "No problem. Maybe some other time."

"For sure," said Ali, trying to sound enthusiastic.

A sense of unease accompanied her as she followed Cassie out of the cafeteria. Gigi was still sick, so there'd be no after-school visit to talk about books. Digger would be cooking or working on his latest project, a sculpture he was creating out of hub caps he found in ditches around the city. That left homework or reading, neither of which appealed to her all of a sudden. Her rules were supposed to make things better. So why did saying no to Cassie not make her feel better? Why did it just make her feel lonely?

Chapter Four
FOG AND
MARINE DISASTERS

The fog has caused many marine disasters in the Bay of Fundy: the brig *Glide* in 1855, the barque *Mauvourneen* in 1866, the tug *Gypsum Kin* in 1899. The Murr Ledges off Grand Manan Island are the resting place of many a ship that failed to find her way in the dense fog.

—PERCIVAL T. SLOANE,
  A History of Fog in the Bay of Fundy (*1932*)

TWELVE

Ali, still out of sorts in science class, was flustered when Mr. Corby reminded the class that today was the day they'd brainstorm their projects.

"You have twenty minutes and can work here or in the library," Mr. Corby bellowed over the screech of desks being shoved together and students shouting to their partners. "By the end of class, you need a topic and a plan. Let me know if you need help."

Ali glanced over her shoulder to where Emily and Taylor sat huddled together and waited for Emily to signal to her. Even though Emily had been nice to her the other day, the idea of working with her still made Ali nervous. Nearby, Cassie and Murray sat with their heads together, whispering. Now and then, they'd lean forward and share a high five. If only Mr. Corby had paired her with one of them. They were having fun. Ali doubted that working with Emily would be fun.

Two long minutes later Emily stood up, smiled at Ali, and pointed to the door. By the time Ali stepped into the hallway, Emily was halfway to the library. Ali raced to catch up and tried not to be offended when Emily didn't slow her breakneck pace.

"We'll work in the library because there's a couch that's way more comfortable than the plastic chairs in the classroom," announced Emily when Ali finally caught her.

They were too late. Two boys were already sprawled on the couch. Ali turned to search for another spot, but Emily grabbed her arm and held her in place.

"Tom," she cooed. "Do you mind if we sit here? I have my heart set on this couch. I love the natural light from the window." Ali and the two boys stared at the window, where exactly zero natural light was coming in thanks to the thick fog.

Ali recognized Tom Power as the boy with the basketball on the first day of school. He also sat next to Emily in class and laughed at everything she said. If anybody was going to give up their seat to Emily, Ali knew it would be Tom. But he wasn't alone.

"We're comfy," Tom's partner replied, a ruddy-faced boy whose name Ali didn't know yet. He was the kind of boy whose words came out sounding like a challenge. But he didn't intimidate Emily at all.

"I know it's silly—" Emily started to say, then stopped. "I'm sorry, I don't know your name and it seems rude to ask you a favor until I do."

"Jackson Mather" was the gruff response.

Emily's smile dazzled. "I know it's silly, Jackson, but I really want to sit here. If you're desperate to stay, fine, but if you don't care, it would be super nice if you'd give it to us."

Ali expected Jackson to say something snarky, so she was surprised when he elbowed Tom. "They can have it." The two boys gathered their things and stood up.

"Awesome!" Emily squealed. "You guys are the best! I won't forget this."

Jackson's defiance was replaced by a bashful smile. He mumbled, "No problem," and scurried after Tom to the other side of the library.

"Wow," said Ali, flopping onto the couch, "I can't believe they moved!"

Emily sat down, opened her notebook, and uncapped a red pen. "My dad says that if you're nice to people, people will be nice to you. Some people forget that."

> EMILY'S RULES
> 1. If you are nice to people, people will be nice back to you.
> 2. You can only be excellent if you put in the work.

Ali made a mental note to create a new category called Emily's Rules as soon as she got home, and make what Emily had just said rule number one. She'd never met anyone so wise.

Emily bit down on her pen cap. "We need to come up with something stellar. I want to get the best mark. Do you have any ideas?"

Ali might have forgotten that today was project brainstorming day, but she'd come prepared. "What about a field study? In my last school, we did a field study of wildflowers. Everyone collected whatever they could find in their neighborhood and brought them to school. We worked together to identify them. It was fun."

"A field study." Emily repeated the words like she was testing them. "How would we do that for the classification of organisms?"

Ali stared at the gold stars scattered across Emily's leggings. She needed to impress Emily. If she didn't, she might be on the outs with the popular kids, and she couldn't afford to do that. It was a relief when the perfect solution popped into her head.

"What if we did a field study of a single block in Saint John? You know, take pictures of everything we see from the five kingdoms and then do a summary about what we saw."

Emily smiled. "Ooh—I love that idea! It's so scientific! We could do the block that runs around the park near where I live!" Her face clouded over. "But how can we see everything?"

"Do you mean monerans and protists, because they're so tiny?" Ali asked.

Emily nodded. "We can't leave anything out. . . ."

Ali did a little bounce on the couch. "All we have to do is research how much bacteria the average plant or person has on them and then do a rough estimate!"

Emily squealed. "That's brilliant! Of course, we can just assume that any boys we see are covered in billions of bacteria, since they smell so bad." They erupted into giggles, loud enough that the school librarian shushed them, which made them giggle more.

"Okay, here's the plan," said Emily. "Come to my house after school next week. We'll do the field research and then decide how to organize our presentation. Isn't it great Mr. Corby made us partners? Usually I have to come up with ideas by myself, but we work so well together!"

Now Ali understood why Jackson had agreed to move. There was something about Emily that made you want to please her, which was probably why she was so popular. "I can't do it Monday afternoon—I have debate team."

"I didn't know you joined the debate team," Emily said, as if she should have.

"Uh-huh. I'm kind of nervous because we start debating next week."

"You'll be great," Emily declared. "I should have joined. I'm going to be a lawyer when I grow up like my dad. He loves debating." Ali was surprised by how wistful she sounded.

"I bet it's not too late for you to join."

Emily shook her head. "I can't. Tuesday is my only free day. I figure skate, do modern dance, take Japanese lessons, and volunteer with my mom at the community center."

"Whoa."

"My dad says you can only be excellent if you put in the work." She wrote her address and phone number on a rainbow-colored sticky note. "Why don't you come home with me on Tuesday? My mom can drive you home afterward if your parents can't come get you."

Mr. Corby popped his head into the library. "Time to come back, everybody!"

Emily linked her arm through Ali's. "We are going to be such an amazing team!"

Ali nodded. They *were* an amazing team, and Emily was exactly the kind of person she wanted to be friends with: popular, smart, and nice. Now all she had to do was make Emily want to be friends with *her*.

THIRTEEN

The thing about moving all the time was that nowhere felt like home. Ali couldn't point to one city, town, or village and say, "This is my hometown. I belong here." In most of the books she read, the main character left home to undertake an epic adventure. Sometimes that adventure was about saving their home, like Frodo in *The Lord of the Rings*. Other times, the adventure was about the main character getting lost and finding their way home, like Dorothy in *The Wizard of Oz*. But in every case, if the main character succeeded, they had a home to go back to.

Not Ali. No place tugged at her heart or made her want to stay. When she walked down the street, there were no familiar faces; she was never anywhere long enough to recognize anyone. Over time, even the people she did remember became so blurred that she couldn't recall where she knew them from. Saint John was her last chance to set down roots. But Saint John depended on Gigi, and things weren't looking good.

Gigi had improved very little in the two days since the doctor's visit. She slept most of the time and subsisted on Digger's homemade broth. Ali peeked in her room several times a day, but had gotten no reaction. Outside her closed bedroom window—as per the doctor's orders—several birds and squirrels sat in the nearby tree and stared in at her. Digger said they were waiting for their regular handouts, but to an emotional Ali, they appeared to be keeping vigil.

"You're so quiet tonight, Ali," her mother said at supper. "Anything wrong? Besides Gigi, I mean."

"What will happen if Gigi gets too sick to live at home anymore, or if she—" Ali tried to keep her emotions in check but couldn't stop the rogue tear that slid down her cheek.

Her mother reached for her hand. "I know it's hard. We just have to hope for the best."

"We have to tell her the truth, Ginger," said a grim Digger.

The room tilted. "What truth?" Ali demanded.

"Digger . . ." There was a warning in her mother's voice, which Digger ignored.

"We're here as Gigi's guests. Once she's not here, we'll have to leave."

Something electric pulsed through Ali and twisted itself into fearful strands of hopelessness. Ali might not be from anywhere in particular, but she had plenty of memories of the horrible places they'd lived in: walls so thin the wind passed through them like they were cardboard; shouting neighbors; mouse droppings everywhere; wondering if the food bank box would last until her mother's next paycheck; the world—or maybe just her parents—waiting to pull the rug out from underneath them. She squeezed her eyes shut. "You mean we'd have to move if Gigi dies?"

Digger grunted. "We wouldn't have a choice. Uncle Andrew will inherit the house, and since this is his childhood home, I wouldn't be surprised if he wanted to move in."

"But I don't want to leave! Where will we go?"

"We'll be fine, Ali-Cat. We always are."

In her perfect Digger voice, she repeated his hollow words back to him. "We'll be fine, Ali-Cat. We always are."

That was the lie they always told her.

Ali's mother cleared her throat. "Let's change the subject, please. I'm like Ali; I don't want to think about leaving. This is the best place we've ever lived. Any good stories from school today?"

> ALI'S RULES FOR HOW TO LIVE YOUR LIFE SO YOU DON'T BECOME A SCREWUP
> 1. Get a job.
> 2. Don't be a Copycat.
> 3. Pay the rent on time.
> 4. Don't bring junk into the house.
> 5. Don't spend money on lottery tickets—you'll never win!
> 6. Get an education.
> 7. Stay in one place.

Ali had gone to ten schools, but lived in three times that many homes. In the last year alone they had been evicted from two apartments because her parents couldn't pay the rent on time. Ali's mother worked hard, but her job didn't pay enough to support a family of three. Digger rarely worked, and no one was interested in his abstract art. When Gigi had phoned and asked them to move in so she could continue to live at home, Ali's mom had said yes, even though she knew Digger didn't want to live in Saint John again. There had been a huge argument. Digger didn't give in until Ali's mom threatened to move with or without him. And since Ali knew her parents didn't like to dwell on the bad stuff, there was no point asking any more questions.

"You wouldn't believe the ugly shirt Alfie wore today. He said it was his dad's."

Digger closed his eyes. "Was it covered in flowers and parrots?"

"Yeah! How'd you know?"

"I was with Teddy when he bought it at the Salvation Army." Digger's voice was so quiet Ali had to strain to hear him. "We were in high school. He wore that shirt all the time. The girls loved it. But then, everybody loved Teddy."

Ali's mother rolled her eyes. "Everybody loved you

too, Digger. Teddy once told me you were quite a hit with the opposite sex."

Digger blushed and ducked his head. "That was a long time ago."

"Lucky for me."

Ali hadn't meant to turn the conversation so gooey. "You guys are grossing me out."

Since it was Ali's turn to do the dishes, her parents took her comment as a sign to get lost. Anxious to check on Gigi, Ali zipped through the dishes and hurried upstairs. She paused outside Gigi's bedroom, pressed an ear to the door, and listened to Gigi's raspy snore. They should never have let Gigi take the first day of school photo outside in the fog. What were they thinking? She decided to take a quick peek, knowing she wouldn't sleep unless she checked on Gigi. The door creaked when she opened it, but the snores continued. Gigi's body was such a tiny bump under the thick duvet that Ali feared she was shrinking. She backed out of the room. The door made a whiny screech, and Gigi stirred. Ali cursed her stupidity and waited for the snores to resume.

Instead, Gigi cleared her throat. "Don't worry, Alison," she whispered, her voice so weak Ali could barely make out what she was saying. "I'll be fine."

Ali ran into the room and planted a kiss on Gigi's cheek. "Promise?"

"Promise."

"I don't want to have to move again." Ali knew she shouldn't say this to Gigi; it wasn't fair. But she needed Gigi to know she was counting on her. Whether or not Ali ever came from anywhere was wholly dependent on Gigi getting well.

"I know you don't. Now let me sleep. I need my beauty rest."

Ali crept out of the room. She didn't shut the door until the snores began again in earnest. This time, they weren't raspy. They were like the sigh of the wind passing through the trees, gentle waves lapping the shore. Hopeful, Ali smiled. Maybe she'd be like the heroes in her books. Maybe her adventure was to find a home at last.

FOURTEEN

By the end of the weekend, Gigi was on the mend, but the household remained on edge. Ali's parents didn't mention the possibility of moving again, but when Ali overheard her mom tell Digger that they should squirrel away a little money "in case," she knew they were worried. On Saturday, when a cruise ship was forced to dock at the harbor because of the worsening fog, Digger rushed down to the wharf and sold six caricatures to the bewildered tourists who'd expected to land in Boston. On Sunday, her mother took a double shift at the nursing home. Ali couldn't think of a way to make money, but she could think of a way they could stay in Saint John:

end the Sloane Family Feud. Gigi's birthday party was now more important than ever.

The last to arrive at debate team on Monday, Ali took a seat in the second row and tried to make herself invisible. When Ms. Ryder called on Ashok and Carolyn, Ali couldn't stifle a loud exhalation of relief.

Ms. Ryder chuckled. "I know the first time you debate can be intimidating, so you can watch a couple of old pros first. Ashok—before you begin, what's the most important thing a debater needs to do during a debate?"

"Listen to your opponent. It's impossible to win if you don't listen."

Ashok and Carolyn's debate was impressive. The resolution was: "Be it resolved that the sky is blue." Ali knew Ashok would win when Ms. Ryder said he'd argue for the resolution, because the sky was blue, wasn't it? But Carolyn was a formidable opponent, and the two went back and forth, trading arguments like two boxers exchanging jabs in the ring. In the end, Carolyn won the day with her points about

sunrises, sunsets, and the color of the sky during vol-
canic eruptions and forest fires. When they finished,
everyone applauded.

"Who's next?" Ms. Ryder asked. Ali sank down in
her chair.

Alfie hopped up. "Want to give it a go, Murray?"

Cassie bit her lip. Was she nervous too?

"Here's your resolution, boys,"
Ms. Ryder read from a card. "'Be
it resolved that Princess Elizabeth
School shouldn't open until ten
a.m. so students can sleep in.'"

> **ALI'S RULES FOR WHAT TO
> DO WHEN YOU'RE FORCED
> TO DO SOMETHING YOU
> HATE**
> 1. Breathe.
> 2. Try to escape.
> 3. If you can't escape?
>   Try to survive.
> 4. I got nothing. Why are
>   you doing something you
>   hate?

Alfie and Murray pounded fists.

"Like taking candy from a baby," said Murray.

"This baby bites," Alfie replied.

Ms. Ryder shook her head. "You two! Okay, you've
got two minutes to prepare."

"I guess we're next," Cassie whispered to Ali, who
swallowed hard.

There was a swagger about Murray when he began.

"Sure, it would be nice for kids not to go to school until ten a.m., but that's not how the real world works. School is supposed to prepare us for life. Most jobs begin between eight and nine o'clock in the morning."

Alfie was equally self-assured. "Actually, your argument is flawed. Lots of people do shift work." He ignored Murray's scowl and continued. "In fact, my mother teaches three nights a week at the university. Research studies show teenagers are biologically wired to stay up late and sleep in. Starting school at ten a.m. means they'd be alert and ready to learn."

Murray refused to be bested. "Point taken, but what about their teachers? My dad teaches at Saint John High. He goes to bed at nine thirty and gets up at five. If school ran from ten to five, our teachers would be exhausted by early afternoon."

"School is about optimizing learning for *students*. Teachers would adapt. And don't forget: if school ended at five o'clock, kids would arrive home at the same time as their parents, so they'd be better supervised and get in less trouble. It's a no-brainer."

Murray's forehead creased as he searched for a rebuttal. Several seconds passed, and then his eyes lit up. "I think Hogwarts begins classes every morning at nine o'clock sharp. Shouldn't we aim to be like Hogwarts?"

Alfie gave Murray a consoling pat on the arm. "You do know Hogwarts isn't real, right?"

Murray groaned and Ms. Ryder clapped her hands. "Very close, gentlemen. Kudos, Murray, for finding a way to bring Hogwarts into the debate, but this victory belongs to Alfie."

Murray and Alfie shook hands and sat down.

"Our last debaters will be Cassie and Ali. Here's your resolution: 'Be it resolved that Princess Elizabeth School is the best school in Saint John.' Ali will argue for the resolution, Cassie against. You've got two minutes to prepare."

Cassie scribbled points on a piece of paper, while a petrified Ali stared down at her notebook, unable to think of a single argument. Alfie turned and gave her an encouraging smile, which made things worse.

Soon he'd know his cousin was the worst debater ever. And why was it so hot in Ms. Ryder's classroom? Didn't she believe in opening a window?

"You start, Ali." Ms. Ryder was chipper, like she didn't know Ali was about to faint.

"The students seem nice in Saint John," a shaky Ali whispered to the wall.

"Ali, it's important to make eye contact with your opponent," interjected Ms. Ryder.

Ali did as she was told. Until this moment, she'd only ever focused on that fact that Cassie was almost six feet tall. But now, forced to stare at her, Ali saw the long sandy curls and the deep blue eyes that were the same color as a blueberry. When Cassie flashed an encouraging smile, there was a sizable gap between her front teeth. She wasn't perfectly put together like Emily was, but there was something about Cassie that made you want to look at her, even if she did dress in baggy overalls and a plaid shirt. Thanks to the smile, Ali began to relax. A warm tingle replaced the earlier panic.

"Many students in Saint John are nice," Cassie replied. "But there's no evidence to suggest that Princess Elizabeth School has nicer students."

Instead of being stung by Cassie's response, her words strengthened the warmth cascading through Ali, as if Cassie's confidence was contagious.

"That's true," said Ali, heartened by how solid her voice sounded now. "But isn't Princess Elizabeth a community school, with lots of local organizations donating time and money to help kids? I think that makes us special."

She smiled at Cassie, whose head jerked back. Ali was pleased. *She's underestimated me.* Seconds ticked by as she waited for Cassie to respond.

Instead, Cassie turned to Ms. Ryder. "Can Ali and I be excused for a minute?"

Ms. Ryder sounded as confused as Ali felt. "I suppose."

Cassie grabbed Ali's hand and pulled her out the door. She dragged her to the closest washroom, checked to make sure it was empty, then marched Ali to the sink. On the verge of tears, she asked, "What *are* you?"

A sense of dread overtook Ali. What was going on? "I don't know what you mean." She searched Cassie's face for an explanation.

Cassie pointed at the mirror. "Open your mouth and look in the mirror."

Heart pounding, Ali did. A gap that shouldn't be there separated her front teeth. But it wasn't just her teeth. Something strange and fiery rushed through her, almost knocking her to the ground. She steadied herself against the sink and watched in horror as her gray eyes turned blue and her dark hair lightened to match Cassie's. Within seconds she was Cassie's twin. Panic-stricken, she turned to the other girl, who had backed up against the bathroom door, eyes wild.

"I—" Ali began, but Cassie cut her off.

"Are you some kind of witch?" Cassie whispered. Not waiting for a response, she fled.

Stunned, Ali stumbled into a stall and locked

the door. This wasn't supposed to happen. Gigi had promised it wouldn't. But it was happening, and even worse, it was happening at school. Ali was a Copycat, and she had no idea what to do.

Chapter Five
THE BENEFITS
OF FOG

Typically, most fogs burn off by lunchtime. A Mrs. Betty Horncastle of Seely's Cove swears that the fog is the key to her spectacular wild roses and that the salty moisture in the air helps her and her chickens sleep.

—PERCIVAL T. SLOANE,
   A History of Fog in the Bay of Fundy *(1932)*

Fifteen

From her hiding spot in the locked bathroom stall, Ali waited to be arrested. She imagined Cassie rushing back to Ms. Ryder's class and announcing to everyone that Ali was a witch. Ms. Ryder would have called the police and asked Murray to lead the debaters out of the school in a well-ordered fashion. She pictured a SWAT team creeping down the hallway toward the washroom while reporters outside said things like "It seems twelve-year-old debater Ali Sloane is not what she seems." No doubt the police had already descended on Gigi's house and arrested her family.

After a torturous hour spent jumping at every footfall and voice out in the hallway, she came to the stunning conclusion that no one was coming. With a shaking hand, she unlatched the door and stepped into the empty bathroom. At first she was too timid to check herself in the mirror, but after ten minutes of dithering, she took a peek and burst into tears when her own face stared back at her. Emboldened, she wiped her tears with a handful of paper towels and poked her head out the door. The hallway was empty. She crept to the nearest exit, ignoring the fact that it was freezing outside and her jacket was still stuffed in her locker, and ran home. She needed Digger.

A half-frozen Ali found him in his basement work-shop, whittling what would soon be a black-capped chickadee out of a pine log, one of the smaller pieces of art that he'd sometimes try to sell for some extra money. As soon as she saw him, she burst into tears.

Digger dropped his carving knife and the unfinished bird and rushed to her side. "What's wrong, Ali-Cat?"

Ali threw herself at him, unable to speak. For

several minutes, they didn't move, as Ali's heaving sobs shook her already-shivering body and soaked both of their sweaters with her tears. She pulled away and spat out, "I'm a Copycat."

Digger flinched. "How do you know?"

"How do I know?" She didn't try to hide her indignation. "I know because I turned into another girl at school!"

Digger grabbed hold of a nearby table to steady himself. "Did anyone see it happen?"

"The girl I changed into saw. We were debating when it started. My front teeth started to change to look like hers and she dragged me to the bathroom. I don't know if anyone else saw it happen. She asked me—" Ali stopped. The memory of Cassie asking if she was a witch was still too raw to talk about. "How did this happen, Digger?"

The last sentence came out as an accusation. Digger ran his hands through his hair and spun around, as if the answer to how Ali had come into

> ALI'S RULES FOR WHAT
> TO DO WHEN IT'S THE
> END OF THE WORLD
> 1. There are no rules.

her Copycat powers could be gleaned from his carving tools or from the outdoor Christmas lights that hung on the wall. He stared up at the ceiling and took a deep breath before he spoke.

"It doesn't make sense. We were sure you weren't a Copycat because they always start to change as babies. My mother said I turned into a baby skunk in my crib after seeing one in a picture book. The only thing I can think is that maybe it's linked to Saint John. You'd never set foot in the city until a couple of weeks ago."

"But not every Copycat lives in Saint John. Gigi says we have cousins all over America."

Digger threw his hands up into the air. "Then . . . honestly? I have no idea."

Weren't parents supposed to know stuff? "What am I going to do? I can't just turn into random people at school. And what am I going to tell Cassie when I see her again? Unless you let me drop out of school," she added hopefully.

Digger exhaled. "You're not quitting school. I bet

Cassie thinks she imagined the whole thing. In my experience, strange things make people uncomfortable, so they find a way to explain it away so life can return to normal. And you won't turn into random people. I'll train you, starting tonight, so you can control your powers. A Copycat out of control is a dangerous thing, both for themselves and everyone else. Once you're trained, everything will be fine."

It sounded so simple. And maybe it would be if Ali had gotten her powers when she was young. But now? Now it was unnerving, because she had no idea if she could control herself.

"I don't want to be a Copycat, Digger. You should have seen how Cassie looked at me. She thinks I'm a freak."

Digger took her hand. "Copycats are *not* freaks. We're just regular people who can do something extraordinary, okay?"

Ali nodded. But she didn't believe him. If Digger didn't think he was a freak, why had he always seemed relieved that she wasn't a Copycat? Something was either good or bad. It couldn't be both.

* * *

They shared the news as soon as Ali's mother got home. Gigi clapped her hands and squealed with delight. Ali's mother was speechless. She hugged Ali hard, like that would make everything better. Which it did, at least for a while.

"What do we do?" her mother asked.

"I'll start training her right away," said Digger.

Ali's mom kept her arms wrapped around Ali as if she expected her daughter to change into a bird and fly away. "Your dad will make sure you're okay."

"Of course he will," said Gigi. "Digger is a very talented Copycat."

Ali knew that was true. But he wasn't talented when it came to getting a real job. Was that because he was a Copycat? And if it was, would she have trouble holding down a job someday too? Ali didn't know what she wanted to be when she grew up, but she was already doubting her ability to do whatever it was.

"You'll live an extraordinary life," Gigi continued.

Her gray eyes shone, as if Ali's news was a tonic for what was ailing her. "I did."

"We have to make sure she's trained well, Digger," Ali's mother whispered. "We can't let what happened—"

Digger cut her off. "It won't."

Ali wanted to ask her mother what she was going to say, but she could tell from Digger's red face that it was a bad idea to ask that question right now.

It was Gigi who changed the subject. "With the three of us helping her, Ali will be the most talented Copycat of all."

Her mother leaned in to Ali and kissed her hair. "You're right, Gigi. Let's order some pizza and then get started. We'll make it a celebration! You know what Maya says: 'If you are always trying to be normal, you will never know how amazing you can be.' This will be awesome, sweetie."

Pizza was ordered with extra pepperoni—Ali's favorite—and the dinner conversation was animated and jolly. It would have been fun, except for one thing:

it felt like they were pretending to be happy to make Ali feel normal. But she wasn't normal.

Gigi raised her glass. "A toast to Ali! Welcome to the world of Copycats! Time to train!"

Ali clinked everyone's glass and prayed she was a better Copycat than she was a debater.

Sixteen

Even though the thermostat in Gigi's bedroom was set to a balmy eighty-five, Ali couldn't stop shivering. She had no idea what was about to happen. What if she couldn't change again? Or worse . . . what if she shouldn't *stop* changing?

Gigi sat on her bed with her back resting against the headboard. Ali was stationed at the opposite end. Ali's mother was downstairs cleaning up the kitchen and would join them soon. Meanwhile, Digger paced. Several minutes passed before he paused and spoke to Ali.

"You get to choose who or what you turn into tonight. When I was learning how to use my powers, I liked to pretend I was someone famous."

Gigi chuckled. "It was odd, walking into a room and finding Abraham Lincoln sprawled on the couch watching cartoons. Of course, it was odder still when Abraham Lincoln spoke and sounded like Digger."

"You can't mimic someone unless you know what they sound like," Digger explained. "I don't know what Lincoln sounds like."

The story would be funny if Ali wasn't so nervous. She weighed her Copycat options. If she turned into a dog, it would seem like she was copying Digger. A squirrel was out of the question. She considered Walter Pidgeon but didn't want Gigi making gooey eyes at her. There were so many choices it was impossible to decide.

"I don't know what to change into," she confessed.

Gigi nodded, as if this was to be expected. "Turn into me. No one's ever turned into me before. It'll be fun." She settled against her pillows and waited.

Ali turned to Digger. "What do I do?"

"Concentrate on her features, imagine yourself becoming her," said Digger.

It was unnerving to stare so hard, but Gigi's encouraging smile made her relax into the task. Ali studied Gigi as if she were memorizing facts for a test: every crinkle and wrinkle; the connect-the-dot age spots; the blue veins that pushed their way above the skin's surface; the fuzzy white hair that reminded Ali of the fiberfill she'd used in third grade to make pretend snow for a diorama; the specks of black in her pale gray irises.

At first nothing happened. Then the same warm tingle she'd felt when she'd stared at Cassie filled her. She didn't need to look to know her body was transforming; the soft crunch of muscles and bones expanding and contracting, and her back curving itself into a hump told her it was happening. The strangest moment was when her clothes morphed from jeans and a sweater into Gigi's purple velour track suit. The only difference between Ali and Gigi was the baby finger on her left hand. It was decidedly Ali's, a smooth outlier in a body covered in wrinkles.

"What do you think?" Gigi's voice asked from Ali's body.

Gigi clapped. "Remarkable!" She leaned forward and took one of Ali's wizened hands. "It's not easy being almost one hundred, is it?"

Ali wanted to agree, but didn't want to be rude. She held up her unaltered pinky finger. "Why didn't this change?"

"Copycats are never fully someone else," Digger explained. "There's always something a little off. I'd say you were a natural. Now let's see how fast you can turn back. It's the reverse of what you did when you turned into Gigi. This time, you think of yourself."

It sounded easier, but it wasn't. Ali tried her best to picture her real self, but it was like the Gigi parts of her didn't want to change back. A wave of panic rolled through her.

"Breathe," said Digger, sensing her fear. He grabbed a photograph of Ali off Gigi's table and passed it to her. "Look at this girl. Remember what it's like to be her, and you'll turn back."

Ali followed his instructions. Bit by bit, the wrinkles smoothed themselves, her spine straightened, and the protruding veins receded. A few minutes later she was herself again, though her forehead and back were slick with sweat.

"It's not easy to turn back when you're first learning," said Digger. "That's why it's so important to practice."

Ali voiced the fear that had held her hostage since debate team. "How do I not turn into other people at school?"

> ALI'S RULES FOR BEING
> A COPYCAT
> 1. Concentrate.
> 2. Don't be afraid.
> 3. Don't let anyone know
>   you're a Copycat.
> 4. Try to have fun.
>   (This will take time.)

"The key is to focus on being yourself and remembering who you are," said Gigi. "Don't think too much about other people. Otherwise, you'll start to change."

Ali's eyes bugged; that was pretty much *all* she did at school.

Digger leaned down so he was looking straight at her. "It sounds weird, but Copycats need to always be themselves."

"But you spend half your day as a dog!"

"Yes, because I need to."

"But why do you need to?" she pressed.

Digger stood up. "I just do." It was clear that subject was closed. "When you go to school tomorrow, focus on *your* thoughts, *your* memories. Don't worry about anyone else. If you start to feel like you're about to change, go to the washroom until the feeling passes. It doesn't last long if you haven't changed."

Gigi jumped in. "In the beginning, you'll be like a foal learning to walk, Alison. Everything will feel awkward. But the most important thing to remember is to not use your powers against other people or for gain."

"What does that mean?"

"Some of us use our abilities for personal gain or for horrible reasons. And we have more than our fair share of thieves. There is a rumor that Jack the Ripper was a Copycat."

The hair on the back of Ali's arms stood up.

"It's a lot to take in," said Digger, anxious to change the subject. "In the end, we have to live by the same rules as Constants: be kind, don't hurt other people, and don't take what you don't need. And for your own safety, don't let anyone know you have these abilities."

"But you told Mom when you met her."

"Not for quite a while, and not until I was sure I could trust her. People can't always be trusted. . . ." His voice trailed off.

Ali sensed there was an untold story, but given Digger's personality, it was unlikely she'd ever learn what had happened. It occurred to her that she didn't need to know the details. Just thinking of the horrified expression on Cassie's face was proof enough that Digger was right. But she wouldn't dwell on that tonight. Not when she'd just discovered that her new skills were also fun. She was itching to change into something else. "Can I turn into something and show Mom?"

Digger beamed.

Ten minutes later, Hermione Granger and her dog joined Ali's mother in the kitchen.

"What am I going to do with you two?" her mother asked. "I am now officially outnumbered in this house."

Gigi, who had hobbled down behind Ali and Digger,

shook her head. "Nope—it's even steven, Ginger. I haven't changed in years."

Ali morphed back. "Don't worry, Mom. I don't think I'm going to be running around as someone else all the time like Digger does."

Her mother reached down to stroke Digger the dog's head. "Oh, he's not so bad."

Afraid things were about to get mushy, Ali offered to help Gigi back to her room. She had so many questions, questions she probably should have asked Digger years ago, and she knew she'd be more successful getting answers from Gigi.

"Why do you think we have these powers?" she asked when she'd settled Gigi in bed.

Gigi patted the spot next to her. "Do you have enough energy for a good story? I know it can be tiring when a Copycat first learns how to use their powers."

Ali dropped onto the bed and cuddled up to Gigi. "Is this a true story or make-believe?"

"I guess that depends upon the person hearing the story. Once upon a time . . ."

Chapter Six
HARNESSING FOG

Since ancient times, the condensation from fog has been gathered using rudimentary fog catchers, typically draped cloth that is later wrung out. There is no record that I can find of the use of such fog catchers in the Bay of Fundy.

—PERCIVAL T. SLOANE,
A History of Fog in the Bay of Fundy *(1932)*

See if G. G. will lend me and Digger some old sheets.

By the way, I'm never getting married—Digger

You better. I'm not taking care of you forever
—Teddy

SEVENTEEN

"The story shouldn't begin with once upon a time if it's the truth," said Ali. Her day had been fantastical enough without Gigi making things up.

"Humph. You're right, but theoretically, even if it's true, it did start once upon a time."

Ali gave her a hard stare.

"Fine, fine. How about this? A long time ago in a galaxy far, far away . . ."

"Gigi!"

"Fine. I'll just jump in. According to Sloane family lore, the first time a Copycat appeared in the Sloane family tree was in 1773. Her name was Euphemia Stewart Sloane. Stewart was her maiden name. She was a domestic servant traveling with a Scottish family named MacKenzie who were emigrating to Canada aboard a ship called the *Hector*. She was so inconsequential, which I suppose a lot of servants were in those days, that her name isn't recorded in the ship's manifest."

"What's a manifest?"

"A record of who and what a ship carries."

"But if Euphemia wasn't listed in the manifest, how do we know she was on board?"

Gigi pushed her glasses down her nose and turned to look at Ali. "We know. Now do you want me to tell the story or not?"

"Tell the story."

"Thank you. The *Hector* was a ship well past her prime, used to transport immigrants to North America. Her boards were rotting, and the people who'd organized the voyage jammed her full of more passengers than she was permitted to carry."

"Did they get in trouble?"

Gigi's face clouded over. "Unfortunately, no one

cared. You have to remember: it was the eighteenth century. Most of the passengers were desperate to start a better life. They didn't complain, at least not at first. But there were more people than berths to sleep in, the sanitation was horrendous, and there was not enough food for everyone."

Ali closed her eyes and imagined what it would be like to be crammed into the hull of a ship. It made her woozy; she hated confined spaces. "What happened?"

"Passengers became ill, and as a servant, it was Euphemia's job to help care for them. She was thirteen years old, and they worked her like a dog. It's amazing she didn't fall sick too."

"Thirteen years old," Ali repeated. "I'll be thirteen soon."

"The sickness spread as more passengers fell ill with chills, fever, diarrhea, and vomiting. It soon became clear that many were suffering from dysentery, a disease often caused by a bacterial infection in the intestines. No surprise, considering the living conditions. And then people started to die."

Ali shuddered. This was turning into a ghost story. "What happened to Euphemia?"

"She soldiered on, helping care for the others, until the ship was surrounded by a fog so thick it was impossible to continue, lest they run aground or ram into another ship. The captain dropped anchor, and they waited."

"How long were they stuck in the fog?"

"Three long days. It was on the second day that Euphemia changed for the first time. She was up on deck, taking a well-deserved rest. As she leaned against the railing, staring at the gray Atlantic waters, two sailors brought up another dead body—the fourth in as many days. It was a young child wrapped in cloth and bound with crisscrossing ropes to secure the fabric so it wouldn't fly off when the sailors tossed the body over. Though Euphemia knew that the dead were being disposed of this way, she had not seen it happen herself. The small corpse being tossed overboard was more than she could bear."

"Did she try to stop them?"

"There are conflicting reports about what happened next. A Mrs. MacKay claimed that Euphemia jumped overboard after the corpse, a story corroborated by a Mr. MacDonald, but one of the sailors swore he saw her run to the far end of the ship."

Ali was no longer cuddled up next to Gigi: she was sitting up, eyes wide, desperate to know how Euphemia's story would end. "Did anyone jump in to save her?"

"It was the eighteenth century; I doubt anyone knew how to swim. One thing was certain: she was gone. The MacKenzies were more angry than sad to lose their servant, but really, no one missed her. The next day the fog cleared, and the *Hector* went on her way. That evening, someone spotted Euphemia on the deck, looking the picture of health."

"How did she get there?"

"You're asking the same question the other passengers asked. She swore she'd fallen asleep inside an empty crate, and slept for two days straight due to exhaustion. Everyone was suspicious, for her cheeks were rosy and she appeared well fed. She began to care for the sick again, but she disappeared twice more before the ship docked in Pictou, Nova Scotia."

Gigi paused to cough, and Ali ran to get her a drink of water. When the spasm passed, the story resumed. "The living conditions in Pictou were not what was promised to the settlers: the housing was wretched or nonexistent, and they had no idea how to live in a land of trees and mosquitoes. According to the other settlers, the trip had changed Euphemia. She was no longer the docile servant who had followed the MacKenzies onboard; she was wild and willful and daring. One morning, while she was out working in a potato field, Euphemia stood up, shook the mud off her dress, and walked into the woods. Search parties sent to find her were unsuccessful. She was gone."

"But how is she a Copycat?"

"She returned six years later with a young son named Botsford, resplendent in silks and wools as fine as those worn by Governor Selkirk's wife. The MacKenzies were flummoxed by her change in status, which she refused to explain. Personally, I suspect she'd used her powers to make a new life for herself. Euphemia and her child stayed for a month, and one or the other of them would often disappear for extended periods of time. A young lad swore he saw Euphemia change into a gull and fly away. One of the MacKenzies' servants claimed that Botsford could change into a dog at will. They were the talk of the settlement, and the talk soon veered toward accusations of dark magic."

Cassie's words rang in Ali's ears. Poor Euphemia! "Did they burn them at the stake?"

Gigi chuckled. "Heavens no, for if they did, you and I wouldn't be here! No, the settlers were simple Scots, not much for putting people to death. One day Euphemia and Botsford woke up, thanked the MacKenzies, and left Pictou forever. But of course that wasn't the end of them. She met a blacksmith named Robert Sloane and moved to New Brunswick. Once a year she would leave her home and travel the world, searching for others who could do what she could do.

Some of the Copycats she met were so taken with her that they decided to settle in New Brunswick too. Even more impressive, she had twelve children."

"Twelve children!"

"Twelve children. Every one of whom was a Copycat."

"I get that we're descended from Euphemia, but you haven't explained—how did she get her powers in the first place?" Ali demanded. "Who were her parents? How many Copycats are there in the world?"

"What I know about the history of the Sloane Copycats comes from Uncle Percy. Remember? He was the one who wrote the book about the fog I lent to you. He was an amazing storyteller."

The dull book filled with useless fog facts. Uncle Percy was *not* a good storyteller.

ALI'S RULES FOR MAKING SENSE OF THINGS
1. There is always a logical, scientific reason to explain why things happen.
2. There is no such thing as magic.
3. But if there IS magic, it requires rules too.

"How or why Euphemia came to have her powers, I can't answer. Maybe the shock of seeing that wee body tossed into the ocean made them spring to life. Some think that moisture in the air has something to do with it. Most Copycats live near the coast and favor foggy locales. And I have no idea how many of us there are in this world." She stopped. "Perhaps the fog triggered *your* abilities. Uncle Percy always said Copycats love the fog; it allows them to change in public if it's thick enough."

Ali slumped back against the pillow. Euphemia's story was interesting, but it raised more questions than it answered—the most important of which was why Copycats could change at all. Despite that lack of clarity, there was one thing Ali knew for sure: the world was governed by scientific laws. That meant Copycats were, too. She just needed to find out what they were.

EIGHTEEN

Ali was exhausted the next morning. She'd struggled to fall asleep, thanks in equal measure to her exhilaration about her new abilities and her dread about what would happen at school the next day. When she did sleep, her dreams were filled with dilapidated schooners and dead bodies. In the middle of the night, when Gigi's grandfather clock chimed four times, Ali woke in terror, tangled in her bedsheets, certain she was about to be tossed overboard. It was impossible to sleep after that, so she spent the rest of the night trying to figure out how to convince her parents to let her stay home from school.

Digger was immune to her pleas. "You'll have to

face Cassie sometime," he pointed out. "You might as well get it over with."

"What am I supposed to say to her?" demanded Ali, nibbling at the piece of cold toast she'd nursed for the past half hour. "Do you expect me to lie?"

"Not lie," said Digger. "Respond with creativity."

Which, as far as Ali could see, was the same as a lie.

"Besides, aren't you supposed to go to Emily's after school today to work on your project?"

Ali had forgotten about her commitment to Emily. "Fine, I'll go. But remember: if they arrest me at school, it's all your fault."

"Duly noted."

She'd almost made it to homeroom when Cassie pounced on her and pulled her into the empty computer lab. Except Cassie wasn't alone; Murray was waiting for them. He closed the door and the two of them faced Ali, who steeled herself for the worst.

"I owe you an apology," said Cassie.

Ali flinched, then shook her head. "Wait—what?"

Murray gave Cassie an encouraging nod, and the

girl continued. "I kind of freaked out yesterday. I shouldn't have. I could tell you were upset, and after I told Murray—"

Ali's eyes widened. "You told Murray?" This was worse than she'd expected.

Murray bobbed his head. "This is the biggest thing to happen at this school ever!"

Ali dropped into a nearby chair and put her head between her knees. On the way to school she'd played out possible scenarios. None involved Cassie and Murray acting thrilled.

Murray crouched down in front of her. "Was that the first time you ever changed? Did you know you *could* change?"

Cassie jumped in. "Could you hear what I was thinking? How did you change your clothes so they matched mine?"

"If I asked you to change into me right now, could you?" Murray asked.

The rapid-fire questions made Ali dizzy. Cassie squatted next to Murray and placed a tentative hand on Ali's arm. "Sorry for throwing all this at you. We're just trying to understand."

Ali's eyes filled with tears. "Well, that makes three of us," she said, then groaned. She'd forgotten that she was supposed to deny everything. Digger would *not* be impressed.

Murray smiled. "It's like you're a superhero or something."

"A superhero?"

"Sure. You are now the most interesting person at Princess Elizabeth School."

In spite of her predicament, Ali smiled. She'd never been the most *anything*.

"You don't drink something to make yourself change, do you, like Polyjuice Potion in Harry Potter, because if you do, could I try some?"

"No Polyjuice Potion."

Murray's shoulders sagged.

"Who else knows about your powers?" asked Cassie.

"Does Alfie?" added Murray.

"Just my family. Please don't tell Alfie."

"Why not?"

"My family doesn't want anyone to know in case we're subjected to weird experiments."

Murray nodded. "Makes sense. Okay, no telling Alfie. Can you turn into something right now, before school starts?"

"Don't turn into me," said Cassie. "I mean, I think it's cool and all," she hastened to add, "but do Murray this time."

The hall outside the classroom was beginning to fill with students. "I can't. Someone might see two Murrays."

Murray seemed disappointed. "You're right. How about something small, like a mouse?"

Ali wasn't a fan of mice. They were dirty and had the nasty habit of terrifying you when they darted out of places they had no business being in, like the cupboard under Gigi's sink. But Murray and Cassie were being so nice that it seemed rude not to try. She pictured the mouse she'd seen in Gigi's house last week, a fawn-colored thing with a tail twice the length of its body. Seconds later, she was perched on her hind legs, looking up at two gigantic faces.

"Wow!" whispered Cassie.

Murray was speechless.

Their gawking was interrupted by the morning bell.

"Change back!" whispered Murray. To Ali's tiny mouse ears, it was like bellowing.

Panicked, Ali struggled to turn back. But the deafening noise of students outside the computer lab, coupled with the flustered looks on Cassie and Murray's faces and her own inexperience as a Copycat, unnerved her.

"Hurry up!" Cassie was halfway to the door.

"Can't you change?" Murray asked.

A mortified Ali the mouse shook her whiskers.

> ALI'S RULES ABOUT WHY YOU SHOULDN'T CHANGE AT SCHOOL
> 1. School is dangerous enough as it is without putting yourself in physical danger.
> 2. No easy escape routes.
> 3. What if you can't change back?????

"We can't just leave her here," said Cassie. "What if someone stomps on her?"

Without asking, Murray reached down, grabbed Ali by the tail, and with one swift move, tossed her into his shirt pocket. "Sorry," he whisper-yelled at where a shocked Ali lay upside down in his pocket. "We'll figure you out later. Can't be late for class."

Cassie's monstrous eyes glanced in at where a squirming Ali tried to right herself. "I hope she can breathe."

"She'll be fine," Murray said, which made Ali furious, because how could he know that?

Ali was pummeled and buffeted like an astronaut blasting off into space as Murray ran toward homeroom. Could mice throw up? Ali wondered. A moment later she discovered they could. At least none of it landed on her.

"Did you just pee on me?" Murray demanded, looking down at the small wet spot in the corner of his shirt pocket.

"I wish I had" was Ali's angry retort, which came out as a squeak.

"Shh!" Cassie admonished. "We're going into class."

Murray took his seat, which was a relief to Ali's seasick stomach.

Ms. Ryder began taking attendance. "Here!" Murray boomed. Why was he so loud?

"Has anyone seen Ali Sloane?" Ms. Ryder asked. "I was sure I saw her arrive at school earlier this morning."

Ali held her breath.

"I don't think she was feeling well," Cassie called out. "Maybe she went to see the nurse?"

"Thanks, I'll go check on her after class. Get out your books, everybody; we'll get started right after morning announcements and the national anthem."

Murray peered into his pocket and smiled. "Don't change back," he mouthed.

"Did you say something, Murray?" Ms. Ryder asked.

Then: the *thwack, thwack, thwack* of the teacher's shoes coming their way, and the *boom-boom-boom* of Murray's racing heart. The footsteps stopped.

"What do you have in your shirt pocket, Murray?"

NINETEEN

At that moment, cowered in the corner of Murray's pocket, Ali made up a new animal rule: *Don't turn into an animal that someone can stomp on.* Now she understood why Digger changed into a big dog. What if Ms. Ryder pulled her out and threw her against the wall? Lots of people—herself included—hated mice. Wait, she didn't hate mice anymore; the last ten minutes had changed her perspective.

Murray made a slurping sound, which Ali realized was him sucking in his breath.

"Well?"

When Murray didn't respond,

> ALI'S ANIMAL RULES (AMENDED)
> 1. It would be nice if the dog in your house wasn't your father.
> 2. Wild animals belong OUTDOORS!!!
> 3. Don't turn into an animal that someone can stomp on.

Ms. Ryder leaned over and peered into the pocket. Her eyes widened, as did Ali's, and she jumped back.

"Why do you have a mouse in your pocket?" she squawked.

The class exploded into three kinds of responses: kids squealing in fear, kids laughing, and kids begging to see the mouse.

Ms. Ryder regained her composure and shouted over the racket. "Why do you have a mouse in your pocket, Murray?"

"I . . . I found it on the way to class," Murray stammered.

"And you decided to bring it here?"

"Uh . . ." Murray was at a loss for words.

Cassie saved the day. "It was my fault. I told him it would be fun to keep the mouse until after lunch and show it to the other kids in science class. We're studying the classification of species."

Ms. Ryder cleared her throat. "Do you think it was kind to trap a poor defenseless mouse in your pocket for hours? I'm sure it's scared to death."

Ali, enjoying Murray being chewed out by the teacher, nodded.

"You'll excuse yourself and go put the mouse outside. And I mean, outside the school, not outside the classroom."

Uh-oh.

Murray stood up.

"Can we see the mouse before he puts it outside?" Emily called.

Ms. Ryder sounded exasperated. "Fine." The intercom crackled, and Principal Birchwood began the morning announcements as Ali was picked up by the scruff of her neck. Terrified of being dropped, she did her best to stay motionless as Murray paraded her around the classroom. Some of the kids recoiled, Tom Power begged to hold her, and Emily leaned over and ran her index finger over Ali's fur.

"It's beautiful," she whispered. "Isn't it weird that the mouse's eyes are gray?"

If Ali weren't so tiny, she might have kicked herself.

"That's enough of today's mouse show," said Ms.

Ryder, pointing to the door. "Take it outside and then wash your hands before rejoining us, please and thank you, Murray."

Out in the hallway, Murray eyed Ali. "Change back. I don't want to put you outside." They began to walk toward the double doors that opened onto the playground.

Ali didn't want to be put outside either, but she couldn't calm down enough to change back. They were almost to the door when the national anthem began. Murray stopped and began to sing along, which, for some reason, seemed so funny to her that she stopped being upset. By the time the song was halfway done she was able to picture herself, and after several deep breaths, she began to change back.

"What the—" Murray shouted, drawing his hand back in fright and dropping Ali the mouse. Fortunately for her, by the time she hit the floor she was Ali the girl again.

An angry Ms. Ryder poked her head out of the classroom. "Keep your voice down, Murray! Oh, there you are, Ali. I assume you got rid of the mouse, Murray?"

A chastened Murray nodded.

"Good. Now get inside, you two; I've had enough drama this morning."

"*She's* had drama," Murray muttered.

Lunchtime was strange. Murray, Cassie, and Ali didn't say much, though they exchanged significant glances whenever Alfie wasn't looking. Alfie seemed oblivious; he was too busy telling them about a movie he'd watched the night before.

"It was so cool," he said, his legs bouncing up and down so hard it made the table jiggle. "It was about this robot from the future that could change into anything!"

Murray raised an eyebrow at Ali and she scowled. She was *not* a robot.

"Anything?" Cassie asked.

"Anything. It kept fooling people because it could look like their friends, their pets, anything. It was unstoppable."

Cassie leaned forward, enthralled. "But if it was unstoppable, how did they stop it?"

"The heroine figured out how to turn him off. We should all watch it together sometime."

"It sounds scary," said Ali. "I hate scary movies."

"It's not that scary. It's more thrilling than anything."

"It would be amazing to turn into other people," Murray mused. "Remember when Harry and Ron turned into Crabbe and Goyle in *Harry Potter and the Chamber of Secrets*?"

Murray was turning into a blabbermouth.

"I've never read a Harry Potter book," said Alfie. His grin was wicked; he knew Murray's head was about to explode.

"YOU'VE NEVER READ HARRY POTTER?" Murray spluttered.

As the two boys got into it, Cassie whispered in Ali's ear. "Want to hang out after school? We could work on your *thing*."

Cassie was too loud. "What thing?" asked Alfie.

"Oh, you know, a school project," said Cassie, shrugging.

"What kind of project?"

Ali saved the day. "I can't hang out; I'm going to Emily Arai's house after school to work on our science project."

Alfie furrowed his brow. "But aren't you and Cassie working on a project?"

"It's a different thing," said Cassie. "I forgot you got stuck with Emily Arai. Poor you."

"You don't like Emily?" Ali asked, surprised. Everybody seemed to love Emily Arai.

Cassie snorted.

"She's not that bad, Cass," said Murray.

"Whatever," Cassie said.

Murray didn't know when to stop talking. "They used to be friends when they were younger, but they don't get along anymore."

Cassie snatched up her lunch box. "I'm leaving."

"Well, that was awkward," Alfie said as the three of them watched Cassie's receding back. "Is there something in the air today? You guys are acting strange."

Murray shrugged. "It's the fog, man. It's making everybody weird."

Chapter Seven
FOG AND MENTAL HEALTH

My mother always put me in my place when I complained of the fog as a child. "The sun is up there, Percy, always. You must trust in that." I have never forgotten her sage wisdom.

—PERCIVAL T. SLOANE,
A History of Fog in the Bay of Fundy *(1932)*

TWENTY

"Murray's mouse" was the number-one topic for the rest of the school day. Opinion was divided about whether Ms. Ryder was right or wrong when she'd made Murray put it outside. There was such a heated debate in science class as to what a mouse's natural habitat actually was—Emily argued that Ms. Ryder had kicked the mouse out of its home— that Mr. Corby said he hoped more animals moved into Princess Elizabeth School. Ali pretended to ignore Murray's and Cassie's constant stares. If they weren't careful, her secret wouldn't survive the day.

Emily was still talking about the mouse on the

bus ride to her house after school. "I'm so sorry you missed it. You would have loved it so much!"

Ali gave a half-hearted nod.

The Arais lived in a massive house overlooking the Bay of Fundy in uptown Saint John. Emily pointed to the bay, shrouded in thick fog. "We usually have an amazing view."

"When I was little, I used to think you could walk on clouds," said Ali, staring into the milky void. "Now it feels like we're living in them." She turned her attention to the house, which was stunning, with its beautiful brickwork, expansive sunroom, and third-floor tower topped with a spiky fence that made you think of a haunted house in a movie.

"It's called a widow's watch," Emily said, like she was used to people admiring her house. "In the olden days, sailors' wives would wait and watch for their husbands' ships to return. A lot of them never did, which is when they started calling them widow's watches."

Ali shivered. It made her sad to think someone

stood up there, waiting for someone who might not have returned.

Emily nudged her. "Let's go in."

Ali followed her inside, stopping again when they stepped into an enormous two-story foyer. A grand staircase curled its way to the second floor, past a chandelier hung with dozens of glass disks that twinkled on the shiny marble floor below. Several fancy rooms opened off the foyer, all of them magazine worthy and so neat it was like nobody used them.

"I'll grab my phone and then we can go. We're going to the park, Mom!" Emily shouted.

"All right!" a voice in the distance called back.

"My mom's into watching some kind of home makeover show," Emily explained. "You'll meet her when we come back." Ali followed her up the stairs, feeling like Cinderella at the ball.

Emily's bedroom was what every teenager's bedroom should look like: canopied bed, vanity table, ruffled curtains. There was even a walk-in closet and a private bathroom!

"Your room is beautiful," murmured Ali as she stared at a picture of Emily on the wall with her arms wrapped around Mickey Mouse at Disney World.

Emily grabbed her phone off her desk. "Thanks, but I think it's kind of over the top. My mom hired a decorator."

Ali thought of some of the places she and her parents had lived in: squalid dumps with broken windows, leaking toilets, and screaming neighbors. Emily's house was so soundproof you couldn't hear the traffic going by. She started when she realized Emily was staring at her.

"What? Do I have something on my face?"

Emily giggled. "I'm worried you won't be warm enough. Want to borrow a sweater?"

Ali had wondered the same thing when she'd stepped off the bus. Her thin windbreaker was no match for the fog's icy tentacles. The idea of borrowing one of Emily's lovely sweaters was tempting, but also humiliating.

Emily pulled open a built-in cupboard where at

least two dozen sweaters were stacked in perfect flat squares like in department stores. "I bet you forgot we were going to be outside today," she said, running her fingers along the edge of the sweaters until she reached a cardigan that was the same color as the vivid geraniums in Gigi's window boxes. She pulled it out, careful not to mess up the other sweaters, and tossed it over to Ali.

"This will look nice with your dark hair and pale skin. You can give it back tomorrow."

Ali ran her hand down the sleeves, mesmerized by the soft yarn. "Thanks."

"It's cashmere," explained Emily. "The only kind of sweater my mom buys. They're made from the wool of some fancy goats in Nepal or something."

Ali pictured goats hopping around Mount Everest dressed in multicolored sweaters like the ones in Emily's cupboard. She was glad Emily couldn't see the secondhand sweaters, with their multiple snags and holes, jammed into her dresser at home. Even after she put on her windbreaker and they left Emily's house, she continued to steal looks at the wonderful cashmere.

The park, King's Square, topped a steep hill and was surrounded by the City Market, the Imperial Theatre, and several tall buildings. Ali knew Emily had made the right choice when she saw all the people and animals. This was the perfect spot for a field study.

"I'll take pictures, and you take notes about what we see," Emily said.

First on the list was an old lady tossing peanuts at a dozen chubby gray squirrels, followed by a young man throwing a Frisbee to a German shepherd. A flock of pigeons sat atop the bandstand; their strangled *ooh-ooh-ooh* calls made Ali smile. A speckled frog hopped among a bed of asters. The list of organisms grew:

- fourteen squirrels
- two chipmunks
- twenty-two pigeons (except they kept flying away, so this was a guess)
- four dogs

- five sparrows
- one worm
- one frog
- one rabbit (someone was carrying it)
- forty-eight trees (then Ali lost count)
- thirty-eight people
- six hundred flowers (Ali guessed the number)

As they walked back to Emily's house, they discovered even more organisms:

- eighteen squirrels
- six chipmunks
- eight crows
- three blue jays
- bacteria (in a puddle)
- three toadstools
- eighty-seven trees
- one hundred-plus bushes
- two hundred-plus flowers in pots or planted
- twelve dogs

- twenty-four cats
- fifty-seven people

They cheered whenever they spotted something new. Despite her fancy clothing, Emily was willing to kneel on the ground to get the perfect close-ups of puddles and toadstools. They laughed so much that Ali was giddy. She realized with a start that she hadn't worried once during the trip, thanks to the magic of Emily. For the first time in days, she was as light as the fine mist in the air.

It seemed Emily felt the same way. "This was so much fun."

Ali smiled. "It was, wasn't it?"

Emily stopped. She turned to Ali, eyes shining. "Are you in a hurry?"

Ali looked at her watch. "No. My dad's not picking me up for another hour."

"Want to go on an adventure?"

"What kind of adventure?" Experience had taught Ali that it wasn't safe to assume all adventures were fun. Her parents called their multiple moves "adventures," when the better description would have been "tortures."

Emily began to hop from foot to foot. "Mom says there's seals at Tin Can Beach."

"I heard that on the radio."

"Want to go see them? I know they're not on the block we're studying, but it would be fun and we could tell the class about them during our presentation. It's only a ten-minute walk, so we can go down, take some pictures, and be back with loads of time before your dad comes."

Time wasn't Ali's concern. "Do seals bite?"

"I bet they're too cute to bite! But if you're worried, we'll keep our distance just to be sure. *Please.*"

Emily's plea overcame Ali's natural timidity. "Okay."

"Yay!" Emily linked her arm through Ali's. "You are so not going to regret this!"

TWENTY-ONE

Tin Can Beach wasn't always named after the garbage that washed aground on its rocky shore. A century before, it had been Rockaway Beach, a favored summer haunt for Saint Johners who swam and picnicked on hot summer days where the south end of the city jutted out into the bay. During World War II, the bathing houses and canteens gave way to a military installation, a watchful presence to guard against a potential Nazi invasion. When the soldiers left, the sugar refinery came. Later it lapsed into a neglected world, surrounded by barbed wire, a desolate spot favored by wildlife, the odd criminal, and a resting spot for what the bay no longer needed. The city was in the process of reclaiming the beach, though it had yet to return to its former glory. But Ali knew none of this as she walked down Sydney Street with Emily; all she cared about was that her new friend wanted her to go on an adventure.

"I've never been to this part of the city before," she confessed as they made their way down the hill, the fog thickening with every block.

Emily was a natural tour guide, although the landmarks she pointed out were shrouded in mist. "There's Rainbow Park, over there are the armories, and that's a construction company. Ahead, where the road turns left, is Tin Can Beach." The two passed through a barrier of garbage cans and picked their way through a patch of scrubby grass that gave way to the rocky shore.

The seal herd was about twenty feet from the water. Ali did a quick count: nine seals, clumped together like they'd just finished playing ring-around-the-rosy and had all fallen down. "They're so big," she whispered. Their fur was a pale brownish beige, and all of them were covered in spots of varying sizes that made it look as if someone had splattered black paint on them by mistake. Ali inhaled, enjoying the smell of wet fur and salt.

The seals weren't the only life on the beach. A group of young boys, their hands in their pockets, stood bunched together eyeing the seals. Of greater interest were the man and woman who circled the seals in matching rain slickers and rubber boots. The woman carried a metal clipboard and was taking notes. The man held an expensive-looking camera with a six-inch lens that he clicked nonstop as he attempted to capture every angle of each seal.

At first the two girls hung back, but then Emily stepped forward and approached the woman, pulling Ali with her. "Are the seals all right?" she asked.

The woman paused to look up and smile. "Most of them seem quite healthy."

The man stopped taking pictures and clambered over the damp stones to join them. "Most of them are sleeping."

Emily crouched down and stared at the face of the closest seal. "Kingdom: Animalia. Phylum: Chordata. Class: Mammalia. Order: Carnivora," she recited.

"Impressive," said the man.

"We're studying classification in science at school," Ali explained. "Today we're doing a field study of all the organisms in uptown Saint John."

"Looks like we have a couple of future marine biologists with us, David," said the woman. Both Emily and Ali puffed out a little.

"I didn't know seals were carnivores," said Ali.

The man nodded. "Don't worry, they eat fish, although they have been known to eat the odd duck. They're also known as pinnipeds, because—"

"They're fin footed," Emily finished.

Ali shook her head. "How do you even know that?"

Emily smiled. "I searched online last night."

"I'm impressed," said the man. "Lots of people have come to see the seals since they came ashore, but none have been quite as educated as you two." He slung his camera over his shoulder and stuck out his hand. "My name's Doctor David McAloon. I'm chief zoologist for the New Brunswick Museum." He nodded to the woman. "And this is Doctor Abby Reynolds. She's a marine biologist who works for the Huntsman Marine Science Center in St. Andrews. It's not every day we have a pod of seals come ashore in the heart of the city. It seems the fog is stranding everyone and everything."

"They're so cute," Emily murmured. She reached out to pat the closest seal. It opened its eyes and made a strange raspy sound, and Emily drew back her hand. Ali stared at the seal. There was a slick ring around its eyes that made it look like it was crying.

"No touching," said Dr. Reynolds. "They seem gentle until they take a chunk out of you."

Emily jumped to her feet and backed up until she was beside Ali. "But they're so sweet!"

Dr. McAloon chuckled. "Being cute doesn't mean they aren't dangerous." Ali had met enough mean kids over the years to know Dr. McAloon was right.

Emily pulled out her phone and took several

pictures while Ali continued to watch the seal. "Why do its eyes look so gross?"

The zoologist smiled. "Seals have a protective ring of mucus around their eyes that keeps them moist when they're out of the water. It works, but it also makes it difficult for our fellow here to see well."

"You'll be interested to know that seals don't see in color," Dr. Reynolds added. "In other words, we look like a bunch of gray blobs to him."

The seal closed its eyes again.

"If they only see gray blobs, how do they find each other on shore?" asked Ali.

"They rely on smell and hearing," the zoologist said.

"How do they find their way home if they're nowhere near other seals?" said Emily.

Dr. Reynolds smiled. "It's a bit of a mystery, but they seem to find a way."

"How long do you think they'll stay here?" Ali asked.

"I suppose until the fog lessens. We suspect they

got lost and ended up here," said Dr. McAloon. "Of course, they can't tell us their itinerary, so your guess is as good as mine."

Ali stared at the herd. Toward the center, one of the seals had a patchy coat, and in places the fur had rubbed off completely. As if it could sense she was watching, it opened its eyes. Unlike the other seals, its eyes were a milky gray and mucus-free. She pointed it out to Dr. Reynolds. "Is that one sick?"

> ALI'S RULES FOR HAVING
> AN ADVENTURE
> 1. Try not to be afraid.
> 2. Don't be shy (or maybe don't be AS shy).
> 3. Keep your eyes and ears open.
> 4. Be prepared to learn something about yourself. Example: the word "outlier" is way better than Copycat!

"We're not sure. The rest of the herd is quite protective of him, so maybe. Another sign of poor health is that he's shedding his fur, which is unusual, because typically seals do that early in the year. We suspect he's blind, because there's no mucus. Of course, there are always outliers."

"Outliers?" Ali asked.

"Something that's different, but may be still normal," said Emily.

Ali could relate. She liked how scientific "outlier" sounded, versus the term "Copycat."

The scientists returned to their data collection. The girls continued to watch the seals for several minutes, neither speaking. Emily glanced down at her watch. "We'd better get going."

They said goodbye to the scientists and trudged back up Sydney Street.

"Wasn't that amazing?" breathed Emily.

Ali nodded. "I'm so glad we went to see them." And she was, though she couldn't stop thinking about the sick seal. It made her sad.

"Wait until we tell everyone at school tomorrow," Emily crowed. "We really are explorers, aren't we? I bet everyone will want to go to Tin Can Beach to see the seals now."

The idea that everyone at school would know that she and Emily had an adventure made Ali smile. Everyone would know who she was and want to hang out with her, too. The day hadn't started well, but the ending was like a fairy tale.

TWENTY-TWO

Like the rest of Emily's house, the kitchen was perfect. It belonged on a cooking show, not in someone's home. Pink-frosted cupcakes were arranged on a fancy footed plate next to two tall glasses of milk and pink linen napkins that Ali was afraid to use. Mrs. Arai, dressed in a silk party dress, hurried into the kitchen and extended her hand to Ali.

"I'm so happy to meet you, Ali. Did you girls have fun?"

"We went to see the seals down at Tin Can Beach!" Emily said. "Amazing!"

Mrs. Arai gave her a distracted "That's nice," then pointed to a laptop sitting on the island. "Your dad just sent over the commercial for us to look at. Do you want to watch it?"

"Yes!" Emily noted the confused look on Ali's face and said, "Every year my dad makes a new TV commercial for his law firm. This year Mom and I are in it too. Want to see?"

Ali licked some pink frosting off her ring finger and leaned over to watch. As soon as Mrs. Arai hit play, Emily's father's face filled the screen.

"One day soon, you're going to need a lawyer," Mr. Arai said, his voice serious but kind. "And when that day comes, I want you to call me. Because I'll treat you with the same love and respect I give my family."

Then the camera cut away, and there were Emily's parents and Emily, walking arm in arm along a sandy beach, laughing and smiling like they were the most perfect family ever.

"There's me!" Emily squealed.

The camera zoomed in on Mr. Arai again. This time his face was super serious. "I'm Joseph Arai, and I won't stop fighting for YOU." He said the word "you" loud, like he wanted the audience to know he meant business. Then the screen changed, and Mr. Arai was replaced by a black screen with the phone number and address of the Arai law firm.

"Wasn't that wonderful, Mom?" Emily asked.

Mrs. Arai's smile was strained when she nodded. Her eyes were pink, as if she'd been crying. Ali couldn't imagine anyone who lived in a house like this could ever be sad.

"Do you need a ride home?" she asked Ali.

"No, my dad should be here any minute."

"Wonderful. I'll leave you girls to your fun." Mrs. Arai disappeared through a nearby door. The echo of her high heels clicking down the hallway sounded glamorous.

Emily dug into another cupcake. "Today was awesome! I wish I wasn't so busy all the time; we could hang out more."

"Me too."

Without looking up, Emily said, "Do you and Cassie hang out a lot?"

"At school." Ali tensed, wondering where this was going.

"I guess she hangs out with Murray most of the time."

"I guess. I don't know them all that well; we just met." As soon as the words escaped her mouth, a pang of guilt made Ali wince. Why had she said that? Besides her family, Cassie and Murray knew more about her than anybody ever had.

Emily's voice was neutral when she responded. "I guess they have a lot in common. Cassie and Murray, I mean."

"I guess."

"What's your cousin like?"

"Nice. I don't know him very well either."

Emily sighed. "It must be fun, having a fresh start. I'd love to move somewhere new."

Clearly Emily had never moved before, otherwise she wouldn't romanticize what it was like to move to a new place and have to make new friends. "It can be hard sometimes," said Ali.

Emily cocked her head, like Ali's comment was unfathomable. "I think it would be great."

Maybe it would be, if you were Emily. Ali suspected Emily would be popular wherever she lived. She realized she was still wearing Emily's sweater and began to pull it off.

Emily held up her hand. "No—wait . . . you keep it. It looks so good on you!"

"I can't." Her parents wouldn't want her to take other kids' clothes.

"Yes, you can! You saw my closet; it's stuffed with so many clothes I don't wear half of the things in there! Wear it tomorrow. It'll be like we're twins!"

Ali left the sweater on. She wanted to tell Emily something interesting. "Guess what? I'm planning a birthday party for my great-grandmother. She's going to be one hundred years old."

"Really? I love parties! My mom throws parties all the time for my dad's law firm, and sometimes she lets me help. What's the theme?"

"Theme?"

"You know, is it going to be a circus party, a cowboy-themed party, a French-style party with all kinds of Eiffel Tower decorations, a movie-star party. . . ." Emily's voice trailed off, and she gave Ali an expectant look.

Taken aback, Ali sifted through the suggestions. The only things she'd planned on were a birthday cake, balloons, and maybe a piñata. An image of the Walter Pidgeon shrine popped into her head. "Maybe a movie-star party?"

"I love movie-star parties! Mom throws one every year for the Academy Awards. All of her friends dress up in fancy gowns and tuxedos and she rolls out a red carpet for them. She even buys little toy Oscars at the dollar store. You can decorate the cake with gold stars."

Ali pictured Gigi cutting into a fancy cake surrounded by miniature Oscars and knew immediately it was a good idea. But she also knew there wasn't a big budget for Gigi's birthday party. In fact, thanks to all the Copycat stuff, she hadn't even talked to her parents about it yet.

"Mom!" Emily hollered.

Emily's mother appeared seconds later, as if she'd been hanging around offstage waiting to make her entrance. "Is everything okay?"

"Can we lend Ali the red carpet for a party she's throwing for her great-grandmother?"

For the first time since they'd met, Ali saw genuine excitement on Emily's mother's face. "Of course! Are you doing a movie-themed party?" she asked.

"Uh-huh. My great-grandmother loves Walter Pidgeon."

"I do too! What fun! I still have a few of those dollar-store Oscars," she mused aloud. "And I think I even have some gold balloons left. You're welcome to all of it."

"Are you sure?" Ali breathed. Getting things for free would help.

"Of course! They're in a closet in the basement. Let me go grab them." She rushed away.

"Your mom is so nice," said Ali.

Emily nodded. "Yeah, though I kind of wish she

had a job. She's always here, hovering."

"Sounds like my dad. On the other hand, I wish my mom was home more. She works long hours at a nursing home."

"Like my dad. He works all the time. Do your parents get along?"

It was an odd question, but Ali didn't want to be rude by not answering. "I guess."

Emily nodded. "Mine too." But she didn't sound certain.

The doorbell rang. "That must be my dad," said Ali, hopping off her stool and popping the last bite of cupcake in her mouth.

Digger stepped inside just as Mrs. Arai came down the hallway carrying a large canvas tote filled with party supplies. When he saw Mrs. Arai, Digger's mouth dropped open.

"Tina?" There was no mistaking the surprise in his voice.

"Digger?" replied an equally flabbergasted Mrs. Arai.

"You guys know each other?" Emily asked.

Mrs. Arai blushed. "Digger and I went to high school together."

Given the blushing, Ali sensed that Digger and Mrs. Arai had been more than just friends in high school. From the way Emily's eyes narrowed, she'd realized the same thing. "You dated Ali's dad in high school?" She sounded scandalized. "Does Dad know?"

Mrs. Arai flicked a piece of lint off her dress. "I don't think your father would care about who I dated in high school, Emily." She passed the large tote to Ali and stuck out her hand to Digger. "It's been a long time."

Digger smiled. "It sure has."

"The last time I saw you, you and Teddy were running Teddy's underwear up the flagpole after graduation."

For the first time in a while, Digger laughed out loud, a real belly laugh that made Ali wish he laughed like that more often.

Emily was aghast. "You ran some guy's underwear up a flagpole?"

"It seemed like a good idea at the time," said Digger, oblivious to Emily's tone.

"This is so weird," Emily grumbled.

Ali didn't say anything, but she agreed with Emily. It was weird.

"What are you doing these days, Digger?" Mrs. Arai asked.

Carefree Digger became guarded. "This and that. We better get going, Ali-Cat. Your mom's going to wonder where we are." He pointed at the tote in Ali's arms. "What's all this?"

Mrs. Arai beamed. "Ali said you're planning a movie-themed party for your grandmother's birthday. I had some leftover party supplies and donated them to the cause."

Digger shot Ali a questioning look and smiled at Mrs. Arai. "We can't take all this."

"You can and you will. It'll just collect dust here. And your grandmother is such a legend. It would be my honor if you used them. The only thing I'd like back is the red carpet."

Digger paused. Ali could almost hear the argument in his head. In the end, he nodded. "Thank you, Tina, that's very generous. I'll be sure to tell my grandmother what you donated. I haven't seen a guest list, but I'm sure your family is on it."

> ALI'S DIGGER RULES
> (AMENDED)
> 1. Don't tell anyone that Digger is a Copycat.
> 2. Don't mention Teddy Sloane.
> 3. Don't force Digger to talk when he doesn't want to.
> 4. Don't complain. It won't change things.
> 5. Don't point out jobs in the newspaper to Digger.
> 6. Digger has MANY secrets!

"Hooray!" shouted Emily. "I love parties!"

Ali gave her a weak smile and wondered how much trouble she was in.

Digger reached for the front-door handle. "On that note, it's time to hit the road."

"I'll walk you out," said Mrs. Arai.

The two adults headed outside. Ali started to follow, but was held back by Emily.

"How strange was that?"

"Strange."

"Just think! You and I could have been sisters if our

parents had stayed together. I always wanted a sister. I hate being an only child."

Ali wouldn't want another mother. But Emily was right: being an only child was no fun. If she had a brother or sister, moving around might not have been so lonely.

Emily brightened. "How about this? As of right now, you are my long-lost sister." She put her arm around Ali's shoulder, pulled out her phone, and held it out in front of them. "Say 'Sisters'!" she cried. "I am so posting this." She captioned the picture SISTERS. "What's your phone number and username? I want to add you to my contacts so we can text."

"I don't have a phone," said Ali. From the appalled look on Emily's face, she might as well have told her she was a Copycat.

Emily eyed the phone in her hand. "Poor you! I couldn't live without my phone! Tell your parents you need one. Everybody has one!"

There was no money for Ali to have a phone. "I can give you Gigi's number."

Emily, who had recovered from the shock of learning Ali was phoneless, smiled and typed Gigi's number into her contacts. "Aren't you glad Mr. Corby put us together?"

Ali was so glad she was on the verge of tears. The truth was, Ali's friendships were fleeting. Over the years, there had been kids she was friendly with, but not *true* friends with, not friends you told your secrets to and had inside jokes with. Maybe she could have that with Emily.

"Mr. Corby is the best," she said, and she meant it.

Chapter Eight
PREDICTING FOG USING SCIENCE

Meteorologists decry their inability to predict the onset of fog with any certainty or to determine its likely duration. If accurate predictions are ever achieved, they might well save many a seagoing vessel.

—Percival T. Sloane,
    A History of Fog in the Bay of Fundy *(1932)*

I always get lost in the fog.
—T

You have no sense of direction.
–D

TWENTY-THREE

Digger was silent during the drive home. Ali assumed he was angry she hadn't told him about Gigi's party. Should she broach the subject with him now, or wait until they got home? In the end, she decided to postpone the discussion, hopeful her mother would be enthusiastic and bring Digger around. But it was a miserable ride home, thanks to the fog that gnarled traffic so badly that what should have been a ten-minute drive took half an hour instead. To take her mind off her father, Ali passed the time daydreaming about the seals down at Tin Can Beach. Were they warm enough? How long would they stay? Would the sick seal be okay?

Her mother was in the kitchen making spaghetti when they arrived. "There you are! Why are you so late?"

"The traffic was a mess," said Digger, dropping into a chair.

Ali's mother gave Ali a fierce hug. "I've been worried about you all day. How did it go with Cassie?"

Digger started. It was clear that in all the commotion at Emily's house, he'd forgotten about the situation with Cassie.

> ALI'S RULES FOR NOT FREAKING OUT YOUR PARENTS
> 1. Remain calm.
> 2. Change the subject.
> 3. Don't tell them you were a mouse at school. Or if you do, make it seem MUCH less exciting than it actually was.

"Good, but she told a boy named Murray about me."

Ali's parents exchanged a panicked look. Her mother pointed to the kitchen table. "Sit. Tell us everything so we know what we're dealing with."

Ali left nothing out: Cassie's apology, Murray's excitement. Now and then her mother asked questions of clarification. Digger said nothing. When Ali got to the part where she turned into a mouse and couldn't change back, he slipped into dog mode and crept under the table.

"But everything's okay," Ali called down to him. "They won't tell anyone."

Ali's mother stuck her head under the table. "Come out, Digger. Ali's right; if they were going to tell someone else, they already would have."

Digger crawled out from under the table and became himself again. "We should have practiced changing into animals last night," he muttered. "There's so much you need to learn."

"We can practice after supper," Ali offered, but her suggestion didn't improve his mood.

There was a splutter as the pasta pot began to boil over. Ali's mother jumped up and raced to turn down the heat. "Did everything go okay with Emily?" she called over her shoulder.

"It was great. We did our organism inventory at King's Square, and then we went down to Tin Can Beach and visited the stranded seals. There were some nice scientists there. They were impressed by how much Emily and I knew about classification systems. And guess what?"

"What?"

"Digger knows Emily's mother."

Ali's mom crossed her arms and smiled at Digger. "Another old girlfriend?"

"A friend," Digger corrected. "If she liked anyone, she liked Teddy. Like I said, all the girls liked Teddy."

"So you keep telling me."

Digger seemed anxious to change the subject. "Do you know what Ali's done? She's decided to throw a birthday party for Gigi. And she got Tina Arai to give her all kinds of party things."

"She wasn't using them!" Ali protested. "Besides, we should throw her a party! Turning one hundred is a big deal!"

Her mother was as enthusiastic as she'd hoped. "That's a great idea!"

"It'll be a movie-themed party. You know, because Gigi loves Walter Pidgeon so much."

"That sounds fun. Her birthday is a week from this

Saturday. Why don't we do it then?" Ali could tell her mother was getting excited. "Who will we invite? Her neighbors, her—"

"Not too many people," begged Digger.

"I invited Alfie," said Ali.

The room went quiet. "What did he say?" asked Digger.

"He wants to come, but he won't unless the rest of his family comes, and they won't unless his grandfather does."

"Then don't expect Alfie" was Digger's bitter reply.

Ali's mother drained the pasta water through a colander and began to heap four plates with spaghetti and sauce. "We should invite them," she said as she placed the plates on the table.

"Alfie's going to ask him," said Ali. Digger snorted.

Ali's mother smiled. "Maya Angelou said, 'And let faith be the bridge you build to overcome evil and welcome good.' My money is on Alfie. Now enough moaning and groaning. Go get Gigi, Ali, and not another word about this birthday party. We can make it a wonderful surprise for her."

* * *

Ali spent the evening learning how to change into animals. They practiced in the living room because Gigi was tired and had gone back to bed right after supper. Her mother knitted in the corner as Digger tried to coach Ali through three unsuccessful attempts to change into a chipmunk.

"Try to focus on its stripes," he suggested.

Ali pictured one of the chipmunks she and Emily had photographed in the park. Which made her think of the beautiful red sweater she was still wearing. After two more tries, she managed to change into one. It was fun, sprinting under the couch, hopping from chair to chair, stuffing bits of cookie her mom held out to her into her mouth until her cheeks bulged to the size of fat acorns . . . but she was glad when Digger talked her through the steps to change back to herself. Chipmunks used a *lot* of energy.

"How did I do?"

"You did great," said her mother. "Except you had a bright red stripe down your back."

Whoops. "How do I make sure that I change perfectly?" Ali asked.

Digger bit his lip, perplexed. "Huh. That's rarely happened to me. I think you need to concentrate harder."

Concentrate harder? That's all she seemed to do these days!

Digger seemed to sense her frustration. "You'll get there. How did you feel when you were a mouse this morning?"

"I kind of panicked," she confessed.

"A lot of Copycats panic in the beginning. They worry that if they don't change back right away, they'll never change back, which just makes things worse."

"Did you ever have trouble changing back?"

"No, but I was encouraged to practice from when I was a baby. Practice makes perfect."

"Maya once said, 'Nothing will work unless you do,'" offered her mother.

Digger nodded. "Maya's right; it's going to take time for you to learn how to transform easily. I want you to practice at least two hours every day. Remember—you *know* you can change back, because you've changed back before and you've seen me and Gigi do it."

Ali placed a hand on each cheek. They were still sore from being puffed out. "Gigi never changes."

"I've never seen her change either," Ali's mother chimed in.

"You're right. I forget that she hasn't changed in years. I think she lost her abilities around the time she turned eighty. Most Copycats stop changing when they get very old. I think it's too hard on our bodies."

"Do you think it makes her sad that she can't change anymore?"

Digger's shoulders hunched a little and he took a deep breath before he responded. "I do. When the day comes that I can't change, I don't know what I'll do. No matter where I am or what I'm doing, there's always the urge to be something else."

Ali didn't like to think that Digger didn't prefer to be his human self. "Has a Copycat ever been stuck as something else for a long time?"

Digger chuckled. "Gigi told me that her uncle Percy was once stuck as a rat for forty-two days, much to his wife's distress. He chalked his inability to turn back into himself up to a bacterial infection he picked up as a rat wandering the Saint John docks."

Ali was glad she'd spent her time as a mouse safe in Murray's shirt pocket. Who knew what kind of disease she might have contracted if Murray had been forced to put her outside!

"Can we turn into *any* living thing? Like a tree?" Ali asked after spending ten minutes as an ant, which was super scary, because she was worried something bigger would gobble her up.

"I tried to turn into a tree once, but it didn't work. As far as I know, Copycats can only turn into sentient creatures." He smiled at the puzzled expression on Ali's face. "Creatures that can feel or perceive things."

"Huh. Does it scare you and Mom that Murray and Cassie know about me?"

The glance her parents exchanged answered her question.

Her mother put down her knitting and joined Ali and Digger on the floor. "We are a little worried," she said, rubbing Ali's shoulder. "I'm sure they're nice kids, but—"

"People are lousy at keeping secrets," Digger finished. "There's been many times in history when persecution arose because someone saw a Copycat change. But lots of humans don't see physical, intellectual, or spiritual differences as bad things. And to be fair, Copycats can be dangerous if they aren't trained or aren't good people."

"Gigi said that too. Did you ever know a Copycat who wasn't a good person?"

"Nope. Copycats guard their secrets well. Most of the time," he added, raising an eyebrow at Ali. "But there are always risk-takers. Okay, enough talk. You need to practice. How about a lion this time?"

TWENTY-FOUR

Ali wore Emily's sweater to school the next day and received five compliments about it before homeroom. The sweater, like Emily, seemed to have magical powers that drew you to it like a magnet. Emily squealed with delight and ran up to Ali as soon as she walked into homeroom. At opposite ends of the classroom, Cassie and Taylor crossed their arms.

"You look so pretty!" said Emily. "Guess what? I told my father all about your great-grandmother's party, and he says we can come. But I have some bad news."

Ali's stomach clenched. "What?"

"I forgot my parents are taking me out to lunch today, which means we can't eat together."

Ali hadn't expected Emily to invite her to eat lunch with her. Being invited to eat with the popular kids was the fast track to becoming popular. That had never happened to her before.

"They take you out to lunch?" Ali could count on one hand the number of times her parents had taken her out to eat.

"We've been doing it since kindergarten," Emily explained. "It's my dad's way of making up for all the hours he works and all the traveling he does. Today we're going to my favorite Indian restaurant, Thandi. Have you ever been there?"

Ali shook her head.

"Anyway, we'll eat together tomorrow, okay? We need to work on our science project." She didn't wait for Ali to respond before she hurried back to her seat. Emily's parting words made her frown. Maybe the only reason Emily wanted to eat lunch with her was to work on the project. *Careful, Ali,* she told herself. *There's no fast pass to popularity.* Still, it was a start.

Ali slipped into her seat. "Hey, Cassie."

Cassie turned. It was clear she was not having a good day. "Hey."

"I practiced my powers last night," she whispered back, surprised when Cassie's response was a lukewarm "Good."

Before Ali could say anything else, Ms. Ryder started talking. Ali tried to pay attention, but all she could think about was how fantastic Gigi's party was going to be and how wonderful it was that Emily wanted to eat lunch with her, regardless of the reason.

Cassie was sitting by herself when Ali arrived in the cafeteria.

"Where are Alfie and Murray?" she asked.

She received a shrug in response.

Ali stopped unpacking her lunch. "Are you mad at me or something?"

For a second, she was sure Cassie was going to tell her off. Then Cassie's chin began to quiver. Her voice was thick when she responded. "I was worried you'd eat with Emily and abandon me too."

Ali's first inclination was to deny the accusation, since getting along with people was important, but decided against it. After all, if Emily hadn't gone out to lunch with her parents, Ali would have sat with her. But would she have sat with Emily if she'd known Cassie had no one to sit with? She liked to think the answer was no.

"You haven't told me where Alfie and Murray are."

"They went to a Dungeons and Dragons game that some guy in grade eight is hosting in Mr. Corby's classroom this week. I could have gone, but how boring would that be?"

"Less boring than sitting all alone?" offered Ali with a quick grin.

"Yeah, well, maybe. How's your project with Emily going?"

"Good. We went down to Tin Can Beach to see the seals."

Cassie's eyes lit up. "What were they like?"

"They're way bigger than I imagined they'd be.

There was a zoologist and a marine biologist there, taking pictures and notes. It was so interesting!"

"I wish I'd gone too. Figures you'd go with Emily."

Ali crossed her arms. "I went with Emily because we were working on our project." Why was Cassie being so difficult?

"I'm sorry," Cassie whispered. "I'm being stupid. I'd like to do fun things with you too."

This was uncharted territory. Ali had never been in demand before. She didn't want to disappoint Cassie. "Maybe we could go this weekend if they're still there."

"Are you serious? That would be great! I bet Murray will want to go too. We'll bike there; it only takes half an hour. Murray and I used to go to Tin Can Beach a lot in the summer, before Alfie arrived."

> ALI'S RULES FOR WHEN
> YOU SUDDENLY FIND
> YOURSELF POPULAR
> 1. Enjoy it.
> 2. Enjoy it.
> 3. Enjoy it.

"Sure," said Ali, pleased she'd made Cassie happy again.

Cassie dug into her lunch with newfound gusto. "So, what did you change into last night?"

Ali leaned across the table. "A chipmunk, an ant, and a lion."

"No way!"

"Yup."

"Which did you like better?"

"For sure the lion. I was terrified someone would step on me when I was an ant, and the antennae felt so strange. Did you know ants use them to smell?"

Cassie nodded. "Em . . . I mean, I did a project about ants in grade two."

"I turned back when I spied a spider in the corner. It was staring at me, like I was supper or something."

"Gross."

"Gross is right."

Cassie sat back in her chair. "You have the most interesting life ever."

Ali leaned back, surprised by the compliment and the look of admiration on Cassie's face. She'd been so worried about becoming a Copycat that she hadn't considered the flip side of her predicament—that she was the only person at Princess Elizabeth School who could do what she could do. It was kind of amazing. There was only one problem: no one besides Cassie and Murray could know. It kind of made her sad. Imagine how popular she'd be if everyone knew. She'd have more friends than she knew what to do with!

TWENTY-FIVE

"Let's talk about evolution," Mr. Corby said in science class that afternoon. "Many, if not all, of the organisms we've been studying this past week have evolved to adapt to their environment."

Murray raised his hand. "I read about this cool moth whose wings look like owl eyes so that its predators will leave it alone."

Mr. Corby smiled. "That is the perfect example of evolution and adaptation to save your species from extinction. Some species are even able to change their gender, like clownfish. Which comes in handy sometimes."

"Some people think my aunt Mia changed her

gender," Taylor said, "because she used to be my uncle Todd, but she says she was always a Mia and her body just had to catch up with the rest of her."

Mr. Corby smiled.

"Do you think people evolve?" Cassie asked. "Like, do you think we could ever change color like a chameleon or make ourselves look like someone else?"

Ali leaned forward, intrigued.

"Perhaps," Mr. Corby mused. "Of course, human beings *have* evolved over time. For instance, we used to be hairier."

"My dad is still pretty hairy," Tom called out. "You should see his back!"

Murray's hand shot up again. "But getting less hairy happened over thousands of years, didn't it? Do species ever evolve quicker than that?"

Ali held her breath, hoping for the answer to all her questions.

"Excellent question, Murray. Charles Darwin believed evolution occurred over tens of thousands of years. But recently, scientists have discovered a phenomenon they call rapid evolution. Some species are changing and adapting much faster than anyone believed possible. Sometimes that's because a new predator is introduced into their lives or they change geographic location by hitching rides on airplanes and the like."

"Do you think humans could ever experience rapid evolution?" Murray pressed. He glanced over at Ali, who smiled. "Could they develop the ability to look like other people?"

"Perhaps if they were threatened or their environment changed quickly enough, they might develop new abilities to compensate," said Mr. Corby. "It's not impossible that, over time, humans might be able to alter themselves at will."

> ALI'S THEORY ABOUT EVOLUTION
> 1. Charles Darwin was mostly right.
> 2. Rapid evolution is weird and makes you worry that the tree in your backyard might walk away if you threatened to cut it down.
> 3. Is the evolution of moth wings and Copycats the same thing?

"But what would be the benefit?" Emily asked. "I wouldn't want to look like anyone else." Emily seemed subdued since her lunch out with her parents. She'd barely said hello to Ali when she'd arrived back.

Cassie rolled her eyes. It was a pain that Cassie disliked Emily. Otherwise, they could all be friends.

"Simple, Miss Arai: surprise. Imagine if you could turn into anything. You could hide in plain sight, and your enemies would never know you were there. Or you could learn secrets by being someone else, or even replace someone in their life. In some ways, if you could be anyone, it would be like becoming an invisible person."

It was impossible for Ali to miss the appalled look Murray and Cassie exchanged. She grinned. Being a Copycat was proving to be more interesting than she'd suspected.

Ali was pleased to find Alfie waiting for her at her locker at the end of the day.

"I talked to my mom and my grandad about going to Gigi's birthday party," he told her as soon as they stepped outside.

Ali's heart leapt. "That's awesome! The party will

be a week from this Saturday!"

Alfie groaned. "As soon as I brought up the subject, Granddad cut me off. He refuses to even consider going. My mom tried to talk to him, but it's hopeless."

"But families are supposed to forgive each other," Ali said. "And I'm planning such a cool party! It's going to be a movie theme. We're even going to have a red carpet!"

"Sounds fun. I think it's stupid that he's so mad. If anyone should be mad at Gigi and your dad, it's me and my mom, not him."

Ali stopped walking. "But I don't get it. What did Gigi and Digger do?"

"I don't really know what happened to my dad. Neither my mom nor Granddad wants to talk about it. I just know that your dad and Gigi were somehow involved."

She dreaded the response to her next question. "*Are you mad at them?*"

Alfie shook his head. "No. I mean, if my mom isn't mad, I guess I shouldn't be either. Besides, I never knew him at all. He died before I was born."

It was just like what they'd discussed in science class. Alfie's mother had been able to adapt to her new circumstances, but not his grandfather. Why could some people change so much and some not at all? What Alfie's grandfather needed was some rapid evolution.

"It must have been hard, not having a dad." Digger might be strange and not work very much, but at least he was always there for her.

Alfie kicked at a stone. "I think about him a lot. I wonder what it would be like if he was alive. Would I have grown up here instead of England? Granddad says my dad played baseball when he was my age. I tried to play last summer at camp, but I was awful. Maybe if he was around to coach me I'd be better."

Ali had to blink hard to stop the tears. "Digger could coach you. He's great at sports."

Alfie began to shuffle along again. "Granddad says this is the worst fog in years."

Ali gazed up. It was impossible to see the tops of

the trees through the heavy mist. "My mom hates the fog. She loves Saint John, and living with Gigi, but she misses the sun."

"Me too. I've felt kind of out of sorts since I moved here. I mean, I'm glad I'm getting to spend time with Granddad, but it's bringing up a lot of stuff." He paused and searched her face. "What about you? Do you ever feel weird living here?"

Ali wished she could tell him just *how* weird she felt since she'd moved to Saint John, but that was impossible. "No. I like it. Maybe it feels weird because it makes you think of your dad."

"A lot of things make me think of my dad these days. . . ." His voice trailed off. Afraid she'd offended him, Ali decided to steer the conversation back to Gigi's party. Alfie needed to understand what was at stake if he couldn't talk Andrew Sloane into attending.

"Digger told me that if something happens to Gigi, we'll have to leave Saint John because your grandfather will inherit the house."

"Why would he kick you out? He already has a house."

"But he doesn't need two houses," Ali pointed out. "And Gigi's house is where he grew up. We couldn't afford to take care of Gigi's house anyway. Digger doesn't work and my mom doesn't make a lot of money." She'd never told anyone that before. What would he think?

There was another awkward silence. Ali was about to say something boring about the weather when Alfie's eyes lit up. "I know how we can get Granddad to come to the party!"

Ali's chest swelled with hope. "How?"

"You invite him."

"Me?" Ali squeaked.

Alfie grinned. "Yes! If you ask him, I bet he'd be too polite to say no. Come by on Sunday."

Ali tilted her head. "Do you really think me asking him will make him change his mind?"

"It has to," Alfie whispered. "I need to meet your dad and Gigi."

They'd reached Gigi's house. Alfie began to shuffle back and forth, getting ready to bolt.

"Fine. I'll do it." She couldn't hide the dread in her voice. Talking to Andrew Sloane would be like having three cavities filled without any novocaine. In other words: excruciating.

The conversation was interrupted by raucous chittering above. A squirrel and chipmunk were squabbling on Gigi's windowsill.

"This house needs a cat," Ali muttered.

Alfie shook his head. "I'm allergic to cats. Besides, I like that she feeds animals. Maybe I can help her feed them someday." He saluted, then hurried away, knapsack swinging.

Ali pictured Alfie in Gigi's window. She'd brave Andrew Sloane to make that happen.

Chapter Nine
PREDICTING FOG
USING FOLKLORE

Residents along the Bay of Fundy have long employed various methods to predict the onset of fog. Matthew Morgan of Quaco swore his wooden leg swelled immediately preceding a particularly pernicious bout of fog, though this was dismissed by his neighbors as "Quaco quackery." Josie Pyle of Chamcook said you could smell the fog coming in, for it carried enough salt to cure a ham. Parker McKenna claimed the seagulls stayed ashore in numbers far exceeding their regular assemblies over land. The most maudlin prediction belonged to my grandfather Barker, who said you could tell the fog was coming when you felt your heart break.

—PERCIVAL T. SLOANE,
    A History of Fog in the Bay of Fundy *(1932)*

TWENTY-SIX

Emily cornered Ali after homeroom the next morning. It was clear she was in a horrible mood. "We need to work on our project today. Meet me in the cafeteria at lunch."

Ali, taken aback, nodded. "Sure." Had Emily forgotten that she'd already invited Ali to eat lunch with her today? Something was up, but she knew better than to ask what it was.

At lunchtime, she stopped to let Cassie, Murray, and Alfie know she couldn't eat with them. Except she'd forgotten that Murray and Alfie were occupied elsewhere and that Cassie would be alone. As she approached the table, Cassie flashed her a relieved smile. Ali gulped, but told herself that Cassie would understand. Besides, Ali knew better than anyone that it was possible to survive eating alone.

She blurted out her explanation. "I can't eat with you today. Emily and I are working on our project."

Cassie blinked several times, glanced over at Emily's table across the room, and then stared down at her lunch. Her lack of response was Ali's undoing; paralyzed, she tried to think of how to make things better. What would Cassie like to hear her say? She knew that telling people what they wanted to hear was the best way to get along.

"I'm just eating with her because of the project. We aren't friends or anything." She recoiled at her words, ashamed.

But her instinct was right: Cassie smiled. "Okay. I guess I can go watch Murray and Alfie play. Are we still going to Tin Can Beach this weekend? Murray can come."

"Sure."

"Will you eat lunch with me tomorrow?"

Ali nodded. Out of the corner of her eye, she saw Emily beckon to her. "See you in science class!" She rushed away, not waiting for a response.

Emily had saved the seat next to her, across the table from Taylor and another girl Emily introduced as Jillian, who wasn't in any of Ali's classes. As Ali unpacked her brown paper bag, she couldn't help but admire Emily's purple metallic lunch box with its multiple compartments and colorful utensils. Unlike the other kids, who were eating sandwiches or chips, Emily was eating creamy noodles and a kale salad.

Emily caught Ali staring. "My mom makes my lunch and wants me to be super healthy."

Ali flushed. "Sorry—it looks yummy."

Emily twirled a noodle around her pink fork and handed it to Ali. "Here, try some. It's a light version of fettucine alfredo and it's actually pretty good. I'm not going to offer you any kale. It's gross." She seemed her normal self again, which was a relief.

Ali took a bite and smiled. "I love it!" Maybe Digger

could try making this instead of spaghetti or plain old mac and cheese.

"Are you wearing Emily's sweater *again*?" Taylor asked, eyebrow raised.

Surprised, Ali ran her hands along the soft wool. "I love it."

Emily smiled. "It's not my sweater anymore, Taylor."

Taylor raised her eyebrows and turned her attention to Jillian.

Emily pulled out her notebook. "I've been thinking about how we should do this. How about we do a PowerPoint presentation of our data, using my pictures and funny videos to make it more entertaining?"

"We can work on it in the computer lab tomorrow." Ali's promise to Cassie was forgotten.

Emily scrunched her face. "Why would we do that? We can just use our own computers."

Ali's cheeks burned. "I don't have a computer."

"Can't you use your parents' computer?"

"They don't have one either."

"What do you mean?" Taylor sounded incredulous. "Everybody has a computer."

Ali gave her stock answer, the one that didn't require her to tell people that her parents couldn't afford a computer. "My dad doesn't like computers."

Emily did a double take. "He doesn't like computers?"

"How do you do your homework without a computer?" chimed in Jillian.

"I borrow one from the school or work in the computer lab," said Ali, desperate to change the subject. "How do you want to divide up the tasks?" she asked Emily.

But the table wasn't finished. "I know a program where needy kids can apply to get used computers for free," offered Taylor. "My mom is on the board of directors."

Ali wished for a black hole to jump into.

"You *need* a computer," Jillian confirmed.

Ali wanted to scream "Of course I do!" but instead said, "I'll ask him again. Maybe he'll change his mind." Everyone gave her an encouraging nod.

As far back as she could remember, most of Ali's

Christmas presents had been donated by the food bank her family frequented. Her skates were supplied by local service clubs. Her mother picked through used clothing stores for the family's wardrobe. Her parents applied for every free thing and program they could because there was never enough money. Ali knew they'd apply to get her a computer if she asked them to, but now that she was older, taking other people's cast-offs was mortifying.

> ALI'S RULES FOR WHEN EVERYTHING YOU OWN BELONGED TO SOMEONE ELSE FIRST
> 1. Make up a story that its previous owner was a princess who just didn't need it anymore.
> 2. Tell everyone that secondhand is better for the environment—reuse, recycle!
> 3. Pretend you have a cousin in Chicago who sends you all her old stuff.

Emily seemed to sense Ali's discomfort. "Forget computers. What do you want to do, research funny videos or do the first draft of the presentation?"

"Whatever you don't want to do."

Emily's brows furrowed. "I asked what *you* wanted to do."

Ali shrugged. Emily should choose.

Emily's expression turned inscrutable. "Fine. I'll

do the funny videos. Bring your work tomorrow and we'll put it together." She peered into her lunch box and frowned. "No cookie!"

Liked they'd rehearsed it, Taylor and Jillian each held out a cookie. The three girls burst into hysterical laughter. Ali laughed too, but didn't know what she was laughing at. Emily took both cookies and blew her friends a kiss.

Jillian caught Ali's confusion. "Emily's mom won't let her eat cookies, so we each bring an extra one for her."

"Oh," Ali said, still missing the joke.

"My mom thinks cookies are unhealthy." Emily didn't try to hide her sarcasm. "She's the queen of diets. Those pink cupcakes the other day? All for show. She likes my friends to think she's a fun mom." Emily gobbled the cookies and stood up. "Want to come to the gym? Tom and some boys are shooting hoops. Maybe we can too."

Ali, a total klutz, hated basketball. "Sure," she said.

As she followed Emily out of the cafeteria, she saw Cassie was still sitting alone. She waved, but Cassie didn't wave back.

TWENTY-SEVEN

Ali was happy to see Alfie at her locker again after school. Unlike her relationships with Cassie and Emily, hanging out with Alfie was easy, comfortable. She didn't feel the overwhelming need to please him like she did with other people. It was like they got each other. Maybe it was because they were cousins. Whatever the reason, it was too bad he couldn't come to Gigi's house and that they couldn't do things together outside of school. But until they fixed the Sloane Family Feud, she'd be satisfied with their walks home.

"Do you miss England?" she asked, shivering from the fog that was so thick it made Alfie look ghostly.

Alfie didn't respond immediately, like he was trying to find the right words. "It's amazing to meet you and Murray, but I miss my friends in London. Plus, I'm tired all the time. My mom thinks it's because we're trying to adjust to a new climate."

Another way she and Alfie were different: he'd left friends behind. She'd left no one.

"Did you see your grandfather much when you lived in England?"

"He came three or four times a year, and we'd take trips together. He took me to see the Colosseum in Rome. Have you ever been there?"

"No." She'd never been outside of New Brunswick. "Do you like your teachers?"

"They're okay. I skipped a grade when I came here. I guess my old school was accelerated."

"I wondered why you were in grade eight when you're only a month older than me. Are the kids in your classes nice?"

"I guess so. I'm making lots of friends. Everyone is quite friendly. How about you?"

Ali considered Cassie and Emily. Were they friends? She wasn't sure. "Uh-huh."

"I bugged my mom for us to come here for a long time. I felt like I knew everything about my mom's family, but nothing about my dad's. I mean, Granddad and Mom have told me all about him, but I wanted to see where he grew up. I knew about your family, and Gigi, and I hoped that if I came back, even for a while, they'd stop fighting."

It had never occurred to Ali that Alfie might not live in Saint John forever. "But aren't you and your mom staying here?"

Alfie stuffed his hands into his pockets. "No. My mom's a professor. She's on this thing called a sabbatical, which means her university gave her a year off to do research. We're moving back at the end of the school year."

It was like the earth tilted on its axis. Until that moment, Ali hadn't realized how much she had counted on Alfie being there. But he wouldn't be, at least not for long.

Her voice was shaky when she responded. "Your mom teaches at the university, right?"

"She does. The university agreed to lend her an office if she'd teach one class."

"Oh."

They trudged on without speaking. When they arrived at Gigi's house, Ali was surprised to see Digger standing in the picture window. She expected Alfie to bolt, but he didn't. Instead, he stared at Digger as if he was in a trance. Then he waved. Digger smiled, then turned away.

"He really does want to meet you," explained Ali, anxious that Alfie would be offended. "But he won't go behind your grandfather's back."

Alfie seemed to be on the verge of tears when he responded. "I wish . . ." He paused. "I just really need to talk to him. I hope Granddad listens to you. I should go."

Ali watched him disappear into the mist, ready to burst into tears herself. Whatever it took, she would convince Andrew Sloane to come to the party.

* * *

Ali should have spent the evening working on the science project, but she forgot all about it when Gigi suggested they train. Gigi was in an extra good mood; Digger said she'd found the bag of decorations, put two and two together, and had given him a long list of invitees.

"This party is getting out of hand," he muttered. "We should just take her out to dinner." But Ali didn't think he meant it. She'd tried to talk to him about Alfie after school, but he'd brushed her off. Should she tell him that Alfie had said he needed to talk? No— that would only make him feel worse. She left him in his workshop and joined Gigi upstairs.

"Tonight, I want you to keep changing so we can see if you can think on your feet," said Gigi. "I'll tell you what to copy."

It was a good idea in theory, but Ali was bested by her first transformation, a snapping turtle. She spent fifteen minutes stuck on her back, turtle feet flailing, when she tripped over a pair of Gigi's shoes. Next, Ali the raccoon was mesmerized by the sunflower seeds on the windowsill and spent twenty minutes eating them one by one, which was unpleasant for a girl who detested sunflower seeds. Ali the hyena was too noisy, Ali the snail was a boring blob, and Ali the big bad wolf bared her teeth at poor Gigi, who huddled under the covers in mock fear. Her last transformation was into Topsy, the lazy cat who lived next door and who spent her days snoozing on the front porch.

"You're improving," crowed Gigi when Ali collapsed on the carpet. "It's remarkable when you consider it's been such a short time."

"How long until I'm as good as Digger?"

Gigi laughed. "Digger is talented, but he can be lazy about practicing. He only bothers to change into three things with any regularity."

Ali could only think of two: a dog and Ali. "What's the third?"

Gigi leaned forward and whispered, "Sometimes he turns into the Incredible Hulk when no one else is around. I came downstairs the other day to ask him a question and found the Incredible Hulk eating a grilled-cheese sandwich and watching a ball game."

Ali sat up. "No way!"

Gigi nodded. "Nearly scared me to death. He used to change into the Hulk all the time when he was a boy. Teddy liked to turn into Spider-Man."

"I can't believe it." She pictured Digger as the Incredible Hulk and burst into laughter.

"It's a good reminder that you need to have fun with your powers. When I was young, I used to go to the woods and turn into a rhinoceros. I've always been partial to a horn."

"I want to be the best Copycat ever," said Ali.

Gigi shook her head. "Be the best Ali. That will be enough."

But hadn't Murray said she was the most interesting person at Princess Elizabeth School? He wouldn't have said that about Ali before she became a Copycat. No, being the best Ali was *not* enough.

Her mother stopped to say goodnight when she got home from her evening shift. "How'd you do?"

"It was so much fun. I'm getting better."

"I'm glad. But don't ignore your schoolwork, okay? You're being careful when you train?"

"Uh-huh. I haven't left the house yet."

"Good. Digger says being an animal out in the world can be dangerous. No going outside unless he's with you. Promise?"

"Promise."

Emily appeared at Ali's locker first thing the next morning. Flustered, Ali blurted out, "I promised Cassie I'd eat lunch with her today. She'll have to eat alone unless I eat with her." She said it fast, like ripping off a Band-Aid.

Emily flinched. "Oh." She held out her hand. "Can you give me your part of the presentation so I can put it all together this weekend?"

How could she tell Emily she'd forgotten to do it? She couldn't. "I forgot it at home," she said.

Emily threw up her hands. "How could you forget it at home? I need to finish it this weekend. You know how busy I am during the week."

Ali knew. "I'm so sorry."

Emily shook her head. "You just made my life super hard, Ali."

Taylor came around the corner. "I've been looking all over for you, Emily. What's wrong?"

Emily didn't try to hide her frustration. "Ali forgot the presentation at home, so now I can't work on it this weekend."

"That's awful," Taylor said, like Ali's forgetfulness was a crime. "But it's okay. I just overheard Cassie and Murray talking about how they're going to Tin Can Beach with her tomorrow afternoon. Ali can drop it off on the way, right, Ali?"

Ali studied Emily's face to see if this was an acceptable proposal. The last thing she wanted to do on a Friday night was homework, but this was her fault, so she would.

But Emily wasn't interested in the project now. "You're going to Tin Can Beach tomorrow?" She said it like an accusation, like Ali was doing something she shouldn't.

Ali's head began to throb. She wasn't sure how to respond, afraid if she said the wrong thing she'd make Emily angrier.

"I—" she began, but Emily cut her off.

"Never mind—I'll do the presentation myself. Like always." Without a second glance at Ali or Taylor, she stomped off.

> ALI'S RULES ABOUT HOMEWORK
> 1. Do it.
> 2. Do it.
> 3. Seriously: do it.

Stunned, Ali turned to Taylor, who shook her head. "She just wants to do well. Her parents expect a lot. You know what that's like."

Ali nodded, but she had no idea what that was like.

Alfie caught up with Ali at lunchtime before heading off to his Dungeons & Dragons game. "I just wanted to let you know I'm not walking home today. My mom's picking me up."

"How come?"

"We're going to a fancy inn in St. Martins for the weekend. Murray told me that you guys are going to Tin Can Beach tomorrow afternoon. I'm kind of bummed that I can't go too, but Mom likes to do something special on her anniversary."

"Her anniversary?"

"She and my dad would be married fourteen years tomorrow."

"Oh." Was it still an anniversary if the other person was dead? Ali wasn't sure.

"Maybe we can go to the beach some other time. But don't worry; I'll be there Sunday."

Ali gave him a blank stare. "Sunday?"

"Remember? You're coming over to ask Granddad to the party?"

Ali's stomach flopped. She'd forgotten. "Oh, right. What time should I come?"

"Three o'clock. This will work, right?" he asked, as if Ali knew the outcome already.

"For sure," said Ali.

Alfie smiled. "I can't wait till we can do stuff together as a family. It's going to be so great. Thanks, Ali."

How could Alfie believe in her when she didn't believe in herself?

Chapter Ten
FOG TECHNOLOGY

A recent advancement in fog safety has been achieved by the invention of a car fog light by the Bosch Company. Though not yet widespread, it promises to reduce the accidents associated with low visibility due to fog.

—PERCIVAL T. SLOANE,
 A History of Fog in the Bay of Fundy *(1932)*

PRACTICE!

Twenty-Eight

"I've been researching you," Murray said, when Ali met him and Cassie in front of the old museum after lunch the next day. She'd told Digger they were going for a bike ride, but had neglected to mention that they were going to Tin Can Beach. She was afraid he'd insist on driving them and then hanging around. Besides, Cassie had assured her that most of the time they'd be biking on Harbour Passage Trail, where there were no cars. Going to Tin Can Beach wasn't a big deal, but Ali knew Digger would try to make it one.

"What?" Ali wasn't sure she liked the idea of Murray researching her.

"I have a theory."

"This I gotta hear," said Cassie.

Murray leaned forward against the handlebars of his bike. "So, you know that humans share a lot of DNA with other things, right?"

Ali nodded.

"And DNA is organized into stretches of individual segments of genes, right?"

"I guess . . ." She'd learned about genetics in fifth grade, but couldn't remember much.

"So, proteins attach themselves to these stretches of genes, which end up coiling themselves into chromosomes."

"Murray, you could make singing 'Happy Birthday' complicated," complained Cassie. "What's your point?"

"I think that when Ali changes into something else, she is somehow able to manipulate the genes within her chromosomes, keeping the genes that make her like what she's trying to change into and suppressing the ones she doesn't need." He gave them a triumphant smile.

"I still don't get it," Ali said.

"Maybe I do," Cassie said. She stared at Murray, like she was studying what was inside his brain, and then turned to Ali. "The genetic differences between people are very small—"

"Point one percent," Murray offered, trying to be helpful.

Cassie rolled her eyes. "The differences between humans and chimps is around four to five percent," she said. "But when you examine those differences, you see that a lot of human DNA is deleted in chimps, and a lot of other genetic codes are duplicated over and over. Somehow, you're able to sense someone else's genetic code and alter your own!"

Murray gave a vigorous nod. "Exactly!"

It kind of made sense to Ali. "But why would my body do that?"

"Remember what Mr. Corby said about rapid evolution?" said Cassie. "One of your ancestors had to change for some reason. Maybe your body makes a special protein that triggers the change."

"I'm like a new species?"

Murray's head bobbed like one of the buoys in the bay. "Yes! Now all we need to do is take some of your blood to a geneticist and prove the theory!"

Ali shook her head. "No way! I'm not a lab rat!"

"But that's how we'll know for sure!" protested Murray.

"No way."

Cassie clipped the straps of her bike helmet together under her chin. "Leave her be, Murray. You can't just throw this stuff at her and then be shocked when she doesn't want the world to know. Think about it: does Spider-Man tell people about his abilities? Batgirl?"

"Batgirl doesn't have any abilities, she's just in really good shape," said Murray.

"Besides, your theory doesn't explain how Ali is able to change her clothes, too. There's no DNA in clothing."

"I think I know," said Ali. "I think I can somehow manipulate atoms." She concentrated on the gray hoodie and black jeans Murray was wearing for a few seconds, and the others watched in amazement as her old blue jeans and windbreaker morphed into an exact replica of Murray's outfit.

"Wow" was all Murray could muster.

Ali changed back and climbed onto her bike. "Can we please stop talking about me and my weird powers and just go visit the seals?"

It was eerie biking around the harbor. Murray and Cassie led the way, and Ali pedaled hard to keep up. Every now and then she fell behind, and they'd disappear into the mist, only to reappear so suddenly that Ali would almost crash into them. A foghorn's plaintive call reminded Ali of Emily's story about the women waiting for their husbands and sons to come home from sea. Thinking about how Emily was mad at her made Ali melancholy.

"My dad says that at least five ships are stuck in port, including a cruise ship," Murray said. "The fog extends five miles into the Bay of Fundy, and all the way up the Kennebecasis River to Hampton. He said the whole world is talking about our fog. We're famous!"

Ali shivered and pulled her windbreaker hood up over her head. She'd rather see the sun and be warm than famous.

There were no scientists on the beach today. In fact, the fog was so thick it took them a while to find the seals, whose gray forms were hard to differentiate from the rocks. When they finally spotted them, Ali was surprised to see only five. What had happened to the rest?

"You said there were a lot of them," said Cassie, taking tentative steps forward.

"The rest must have gone back into the bay, unless they're farther down the beach?"

"I'll go check," said Murray. Seconds later, he was swallowed up by the fog.

Cassie crouched down to watch the seals. "They're beautiful."

Ali took a seat on a nearby rock. "That one's sick." She pointed to the one in the middle of the herd, the blind one with the patchy coat. All of the seals appeared to be asleep.

"I hope the zoologist is helping it," Cassie murmured.

Murray emerged from the mist. "I don't see any more on the beach." He smiled at Ali. "Will you do me a favor? Change into a seal. I'd like to really watch how you change. It'll help me build my theory."

"Your theory that the world will never know about," reminded Ali.

Murray shrugged. "Whatever. My genius theory that the world will never know about until you give me permission to share it. Now will you please change?"

Since the beach was deserted, Ali dutifully became a seal, focusing on one of the healthier ones in the herd. She tried to move slowly, but once the change began in earnest, she discovered that her ability to control the speed was nonexistent. When she finished, she used her flippers to shuffle over to Murray.

"Can you understand me?" he asked her.

She bobbed her head and barked yes.

"Cool," said Cassie, turning her attention away from the seals to look at Ali the seal. "She understands us perfectly, but sounds like a seal when she tries to speak to us."

"Did you notice how the seals acted when Ali changed?" asked Murray. "They were watching her. But that one in the middle with the patchy fur made a weird grunting sound, like it was scared."

"Ali says that one is sick."

Murray leaned over. "She's right. Look at its coat. And its eyes are seriously messed up."

Ali managed to turn herself around and shambled closer to the herd. It was hard to see the sick seal from her current point of view; the other seals were much bigger than she was. And the idea of trying to crawl onto another seal to take a better look was not appealing.

"Ali, change back," Murray ordered. "I want to see the process in reverse."

Ali barked and concentrated on becoming herself again. Halfway through her transformation, a dark shape caught her eye. Someone was coming!

"I saw someone," she panted when she was herself again. "Over there!"

Murray ran in the direction she pointed, Cassie in his wake. Ali stayed with the seals and cursed her stupidity for agreeing to change in public. She studied the sick seal. Its eyes were still open. Now and then, it gave a piteous bark. It didn't seem to be getting any better.

"I'm sorry, fella," she whispered. "I hope you feel better soon."

The seal groaned and closed its eyes.

"We couldn't find anyone," said Murray when they came back.

"Are you sure you saw someone?" Cassie asked.

"I think so. Maybe," said Ali. "But I may have been seeing things. One of the scientists said seals can't see very well when they're out of the water." She felt stupid for making them chase after nothing. "I'm freezing; can we go home?"

"I need to pick up a book at the library first," said

Murray. "Let's bike over to Market Square, get a hot chocolate, then I'll grab my book and we can head home."

Ali didn't want to go for a hot chocolate; she had no money. But she couldn't tell that to Murray and Cassie. "Okay, but I think I'll pass on the hot chocolate."

Cassie squished her eyebrows together. "You just said you were freezing. Why don't you want a hot chocolate?"

"I'm getting toasty again," she said, then shuddered.

Murray and Cassie exchanged a look.

"Cass, I forgot to bring money," Murray announced.

Cassie nodded. "No problem. Do you need me to lend you money for a hot chocolate, too, Ali?"

Ali gave in and nodded. She didn't mind borrowing money if she wasn't the only person to do so.

"It's no big deal, you guys," said Cassie. "That's what friends are for, right?"

"Right," Murray said.

"Right," Ali echoed, surprised by how happy she sounded.

As she climbed onto her bike, Ali took a last look at the seals. She suspected they'd be leaving soon. Would they take the sick seal with them or abandon it? She was putting on her helmet when he opened his eyes again, almost as if he knew what she was thinking.

"Good luck," she whispered. She didn't want to think about him anymore; it was too sad. One of her mother's favorite Maya quotes came to her: "I know for sure that love saves me and that it is here to save us all." She couldn't help the seal, but she could send him good thoughts. She closed her eyes, sent the seal all the love she could muster, then sped away to catch up with the others.

TWENTY-NINE

Cassie treated them to hot chocolate and doughnuts. Half an hour later, the three were sprawled across some comfy chairs in one of the library's reading rooms, waiting for the doughnuts to digest before they biked home.

Murray, who was thumbing through a Spider-Man graphic novel, glanced over at Ali. "I'm sorry I bugged you about my theory. I just think it's cool how you can transform into anything."

"That's okay. I know you're only trying to help me." She was surprised to discover that it *was* okay, that she wasn't just saying it to get along.

"Are you still practicing your powers a lot?" Cassie asked.

"Every night. My dad says it's important for me to get good at it so I can control my powers. It's the opposite at school. I do everything I can not to change."

"Do you think you could turn into him?" Cassie pointed to the author's picture on the book she was skimming.

Ali leaned over. "You want me to turn into C. S. Lewis? He's, like, one of the most famous authors ever. And also: he's dead."

Cassie beamed. "Exactly! You won't have to worry about him coming around the corner or anything. Plus, it would be funny to see you change into an old man. Come on. Try."

"Right now?"

Murray grabbed the book from Cassie and passed it to Ali. "It'll be funny!"

Cassie jumped up and went to the doorway that separated the reading room from the rest of the library. "I'll keep watch."

Ali knew what she was about to do was dangerous,

that Digger would be furious if he found out. But Murray and Cassie were being so nice to her. She stared at the photograph. The author had a kind face. She concentrated hard and then closed her eyes. It took a couple of minutes until the warm feeling began, but this time, the change was almost instantaneous.

"Whoa," murmured Murray.

"Amazing," Cassie added.

Ali opened her eyes. She was still sitting, but her body extended well above the back of the chair and she was wearing a tweed suit and a plaid tie.

"You look just like him," Murray said, his voice filled with awe. "I mean, seriously, you look just like him."

Ali stood up and walked over to the window. The reflection in the glass was of an older, balding man.

Cassie glanced out the door. "Oh no! It's Ms. Ryder! And she's coming this way!"

Ali continued to stare out the window, doing her best to stay calm. As long as she didn't try to talk, everything would be fine.

Ms. Ryder stepped into the room. "Hi, guys! I saw you come in a few minutes ago." She paused. "Didn't I see Ali come into the library with you?"

"Uh, she's in the bathroom," Murray said. "Want Cassie to go get her?"

For someone capable of creating complex genetic theories, Murray was a lousy liar.

"Goodness, no," said Ms. Ryder. "I just wanted to make sure I wasn't seeing things. Is this your father, Cassie?" she asked.

"It's . . . my . . . uncle," a flustered Cassie replied.

Ali wanted to keep looking out the window, but that would be rude. She turned and smiled her C. S. Lewis smile and extended a hand, hoping her teacher wouldn't find it odd that Cassie's uncle didn't say hello.

Ms. Ryder took Ali's hand. "Nice to meet you, Cassie's uncle. Have we met? You look familiar."

Ali shook her head. Behind Ms. Ryder's back, Murray's eyes bugged out and Cassie turned a strange grayish pink.

Ms. Ryder seemed rattled. She gave C. S. Lewis an uneasy smile and backed up, bumping into Murray.

"Uh, I guess we should go, Cassie," said Murray, trying to sound normal, but sounding more like the mechanical voice on the telephone that prompted you to press one if you wished to speak to a customer representative.

Cassie's voice was equally odd. "Yes, we should go. Uh, Uncle, can we go now?"

Ali nodded, and followed them out of the room. They didn't speak until they were riding the escalator down to the main level.

"Most. Awkward. Conversation. Ever!" Cassie groaned.

Ali forgot she was still C. S. Lewis and said, "I didn't know what to say!" in her Ali voice.

> ALI'S RULES TRANSFORMING INTO SOMEONE ELSE
> 1. Don't do it in public!
> 2. Try to pick someone whose voice you know.

"Let's go down to the parking garage," said Murray. "There are plenty of hidden spots where Ali can change back."

Five minutes later, Ali was herself again. It was only

when she was unlocking her bike that she realized things weren't as they should be. Murray, standing next to her, made a strange choking sound.

Cassie turned to look. "Whoa."

They all stared down at Ali's hands, which weren't Ali's hands at all, but C. S. Lewis's hairy knuckles. And then Murray began to laugh, and despite her predicament, Ali did too. Cassie tried to keep it together, but finally succumbed, laughing so hard tears ran down her cheeks.

"I'm sure they'll change back by the time I get home," Ali managed to say between hiccupy laughs. "Who knows? Maybe C. S. Lewis's hands will help me get a better mark in language arts. Or write another Narnia book. Or maybe Aslan will come see me. I mean, these hands could come in handy."

"Funniest thing ever!" gasped Murray.

For the first time, Ali's abilities seemed almost normal.

"Did you have fun with Murray and Cassie?" Ali's mother asked at dinner that night.

Ali examined her now-normal hands and nodded. Even though she was still smarting from Emily being mad at her, she'd had a great day. Cassie and Murray were fun to be with. They weren't glamorous like Emily, or homey like Alfie, but they were smart and funny, and best of all, they'd kept her secret.

"How's Gigi?" she asked.

"She didn't cough once," said Digger. "Oh—your friend Emily called a little while ago."

"Why didn't you tell me that as soon as I got home?" Ali demanded.

"I forgot. She said to call when you had time."

Ali hopped up.

"Wait until you finish eating," her mother called after her, but Ali couldn't wait. She'd already disappointed Emily once this week. She didn't want to do it again.

Emily picked up on the first ring. "I just wanted you to know I finished the presentation. It actually didn't take that long."

"I'm sorry I forgot to bring it with me yesterday."

There was a pause on the other end of the line. "I'm sorry I lost my temper. It's just I always end up doing all the work when I partner with people and sometimes I get frustrated. I'd hoped it would be different with you."

Emily did sound sorry. So why did her apology make Ali feel even worse?

"Anyway, we can go over the presentation Monday at school. I asked Mr. Corby and he said we'd probably present on Tuesday or Wednesday and he's giving us class time to finish up." She paused, then added, "Did you have fun with Murray and Cassie?"

Ali did her best to sound neutral. "It was okay."

"Anything exciting happen?"

Besides Ali turning into a seal and C. S. Lewis? "No. We went to Tin Can Beach and then to the library."

"Oh. That's it?" Ali recognized the disappointment in Emily's voice.

"Uh-huh."

"Did Cassie and Murray tell you what they're doing for their project?"

"Nope." It hadn't occurred to Ali to ask.

"If you see them again before the end of the weekend, ask, okay? I always like to size up the competition. Taylor told me what she and her partner are doing, and believe me, our project is *way* better."

Ali just wanted to survive the presentation; she couldn't worry about the other teams too.

"Ali! Come back to the table!" her mother shouted from the next room.

"I'm sorry, Emily, I have to go."

"Whatever." Emily hung up before Ali could respond.

Ali stared at the phone. She had to stop disappointing Emily. But there was still a chance to redeem herself if she could ace her part of the presentation. They would get a good grade, Emily would be happy, and everything would be perfect.

THIRTY

Most Sundays Ali slept late, but not this one. Today was an important day in her quest to reunite the Sloanes. She got up early, ate a big breakfast to soothe her nervous belly, and wrote out a detailed list of the points she wanted to use to convince Andrew Sloane to come to Gigi's party. The rest of the morning was spent turning into superheroes to give herself courage. It was too bad she couldn't visit Andrew Sloane as Captain America. No one could say no to Captain America.

At exactly two forty-five, she slipped out of the house. She'd decided not to tell her parents about her mission in case they tried to stop her. Plus, it wasn't like anyone would notice she was gone; her mother was at work, Digger was down in his workshop, and Gigi was fast asleep. She'd be back before anyone knew she was missing.

It was a short walk, past the old museum and Riverview Memorial Park. When she reached Harbour View High School, she turned right on Brunswick Place and climbed until she reached the last house on the dead-end street. The house was an imposing two stories, with a large porch, a bowed window, and a stone wall separating its narrow driveway from the yard of the house next door. She stared at the house for a full five minutes, listening to the cries of the seagulls fishing in the nearby river. "Go home! Go home!" they seemed to say. Instead, she climbed the eleven steps to the door and rang the bell.

A lady about her mother's age opened the door. "Hello?"

"I'm Ali Sloane," Ali blurted out.

The woman's face crumpled like she was about to burst into tears. She took a deep breath, regained her composure, and gestured for Ali to come in. "I'm

Alfie's mother, Colleen. I'm so happy to finally meet you," she said.

Ali stepped inside, relieved when Alfie bounded down the stairs.

"Hey." He sounded nervous but excited. "Ali's here to talk to Granddad, Mom."

Colleen frowned. "Does he know she's coming?"

Alfie shook his head.

His mother sighed and closed her eyes, then opened them and smiled. But it was an anxious smile, which made Ali's queasy stomach lurch. "He's in his study. I'll tell him you're here."

Alfie pulled Ali toward a nearby wall covered in family photographs. One pictured three couples: an older man and woman, along with two younger couples. They all wore red sweaters and big smiles. Ali studied the photo for a few seconds, surprised to realize it had been taken at Riverview Memorial Park; she could see the old museum in the distance. The idea that the Other Sloanes were taking family photos down the street from where she now lived made Ali's heart squeeze with loneliness.

"Which one is your dad?" she asked Alfie.

"That's him there."

Ali leaned in. Teddy was a mixture of Alfie and Digger and shared their same lopsided grin.

"His real name was Edward," said Alfie. "He was named after Gigi's first husband, Edward Montgomery, who was Granddad's real father. He died in the war."

Ali stared at him in surprise. "I never knew Gigi had a husband who died in World War II."

"Yeah. My granddad never met his real dad."

Just like you never met your dad.

"Gigi's second husband, Richard, was a distant Sloane cousin and became his stepfather. But he was more like a dad, because Gigi married him when my granddad was three years old."

How did Alfie know all this? Ali slumped forward as she continued to stare at the photograph. It was like she didn't know anything about her family.

"How old is your grandfather?" she finally asked.

"Almost seventy-six. My grandmother died a couple of years ago." He pointed to the picture. "That's my aunt Karen. She and my uncle Tim live over on the west side. They have eight-year-old twin girls named Jennie and Jordan. They're funny. My mom calls them the life of the party."

The word "party" brought Ali back to the task at hand. "I hope your granddad agrees to come to Gigi's party."

"Me too."

"Ali!" Colleen called from somewhere at the back of the house. Ali bugged her eyes out at Alfie and walked toward the voice. Colleen gave her an encouraging smile as they passed in the hallway. "First door on the right," she whispered. "You'll be fine; he's nice."

Ali swallowed. If Andrew Sloane was so nice, why did he hate Digger and Gigi?

When Ali stepped into Andrew Sloane's study, the first thing she observed, even before she saw the old man on the leather recliner, was all the photographs.

They were everywhere and told the story of Andrew Sloane's life, one picture at a time. There was a black-and-white photograph of a man in a uniform, who she assumed was Edward Montgomery. It made her catch her breath to look at him. If Edward Montgomery had lived, Alfie would be Alfie Montgomery, and Ali and Digger would never have been born. The rest of the photographs were of Andrew Sloane and his family through the years. There were tons of photos of Teddy. But the most surprising thing was that Gigi and Digger were in some of the pictures. Ali hadn't expected that.

"You going to look at pictures all day, or are you going to come introduce yourself?"

Ali started, and stumbled her way over to where Andrew Sloane sat in front of the muted television set. On the screen, a man struggled to get his golf ball out of a sand trap.

"I'm Ali."

Andrew Sloane nodded. He had a full head of thick white hair, a bulbous red nose, and the Sloane gray

> ALI'S RULES FOR MAKING YOUR CASE
> 1. Be prepared with well-thought-out arguments.
> 2. Don't show any emotions.
> 3. Always expect the other person to say no.

eyes. He wasn't smiling, but he also wasn't scowling, which she took as a good sign. He motioned for her to take a seat on a small chair nearby. For several minutes, neither spoke as they watched the golfer try to sink his ball in the hole.

Andrew Sloane's gruff voice broke the silence. "You look like her."

Ali turned to him. "Like your mother?"

He shook his head. "No, like my grandmother. She lived with us during the war." He picked up a bowl of pretzels from the table next to him and passed it to her. Even though she wasn't hungry, Ali took one.

"Her name was Carrie, and she could spin a yarn. You look just like her. So . . . did my mother send you or did Digger?"

"Neither. They don't know I'm here."

Andrew Sloane nodded. "You're brave."

Ali pulled a scrap of paper from her pocket. Andrew Sloane pointed at it. "What's that?"

"I wrote down a list of things I want to ask you so I don't forget."

There was a flicker of smile. "Go ahead."

"Number one: I'm throwing your mother a hundredth birthday party, and I want all the Sloanes to be there."

She chanced a glance. Andrew Sloane shook his head. "The answer is no."

His refusal sucked the air out of the room. Ali struggled to catch her breath, and tried to come up with an argument that might change his mind. The answer couldn't be no. The only rebuttal she could think of was the one thing she didn't want to say. "She's going to die soon."

"We haven't spoken in years. If I go to her birthday party just because she's going to die soon, what kind of person would I be?"

"The forgiving kind?" Her response made him flinch.

She tried the next thing on her list. "Number two: could Alfie and the Sloanes come? Alfie wants to meet her and Digger."

"If my family doesn't want to disrespect Teddy's memory, they shouldn't go either."

Stunned, Ali let Andrew Sloane's horrible words sink in. She'd come for nothing. There was not going to be a happy ending. A tear rolled down her cheek and she quickly brushed it aside. She would not let Andrew Sloane see her cry.

"What's next on this list of yours?"

Number three asked if he'd let her family stay in the house after Gigi died. Ali crumpled the paper. "Nothing." A Maya Angelou quote popped into her head: "It's one of the greatest gifts you can give yourself, to forgive. Forgive everybody." She knew Andrew Sloane's inability to forgive Gigi and Digger must be chewing up his insides, because his refusal made her stomach feel like she'd swallowed poison.

"You need to forgive your mother and Digger, not for their sake, but for yours. Maya Angelou said it's the greatest gift you can give yourself."

"Is that what Maya Angelou said?" Andrew Sloane's tone was mocking. He stood up and loomed over her, his face twisted into a sneer. "I'll never have peace; why should they?"

Ali didn't have an answer. She didn't know Andrew Sloane, but she knew the smiling man in the photos was gone forever. She stood up as well, not wanting to stay another minute.

But Andrew Sloane wasn't finished. "Whatever they've told you about your abilities? It's all lies. The Sloanes are cursed. Nothing noble ever came from using unnatural powers."

"Unnatural powers?" Ali stammered. She backed up until her hand was on the doorknob. She'd thrown a stick of dynamite into the room, inviting Andrew Sloane to Gigi's party, and it had blown up in her face.

Andrew Sloane wagged a finger. "Just because you can do something doesn't mean you *should*."

She recognized the words immediately: they were the same ones Digger had used when Ali had suggested he meet Alfie, but now they were tinged with hatred, not love. It all made sense now. Andrew Sloane believed Copycat abilities were wicked, while

Gigi and Digger considered them gifts. Nothing Ali could say would change his mind.

Ali flung open the door and fled. Past the living room, where she ignored Alfie when he called her name. Past the park, where the other Sloanes once took happy family pictures. She ran until she was back in her bedroom, huddled in bed with the blankets over her head. The Sloanes would never be reunited. Which meant Gigi and Digger would never meet Alfie and she would have to move again. She had failed.

THIRTY-ONE

Ali didn't tell her parents about her run-in with Andrew Sloane. She spent Sunday evening locked in her bedroom, replaying the afternoon's events over and over instead of doing her homework. Could she have said something to make him change his mind? Mostly, though, she rehashed his horrible comment about Copycats. Gigi was right; there was no way Alfie knew. If he did know about the Copycats in the family, he'd probably been taught that they were abominations. Which meant Alfie would never get to know the real Ali, the one who was learning how thrilling it could be to walk in another's shoes, or paws. It made her sad, knowing there would always be a wall between the two parts of the family.

In homeroom the next day, Emily waved at Ali, but kept her distance. There was no mention of eating lunch together again. Ali was disappointed, but also relieved. For the first time in a week, she hadn't worn Emily's sweater to school. She wondered if Emily regretted giving it to her now. But she couldn't think about that. Her stomach was a jumble of butterflies about Alfie. They hadn't spoken since she'd raced out of his house. She hoped she hadn't gotten him in trouble with his grandfather.

Alfie was staring at a plastic container filled with drool-worthy nachos when Ali sat down at the table. Next to him, Murray was almost finished stuffing nachos into his mouth and was beginning to eye Alfie's container. He smiled at Ali and pointed at her hands. She waved them in the air and he snorted.

"Those look yummy," Ali said, pointing at the nachos.

Mouth full, Murray said. "I'm fulfilling the losing end of the Hawaiian shirt bet. My dad made them this morning, but this guy hasn't even tried them yet." He swallowed, took a slug of water, and leaned in to Alfie. "What, are my dad's nachos not tasty enough for you?"

Alfie picked up a chip and began to nibble. "Sorry— just a bad day."

Ali reached across the table and nabbed a chip. "Is it the Sloane Family Feud?"

Alfie nodded.

Murray frowned. "What's the Sloane Family Feud?"

"Is it okay if I tell him?" she asked Alfie. He nodded again.

"Alfie's grandfather is mad at my dad and our great-grandmother. They haven't spoken in years."

"Whoa. That's a lot of anger," said Murray.

"Uh-huh. Yesterday I went to see him, because I'm throwing our great-grandmother a one hundredth birthday party this coming Saturday, and I want to reunite the family."

"Let me guess—he turned you down."

Alfie picked up the story. "He turned her down, and he's furious at me for hanging out with her. Said I should have told him. He thinks I'm being disloyal to my dad's memory by even talking to you," he said, turning toward Ali. "We had a big argument. Then he and my mom had an argument, and now he's not talking to either of us."

Making things worse was not part of the plan. Ali slumped back in her chair.

"What does your dad have to do with the feud?" Murray asked.

"He's the reason they're fighting. My grandfather thinks Ali's dad and our great-grandmother caused his death."

"Seriously? Wow, this is like a movie or something. Did they?"

"I don't know," Ali said. "I don't actually know how Alfie's dad died."

Alfie stared down at his food. "My mom told me everything last night." His voice was low, but to Ali, it sounded like he was shouting. "Our dads always wanted to take a boat through the Reversing Falls at high tide; you know, run the rap-

> ALI'S RULES WHEN YOU FIND OUT DEEP DARK FAMILY SECRETS
> 1. Wish you didn't know the truth.

ids. I guess it was on their bucket list or something. Anyway, on my dad's thirtieth birthday, they did it. Then the boat flipped over and my dad drowned."

Ali gasped. How could Digger have been so stupid? "But why is he mad at Gigi?"

"She bought my dad the boat as a gift. Granddad says she was always encouraging your dad and mine to be adventurous, even if what they wanted to do was reckless."

Murray nodded. "I get why your grandfather is mad, but it sounds like an accident."

Alfie nodded. "Plus, no one made my dad run the rapids. He *wanted* to go."

Murray popped another chip into his mouth. "How long ago did this happen?"

"A few months before I was born."

"How did Ali's dad survive?"

Ali had a pretty good idea of how Digger had survived. She pictured him turning into a fish and swimming away. Why hadn't he saved Teddy?

"I dunno," said Alfie. "Luck? I just wish our family would let it go. Fighting about it won't bring my dad back."

"Were you living in Saint John then?" Murray asked Ali.

"Nope, I wasn't born yet. I'd never set foot in Saint John until a couple of weeks ago. After Alfie's dad died, my parents left town. My dad refused to even visit Saint John, which makes sense, now that I know the whole story. He must have felt so guilty. They were best friends."

Cassie arrived in a flurry. "Sorry I'm late," she said, plopping down beside Ali. "I was talking to Ms. Ryder about debate team. Mind if I try some?" she said, reaching out to grab a handful of Alfie's nachos, oblivious to the table's somber mood.

"What about debate team?" Alfie asked. Ali could tell he was ready to change the topic.

"So, my mom is a member of Toastmasters International—"

"What's that?" Ali asked.

"It's an organization that helps its members become better public speakers. My mom joined when she got promoted to vice president at the YMCA. Anyway, her chapter has invited our debate team to come to their meeting on Saturday and practice debating with them. How fun is that?"

Ali shook her head. "I can't. We're having my great-grandmother's birthday party this Saturday." She glanced over at Alfie, who kept his eyes fixed on the table.

"What time is the party?"

"Four o'clock."

"Well, it will be over by eleven o'clock, so you're okay. Plus, I need you to be there. We'll be in teams of two, and you can be my partner. Murray?"

"I'll check with my parents." Ali could tell from the way Murray spoke that he was in.

"Alfie?"

"Sure. I don't have anything going on this Saturday."

"Aren't you—" began Cassie, then stopped when Murray flashed her a "Zip it!" look.

Debating in front of a bunch of strangers was not in Ali's future. "I promised to help my mom get things ready for the party."

Cassie refused to take no for an answer. "You have to be there. How about I come to your house afterward and help you and your mom?"

Ali knew from the way Cassie glared at her that she was not going to drop the subject. "Fine, I'll be there." What did it matter if she was the worst debater ever? Things were awful anyway. She might as well go down in flames.

Chapter Eleven
FOG AND WEATHER

One popular belief is that the number of fog days in the summer equals the number of snow days in winter, though, so far as I know, this remains unproven.

—PERCIVAL T. SLOANE,
  A History of Fog in the Bay of Fundy *(1932)*

THIRTY-TWO

Emily dragged Ali to the computer lab as soon as Mr. Corby said project teams could break off to work on their presentations. Emily stuck her flash drive in the laptop, and they waited for the file to open. Ali could tell Emily wanted her to say something.

"I'm sorry again about Friday," Ali offered, hoping that would ease the tension.

"No biggie." But it felt big.

The presentation appeared on the computer screen.

"It looks great!" said Ali, admiring the first slide, which was covered in images of the various organisms they'd encountered on the field trip.

"I'm still working on it," Emily said. "It can be better." She pressed the return key and the images swirled away, replaced by a cartoon of a cell on a microscope slide and the words: WHY DID THE GERM CROSS THE MICROSCOPE? TO GET TO THE OTHER SLIDE.

"That's so funny!" Ali exclaimed.

Emily gave her a pleased grin, then turned serious again. "We should speak to alternate slides, don't you think?"

"Whatever you think."

Emily frowned. She read the germ joke and pushed return. A new slide explaining the methodology for the field study filled the screen. Ali read it quickly, self-conscious in front of Emily. When she finished, Emily held up her hand.

"Your delivery was flat. We need to keep people interested."

Ali tried again. Emily shook her head. After Ali's fourth try, Emily gave her a half-hearted nod. "I guess that's okay."

Ali knew it wasn't okay, because Emily had pressed

her lips together into a tight line. "Show me how you'd do it," Ali said.

Emily pressed restart. Ali listened with rapt attention as Emily made each slide interesting and funny.

"Let me try," Ali said, sure she could mimic Emily's delivery. "If I'm not better, then you can present by yourself tomorrow and I'll push the buttons, okay?"

She could tell Emily believed she'd be the button pusher. They began again, and this time the smile Emily gave Ali when they finished was genuine. "That was awesome! You sounded just like me! Let's do it again to be sure."

After four more run-throughs—Emily said a person could never practice too much—they were a well-oiled machine.

"We'll be the best," Emily told Ali as they headed back to the classroom.

Ali sure hoped so.

Ms. Ryder handed out forms as soon as they arrived at debate after school. "These information sheets explain the Toastmasters event this Saturday. It's wonderful that Cassie's mom has arranged this great opportunity for us. Debating in front of strangers is hard at first, but at least you know the Toastmasters will be rooting for you. I spoke with your mom at lunch, Cassie, and we've decided to have teams of three, not two." She turned on the Smart Board. "Here are the topics: 'Be it resolved that the age at which a person should vote should be lowered from eighteen to sixteen' and 'Be it resolved that students at Princess Elizabeth School should wear school uniforms.' You'll debate each topic for twenty minutes, followed by ten minutes of helpful suggestions by the Toastmasters. The entire event, including the reception afterward where you'll be able to interact with the Toastmasters, will last two hours."

Debating *and* talking with strangers? Ali clutched the seat of her chair.

"Team one is Alfie, Ashok, and Carolyn. They'll argue for lowering the voting age and against school uniforms. Ali, Cassie, and Murray will do the opposite.

I realized when I pulled the names out of the hat that it's a bit of the newbies versus those with experience, but I have faith in you, Cassie and Ali! Any questions?"

Ali raised a trembling arm. "I'm not sure I can make it on Saturday."

Cassie spun around and glared at her.

Ms. Ryder was more understanding. "It'll be too bad if you can't make it. Please just let me know before end of day Friday so I can adjust the teams, okay?" Ali nodded.

Ms. Ryder clapped her hands. "Let's divide into groups and work on your arguments."

Ali followed Murray and Cassie to the back of the classroom.

Cassie didn't try to hide her unhappiness. "You said you would go. My mom's gone to a lot of trouble to organize this."

Ali swallowed hard. "I need to ask my parents." She didn't want them to be mad at her.

"But—"

Murray jumped in. "Stop bugging her, Cass. I told

you I have to ask my parents, too."

Cassie gave a begrudging nod. Drama over, Murray opened his notebook to take notes. "We need to make a list of reasons the voting age should stay at eighteen. Go."

Ali's mind was a blank, but Cassie jumped right in. "Eighteen-year-olds are more responsible than sixteen-year-olds. They know more about life."

"And eighteen is the age that the government considers people adults," Murray added as he wrote. "Eighteen-year-olds can marry without their parents' permission—"

"And there's research that proves that our brains are still developing when we're teenagers," said Ali, relieved to add a point. "The closer to adulthood a person is before they can vote, the more they'll under-stand what's important and not important to vote for." She was happy to see Murray write down her point word for word.

"What kind of arguments do you think they'll use to counter?" Murray asked.

"I think they'll argue that if you can drive a car at sixteen, you can vote," said Ali.

"And that teens have interesting opinions and could shake up politics," Cassie added.

Murray got excited. "Yeah! Like the kids fighting for gun control and the environment or against racial profiling. Think of the difference they'd make if they could vote."

"We should do some research on other countries' voting ages," Ali suggested.

Murray pulled out his phone and did a quick search. "Interesting—the voting age used to be twenty-one. But the majority of countries use eighteen as their voting age now. A few countries have even older voting ages: twenty in Taiwan and twenty-one in Samoa. So we should argue that world opinion is that eighteen is the right age." He reread his notes. "Okay . . . how about Cassie and I work on the arguments that support our proposition, and Ali works on ways we could tear apart their counterarguments? We'll review it at school on Wednesday, okay?"

Ali nodded. She wouldn't forget this time.

They went through the same exercise with the second debate topic. Ali was still terrified, but it was to fun to brainstorm ideas with Murray and Cassie.

"One more thing," Cassie said to Ali as they got up to join the other debaters. "You have to control yourself on Saturday. No changing."

"I wouldn't change!" Ali protested.

Murray rolled his eyes. "Hello, C. S. Lewis's hands. Keep it together, Sloane. We can't afford to be disqualified because one of our members turns into a Toastmaster."

Ali was in such a hurry to get home and practice for the next day's presentation that she forgot to wait for Alfie. She was startled when he called her name and ran to catch up with her.

"You don't want to debate, do you?" he asked.

"Debating in front of strangers scares me to death."

Alfie smiled. "I think it's scary too, which makes me want to do it."

"You know that doesn't make any sense, right?" Ali picked at a piece of lint on her jacket so she didn't have to look at Alfie when she said, "The more I think about your dad's death, the angrier I am at Digger."

Alfie's shoulders drooped. "My mom says that's why they call them accidents; people don't mean for them to happen. And there are boat tours at the Reversing Falls all the time. But yeah, I think your dad and mine were stupid. They should have known better."

It was more than just stupidity. Ali wished she could tell Alfie that Digger was a Copycat. Then he'd understand. Digger should have turned into a giant eagle and plucked Teddy from the water. Why didn't he?

"I'm sorry I couldn't convince your grandfather to come to the party."

"You did your best. I just wish . . ."

"That you could meet Digger and Gigi," finished Ali.

"Yeah. I keep trying to figure out how I can, but I don't want to go against my mom and my grandfather. They're all I have."

"I know. I wish I had a magic wand; I'd turn back the clock so none of this awful stuff would happen."

"I wish you could. Hey . . . I heard you're doing your science presentation tomorrow. So are Murray and Cassie."

"Another thing to worry about! Emily wants ours to be the best."

"Wait until you see what Cassie and Murray have up their sleeve. It's epic."

"Uh-oh. What are they doing?"

Alfie shook his head. "I'm sworn to secrecy."

"But I'm your cousin!"

"I'm still sworn to secrecy."

Ali kicked at a stone on the sidewalk and sent it flying. "Emily will be so mad at me if they get a better grade than us."

Alfie laughed. "I don't know Emily, but she needs to relax. Like my mom always says: There's no I in TEAM."

"Yeah, but there's an E for EMILY."

"And an L for let it go. Don't worry; I bet you guys will be awesome."

Ali sighed. "You're right." She glanced up at the gloomy sky. "I'd give anything for one sunny day. Digger says the fog won't lift until it's ready to and that wishing for something doesn't make any difference."

"He's right about that," said Alfie.

THIRTY-THREE

Ali's parents were whispering at the kitchen table when she came downstairs the next morning. Their expressions were so glum it made Ali's breath catch.

"Is Gigi okay?"

Digger motioned for her to take a seat. Ali braced herself for bad news.

"Your mother and I were just talking about Gigi. We're worried about her. I couldn't get her to leave her room at all yesterday. She seems distracted, and when I took her dinner up to her last night, she was talking to herself. We love living with Gigi, but we're worried that at some point we won't be able to care for her."

"But Mom knows how to care for elderly people; that's her job!"

Her mother winced. "You're right. But at work we have special equipment, and alarms that tell us when a resident has left their room or is hurt, and there are lots of staff to help. At home, it's just your dad."

"I can help Digger after school and on the weekends. Please don't make her leave."

Digger's voice was thick with emotion when he responded. "Ali, we're not saying she's going to have to go into a home, at least not yet. We'll monitor her for a few weeks and hope things get better."

"Can't we hire a nurse?"

"Gigi doesn't have money for a nurse. That's why she asked us to move in with her. But we didn't realize how unwell she was until we got here."

"Where would she go if she couldn't live here?"

"If it comes to that, I'll try to have her placed in my nursing home soon," said Ali's mother. "I'll talk to the administrator. We'll likely need to get Gigi assessed in advance."

"No!" Ali didn't mean to shout, but Gigi stuck in a home with a bunch of sick old people made her frantic. "She'd hate it there, you know she would! The food would be awful, she wouldn't have her things, and how could she feed her birds and squirrels?"

Her mother drew in a breath and reached for Ali's hand. Ali jerked back and jumped to her feet. "She asked us to come live with her so she could stay at home. It sounds like you're giving up on her. It's not fair. You guys never try; you just move on when things get hard!"

"Ali." There was a warning in Digger's voice.

"Whatever," Ali said. "I should go pack my things now. Nothing ever changes with you two." She grabbed her knapsack and slammed the door on her way out. She didn't care that school didn't start for forty-five minutes or that she hadn't eaten breakfast: she couldn't bear to be in Gigi's house a minute longer. Her parents were ruining everything again.

Ali avoided people all day. When Cassie pressed her about Toastmasters in homeroom, she muttered,

"Probably," even though she hadn't checked with her parents. Not that they'd care one way or another. They didn't care about her at all.

At lunchtime, she turned into a moth and hid in a crack in the wall behind a bookshelf in the library. She was too sad about Gigi and too mad at her parents to talk to anyone. It was only when she walked into science class that she recalled it was presentation day.

Emily cornered her straightaway. "Where were you? I looked for you at lunch. We needed to practice!"

"Sorry. I had to do something." Emily had dressed up in a seafoam-green sweater dress and her hair was done up in elaborate French braids. Ali's faded jeans and T-shirt were shabby in comparison.

Emily crossed her arms. "But you're ready, right?"

Ali nodded. She'd read over her notes the night before, but now, knowing she had to speak in front of her classmates, she was a jittery mess. She took her seat, trying to swallow the lump that kept rising in her throat.

Mr. Corby clapped his hands. "Our first two presenters have done an interesting field study pertaining to the classification of organisms. Come on up, Ali and Emily."

When the first slide popped onto the Smart Board everyone clapped. Emily had made it even better than what Ali had seen the day before. She'd changed the title to CLASSIFIED, and used a font to make it seem like their presentation was top secret. Everybody laughed. It must have taken her all evening to make it look so good. Ali had spent ten minutes reviewing her notes, then read until she fell sleep. No wonder Emily did so well in school.

Emily fixed her brightest smile on the class. "For our project, Ali and I did an inventory of all of the living creatures in a one-block radius of King's Square in order to see how many of the kingdoms we could observe."

Ali was next, but her nerves made it impossible to deliver an Emily-worthy performance. Her

ALI'S RULES FOR PRESENTATIONS
1. Try not to do them.
2. Actually help.
3. Seriously, don't do them.

words came out in a monotonous ramble. "We dis-covered that even though Emily lives in the heart of the city, she's surrounded by tons of different organ-isms. For example, we saw almost a hundred people. Each of them was covered in bacteria, fungi, and archaea, which are single-celled organisms. We have ninety trillion of them in and on our bodies, which means that those hundred people had nine quadril-lion things crawling on them."

"I'm going to throw up," said Tom.

"Cool," said Cassie.

"Anyone else feel itchy?" asked Mr. Corby. The whole class, including Emily and Ali, cracked up.

Emily clicked through the presentation. She and Ali went back and forth, describing what they'd seen and identifying the correct classifications. Every time Emily spoke, people paid attention. They loved her funny pictures and videos. Ali didn't get the same reaction. The longer she stood at the front of the classroom, the more rattled she became. Her delivery was so flat that during her last slide, a couple of kids yawned and Emily appeared ready to cry.

Still, if anyone could save the day, it was Emily with their closing remarks. "I guess to sum up, when we first started studying the classification system in class, it was kind of dull." She grinned at Mr. Corby, who pretended to look offended. "But once we started to look around, we realized how cool it is to be able to organize the world into categories. Science helps us make sense of the world around us and allows us to talk in a common language."

"Excellent," said Mr. Corby, "Ali, anything to add?"

Ali shook her head and smiled weakly at Emily.

"Who was responsible for which part of the project?" Mr. Corby asked.

Emily took a deep breath. "We did the inventory together," she began.

Ali waited. This wasn't going to be good.

"And . . . ," Mr. Corby said.

Had Emily already told him that she hadn't pulled her weight? Emily paused. "And I did the rest." She said it fast, like it pained her to say it.

Taylor gasped dramatically. Mr. Corby, face inscrutable, thanked them and told them to sit down.

"Can I say one last thing?" Emily asked.

"Of course."

"I just want to say that I learned so much, like how to decide how to classify what you see. You think things are one way, and then they turn out to be something else altogether." Without so much as a glance in Ali's direction, she hurried to her seat. Ali slunk back to hers, wishing she could disappear.

"Next up: Cassie and Murray," said Mr. Corby.

THIRTY-FOUR

Ali was disheartened to realize that Murray and Cassie had also dressed up: Murray in a tad-too-big gray suit and Cassie in a sky-blue dress. Clearly, Ali was the only one who hadn't gotten the memo. Murray pressed start with a flourish, and the title slide burst onto the Smart Board like a firecracker. Music filled the air. Even Ali, who didn't watch much TV, recognized the familiar theme song right away.

"This is Classification Jeopardy!" Murray boomed.

Everyone, including Mr. Corby, clapped and stamped their feet.

Cassie took over. "Now entering our studio: this eleven-year-old boy plays basketball and is addicted to Minecraft. Please welcome Tom Power!"

Tom raced to the front of the classroom, high-fiving everyone in his row along the way.

"This twelve-year-old girl plays the clarinet, loves lip gloss, and says her favorite place to visit is New York City. Please welcome Taylor Marshall!"

More clapping. Ali could tell from how they acted that Tom and Taylor had agreed to participate before the class started. Why hadn't Cassie and Murray asked her?

"And please welcome our last contestant, who wants to be a professional hockey player when he grows up and whose current team, the Vito's Pizza Vipers, was undefeated last season. Please welcome Jackson Mather!"

Jackson lumbered to the front of the classroom, grinning, his ears a bright red. Cassie handed each of them a small metal clicker.

"Welcome, everyone," said Murray, "Now let's play CLASSIFICATION JEOPARDY!"

The screen dissolved into the familiar game board

featuring five categories: CELL-O: IS IT ME YOU'RE THINKING OF?; HAIR TODAY, GONE TOMORROW; EYE GOT YOU; CREEPY-CRAWLIES; BRINGS OUT THE ANIMAL IN ME.

"Very clever," said Mr. Corby.

"We did a coin toss earlier," said Cassie. "Jackson, you get to go first."

"I'll take Cell-O, Is It Me You're Thinking Of? for one hundred, Alex, I mean, Murray," Jackson said.

"I'm the simplest organism kingdom and my members have one cell," read Murray.

Taylor clicked first. "What is Monera?" she shouted.

"Very enthusiastic response, and correct," Cassie responded. She wrote one hundred on a piece of paper under Taylor's name. "You get to choose the next category, Taylor."

"I'll take Eye Got You for three hundred, please."

"I'm a crustacean with one eye, proving what?"

Tom clicked first. "What is, not every species in the Animalia kingdom has two eyes?"

"Correct!"

The game went on for fifteen minutes, and as the three players amassed ever higher scores, the class became more enthusiastic. Not everyone, though. Emily sat stone-faced, arms crossed. Ali could tell Emily thought Cassie and Murray's presentation was better, and she was right. Not only had Ali messed up her and Emily's presentation, for some reason Cassie and Murray hadn't asked her to play Classification Jeopardy. She tried to tell herself it was no big deal, but it was.

In the end, Taylor prevailed and received a gold plastic trophy, which she held aloft like it was an Olympic medal as she returned to her seat.

Mr. Corby motioned for quiet. "First, congratulations, Cassie and Murray: you've invented an excellent teaching tool to help students learn about classifying organisms. I might borrow it myself for next term."

"For a small fee," Murray said. Ali couldn't tell if he was serious or not.

"We'll negotiate later." Mr. Corby chuckled. "And congratulations to Taylor for paying attention to my riveting lectures."

Taylor waved to the class like she was the queen.

"Best presentation ever!" someone shouted.

Emily stared straight ahead, expressionless.

As soon as the bell rang, Ali bolted. She wanted to avoid Emily for as long as possible. She hid in the same bathroom stall she'd used the day she became a Copycat. So much had happened since then, and none of it was good: Gigi's poor health, Ali's inability to end the Sloane Family Feud, and now, this horrible day. Saint John was supposed to be a fresh start, but like always, nothing had worked out. In the past, she would have blamed her parents for everything. But now she had to admit the truth: she was part of the problem. Maybe she was incapable of making friends.

The door opened, and Emily's and Taylor's voices filled the bathroom.

"Our team was awful!" Emily wailed.

Could Copycats turn invisible?

ALI'S RULES FOR WHEN YOU DON'T FIT IN
1. Move.
2. Change again.
3. Try to find other friends.

Because right now, being invisible was the best idea ever.

"Your presentation was fine," said Taylor, her voice soothing.

"It was no Classification Jeopardy! You know Ali didn't even help me?"

"I know. That's so unfair."

Ali's mother had once said what people think about us is none of our business. As she listened to Emily and Taylor talk about her, Ali agreed.

"I worked for hours on it. She just hung out with her friends and didn't care about me."

Not care about Emily? How could Emily think that?

"I thought you guys were getting to be good friends."

Emily sounded like she was crying when she responded. "Me too. But then she left me to do the project, and she's always ditching me for Cassie. Plus, I don't get her. She's so annoying; it's like she has no opinions of her own. It's always 'Yes, Emily,' 'Whatever you want, Emily.'" She paused. Ali hoped she was finished but she wasn't. "Everything about her is a lie, and I don't need people in my life who I can't trust. I guess I'm lucky I found out early on, before she hurt me like . . ." Her voice trailed off, and Taylor clicked her tongue in sympathy.

It was all Ali could do not to burst into tears. A sick, sinking sensation settled in her stomach. Usually kids liked it when she acted like them and agreed with their opinions, didn't they? Then why wasn't that working here? One of her feet started to slip off the toilet seat. She grabbed the metal toilet paper dispenser to steady herself and winced when it clanged. The bathroom went quiet.

"Someone's in here," whispered Taylor.

"Hello?" Emily called.

Ali was trapped.

"I think it came from the last stall," said Taylor.

Then . . . footsteps and a sharp rap on the stall door. "Anybody in there?" Taylor asked.

Please let the bell ring, please let the bell ring.

Ali began to slip again. The toilet paper dispenser's lid clanked as she tried to hang on.

"There *is* someone in there," said Taylor. "Hold my bag; I'm going to take a look."

Ali sucked in her breath.

"You are not going to believe this," Taylor said.

THIRTY-FIVE

Ali let loose a plaintive meow.

"Here, kitty, kitty," Taylor cooed.

"There's a cat in the bathroom?" Emily sounded incredulous.

"It's so cute!" said Taylor. "I'm going to try to catch it." She began to wriggle her way into the stall. Frantic, Ali jumped from her perch and slipped under the metal wall.

"It's in the next stall!" Emily shouted.

Taylor began to crawl backward, bumping her head. "Ouch! Grab it!"

"I'm not grabbing that cat!"

"You have to! It must be lost!"

Their gym teacher, Ms. Morton, stuck her head in the bathroom. "What's all the yelling?"

Ali saw her chance and slipped between Ms. Morton's legs. The teacher gave a startled screech. Ali needed to get out of this building—fast. But how?

"There's a cat in the school!" someone shouted.

A hand reached for Ali. She veered left. She had to get away before she could turn back into herself. She ran on, but came to a sudden stop when Ms. Ryder came around the corner, dangling something that smelled awfully good.

Ms. Ryder crouched and extended an open palm. "Here, kitty, kitty, kitty." Ali wanted to run away, but she couldn't. As Ms. Ryder drew closer, she understood why: Ms. Ryder held a piece of turkey. Ali took a deep sniff and slunk closer. As she leaned in for a bite, Ms. Ryder scooped her up. "Naughty kitty!" she cooed.

Principal Birchwood stepped out of her office. "Ms. Ryder, why do you have a cat?"

"The poor thing must have slipped into the building," said Ms. Ryder. "I was about to put it outside."

Principal Birchwood sniffed. "Do so right now. I'm allergic to cats, and my asthma will be out of control."

As they made their way to the nearest entrance, kids begged Ms. Ryder to let them pet Ali, which was kind of nice but also kind of creepy. Ms. Ryder pushed the door open with her back and set Ali down. "Go home, kitty. Thanks for visiting Princess Elizabeth School." She closed the door, and Ali was alone.

For a brief moment, Ali considered turning back to herself. But someone might see her and make her go back to school. There was no way she was doing *that*. She could never face Emily again. She would go home and try to convince her parents to homeschool her. But to do that, she'd have to stay a cat.

Until this moment, Ali had believed cats had it easy: they went where they wanted to go, caught the odd mouse, curled up in sunny windows for long naps, were fed and petted by adoring owners. She was wrong. She was outside Princess Elizabeth School for all of three minutes when some boy she didn't recognize tried to grab her. She wiggled free, scratching him in the process, and raced off. Right into the parking lot, where Vice Principal Campbell, who was just pulling her massive truck into her parking space, almost ran her over. But Ali the cat was fast; she flung herself under the next car.

She hadn't reckoned on the sensory overload. The sound of Vice Principal Campbell slamming her truck door was the rumble of an earthquake. A screeching seagull was fingernails on a chalkboard. Her hiding place was a sickening blend of motor oil, asphalt, and already-chewed gum. Her eyes were magical; even in the dim light she could see ants scurrying by, the miniscule writing on a balled-up fast-food wrapper, the movement of a tiny mouse six cars over. And though her cat instincts were desperate to chase the mouse, she held herself in check. There was only one objective: home.

She crawled out from underneath the car. What was the best way home? Her normal route was straightforward: a residential neighborhood, followed by a shopping plaza, more businesses, a couple of churches, a few busy intersections, and then Douglas Avenue. It was easy for someone in seventh grade, but for a cat it seemed impossible. Still, what choice did she have? It wasn't like she could call home and meow for help. But after the first car roared past her, she decided to alter her route and go through backyards instead.

It was a good idea until house number four, where she encountered an enormous sleeping Rottweiler. She'd almost made it to the opposite fence when he opened an eye and, in a flash, was on his feet and headed straight for her, teeth bared. The only way out was up, so Ali hurled herself at the fence, digging her claws into the cedar planks until she was within jumping distance of an overhanging branch. She froze. Would it hold her? But the warm stinky breath of the Rottweiler as it sprang ever closer convinced her to try. She leapt.

> ALI'S FELINE FOUR
> 1. Beware of dogs.
> 2. Beware of people holding turkey and other yummy things.
> 3. Be careful. Not everyone likes cats!
> 4. Take your time to smell the catnip. Being a cat is cool!

There was a dreadful creak when she landed, followed by a horrible crack as the branch broke away. She leapt again, and though she missed the tree trunk, her momentum propelled her forward, and she landed in a prickly holly bush on the other side of the fence from her attacker.

Even though she was scratched and bleeding, Ali was ecstatic. She was alive! And surprised. When she'd practiced turning into animals or people before, she'd only stayed like them for a couple of minutes. Now, fifteen minutes into her Ali the cat transformation, she realized she hadn't taken enough time to experience what it was like to be someone else before. Being a cat was fun! The heightened senses. How easy it was to jump and climb. It was like she was born to be a cat. No wonder Digger was a dog so often. There was something freeing about being an animal that wasn't trying to impress anyone. Maybe that was the solution: stay a cat forever.

But first she needed to get home. It was time to return to her usual route. Except that was even more dangerous. Ali was almost taken out twice by bicyclists using the sidewalk (wasn't that against city bylaws?) and another time by a jogger who kicked at her as he ran past. Everything she encountered was a new peril, which made the going slow. A route that normally took twenty minutes took an hour. By the time she saw her house in the distance, she was like an exhausted soldier home from the war.

There was still a huge problem: she couldn't change back and walk in the front door. Digger might see her and make her go back to school. No, the only one way to get into the house unseen was via the tree next to Gigi's window. Thanks to her Rottweiler experience, it was an easy climb. When she reached the branch across from Gigi's window, she took a deep breath and jumped, hoping Gigi was asleep.

She was. Ali the cat crept across the room, thankful the bedroom door was ajar.

"Hello, Ali."

Ali froze. "Gigi?" she whispered, but it came out as "Mrow."

"I hope you had a good day." Gigi rolled over and went back to sleep.

Relieved, Ali hurried to her bedroom. She'd hide in her closet until school was over, then sneak downstairs and pretend she'd just arrived home. Simple. Except nothing was simple anymore, and probably never would be again.

Chapter Twelve
FOG TREASURES

Mrs. Mabel McLaughlin of Maces Bay once discovered a full casket of wine on the shore in front of her home after three days of thick fog. Alexander MacLeod of St. Andrews wrote in his diary in 1931 that he'd found three barrels of gunpowder and a brass bowl after a week of fog.

—PERCIVAL T. SLOANE,
  A History of Fog in the Bay of Fundy *(1932)*

THIRTY-SIX

When Ali pretended to arrive home an hour later, she found Digger at the kitchen table. She was surprised to see party invitations and envelopes, along with Gigi's address book, in front of him.

"Weren't those supposed to be mailed last week?"

Digger was sheepish. "I forgot. I'm almost finished, and then I'll deliver them before supper. Most are for the neighbors since so many of Gigi's friends are no longer alive."

"I guess that's what happens when you live to be one hundred," said Ali. It must be sad when all your friends pass away. Not that Ali knew anything about friends. She leaned over his shoulder, surprised when she saw whose name he was writing on the envelope: Andrew Sloane.

"You're dropping off an invitation for Andrew Sloane?"

"She wants me to invite all the Other Sloanes, so I am."

A contrite Ali took a seat across the table. "I need to tell you something, and you're not going to like it."

Digger stopped writing. "What?"

"I went to see Andrew Sloane on Sunday afternoon."

"Without asking permission."

Ali nodded. "I know I should have asked you first, but I knew you'd say no."

"I would have."

"I had to go. Alfie was sure he'd agree to come if I asked him."

"Let me guess. He said no."

Just thinking of their conversation made Ali's eyes well up. "He said more than no. He said our powers are unnatural. He said you and Gigi killed Teddy. And Alfie told me how it happened."

Digger took a deep breath, then did something unexpected: he finished addressing the party invitation to Andrew Sloane.

"Wait—you're still going to invite him?"

"Uh-huh." Digger licked the envelope and picked up the last unaddressed party invitation. "Look. I'm not happy you went to see Uncle Andrew without talking to me first. And I'm not happy that he said those things to you. But if Gigi wants him here, he gets an invitation."

"But what about the awful things he said?"

"He's entitled to his opinion. As for Teddy's death? I happen to agree with him, at least in terms of my involvement."

"But it was an accident!"

Digger shook his head. "A car accident is an accident. Neither Teddy nor I knew anything about going through rapids, and Gigi shouldn't have bought him a boat so we could try. It was sheer stupidity."

Ali didn't add that she'd also thought Digger had been stupid when Alfie had told her what had happened. "Is that why you left Saint John and never wanted to come back?"

Digger nodded, then picked up his pen and finished filling out the invitation. "I owed it to Uncle Andrew to leave town and never come back."

"But if we'd never come back, I'd never have met Alfie!"

"Maybe that would have been for the best. All this talk about Alfie and her birthday party has given Gigi hope for a reconciliation that's never going to happen."

"Maybe Uncle Andrew will get the invitation and change his mind!"

"Don't count on it." He sealed the last envelope and stood up. "I'm off to make my deliveries. Do you mind keeping an eye on Gigi?"

"Okay."

The phone rang as Ali headed upstairs to check on Gigi. The display read PRINCESS ELIZABETH SCHOOL. Great. When the voice message button began to light up, Ali picked up the receiver and entered the code.

"Hello, Mr. and Mrs. Sloane, this is Principal

Birchwood. Ali didn't attend her afternoon classes. I'm assuming she went home sick, but just wanted to make sure. Can you call or send me an email to let me know you got this message?"

Ali hit delete.

A few minutes later, Ali rapped on Gigi's door. There was no response. Ali decided to let her be. She didn't want to watch Gigi sleep. In her heart, she knew Digger and her mom were right; Gigi needed more help. At least she would have her birthday party, even if the Other Sloanes weren't there, and Ali would do her best to make it the best party ever.

Her wish to be invisible came true at school the next morning. Emily didn't acknowledge her when she walked past. She saw Murray and Cassie talking to Tom Power farther down the hallway and waved. Murray's wave was half-hearted, and Cassie didn't wave at all. What was going on? She waited for Tom to leave and then joined them.

"Hi, guys."

Cassie and Murray exchanged a look she couldn't decipher.

"Apparently, a cat was on the loose in school yesterday," said Murray.

Ali did her best to sound nonchalant. "Oh yeah?"

Murray crossed his arms. "Spill it, Sloane. Why did you turn into a cat?"

"I didn't—"

Cassie interrupted her. "Ali, we know it was you. Emily and Taylor said the cat was in the girls' washroom."

Before Ali could respond, Murray added, "Plus, you weren't in last class. Did you turn into a cat so you could ditch school? Were you that mad that our presentation was better than yours? 'Cause it sure seemed like it to us. You didn't smile or laugh at all. We didn't do that to you."

"Yours was great!" Ali hated how shrill she sounded.

Cassie shook her head. "I don't believe you."

It was embarrassing to tell them she'd changed because she'd didn't want Emily and Taylor to know

ALI'S RULES WHEN YOU'RE
CORNERED
1. Don't let people know
   you're upset.
2. Try to escape.
3. Come out swinging.

she'd overhead them talking about her and that she hadn't smiled during their presentation because it hurt her feelings that they hadn't picked her to participate. Not that they'd believe her, based on the angry looks they were sending her way.

She shrugged. "I don't know what the big deal is. It was fun when I changed Saturday afternoon."

"That was different!" said Murray. "You were testing your powers, not ditching school."

"I wasn't! I didn't have time to change back before Ms. Ryder put me outside!"

Cassie rolled her eyes. "You expect us to believe you? First you say you didn't turn into a cat, now you say you did, but you got put outside against your will. Which is the truth?"

It was like Ali was cornered by the Rottweiler again. She knew she should try to make them understand, but Cassie's condescension smarted. "I don't like being interrogated!" she said. "We're supposed to be friends. Imagine how stupid I felt when you picked other people to play Jeopardy and not me."

Cassie's eyes widened. She started to say something, but Ali wasn't done. "You think my abilities are cool when I do what you want me to do, but you never ask what it's like to be me, what it's like to go through this. I'm a person, not a freak! And by the way: I'm not going to the stupid Toastmaster event on Saturday. I'm quitting debate!" She stomped away, too angry to even look back.

She was almost to class when Ms. Ryder cornered her. "Ali, did your parents get my phone message last night about Saturday's event?"

Ali pictured herself deleting that message, too. "Uh-huh. I think they're going to call you later. They're both really busy today. I'm still not sure I can go."

Ms. Ryder looked her straight in the eye. "Did you go home sick yesterday?"

Ali nodded. "I was in the bathroom and all of a sudden I felt sick. I'm sorry I forgot to tell the secretary."

"Don't forget again, okay? We have those rules so we know our students are safe."

"I won't."

For the rest of the day, Ali avoided everyone. It was just as well; her family would be moving soon. She couldn't wait to leave Saint John. There was nothing here but fog, unhappy memories, and loneliness.

THIRTY-SEVEN

Ali was surprised to see Gigi at the breakfast table the next morning. When she'd knocked on Gigi's bedroom door the previous night, she'd overheard the old woman having an animated conversation with herself. Much as she hated to agree, maybe her parents were right: Gigi was losing it. But this morning Gigi was alert and happy. She wore her favorite peacock-blue dressing gown and was enjoying a slice of toast and a cup of coffee with Ali's mother.

"Have you seen my gloves, Alison?" Gigi asked when Ali joined them.

"What gloves?"

"My blue satin party gloves. For Saturday's party."

"I'm sure they're in your bureau," said Ali's mother. "I'll look for them when I get home later."

"Don't worry, I'll find them myself."

Ali's mother started to get up. "I'll run and check now."

Gigi put her hand on Ali's mother's arm, looking guilty. "Go to work, Ginger. Digger and I will find them. To be honest, I haven't even looked for them yet. I was being lazy, asking Ali where they were."

Ali's mother laughed. "Oh, Gigi, what would we do without you?"

"I hope you never have to find out," said Gigi.

ALI'S CHOICE FOR THE BEST LITERARY ANIMALS TO TURN INTO
1. Charlotte the spider. √
2. Stuart Little. Note to self: make an outfit for the next time you become a mouse.
3. Mole from The Wind in the Willows.
4. Aslan.
5. Hedwig the Owl.
√ indicates you have done this

Ali hid out in the library again at lunchtime, this time as a spider. She spun a tiny web between the photocopier and the wall, going so far as to include a word, just like Charlotte had in *Charlotte's Web*. Only her word was PATHETIC, because she was. The morning had been awful. Murray and Cassie gave her a wide berth. Emily, who seemed on the verge of tears throughout homeroom, ignored her too. It still hurt that Emily believed she had no opinions of her own. She had plenty of opinions, including the opinion that Cassie, Murray, and Emily were awful people.

When the five-minute warning bell rang, Ali the spider crawled to a private corner and changed back, brushing cobwebs off her jeans and hair. As she gathered her things to leave, she saw Emily huddled against a wall near the library's entrance. Her back was to Ali as she whispered into her phone.

"Daddy, I need you to come get me. No, Daddy, I mean it. I can't stay at school. I want to go home."

There was a pause. Ali started backing up. She had no right to hear this conversation.

"Please, Daddy." She didn't need to see Emily's face to know she was crying. "Please come get me. Please." Then: "Okay, I'll wait in the office for you."

Emily hung up and turned before Ali could duck out of the way. "Were you eavesdropping?" she demanded. Her face was blotchy, her hands clenched into tight fists. "It's bad enough that you came up with an awful idea that was nowhere near as good as Cassie and Murray's, now you have to be nosy too?"

Ali flinched. "No. I—"

"Don't lie. That's all you do. I suppose you're going to tell everybody that my dad's left my mom and moved out?"

"I wouldn't do that!" Ali protested. "I didn't even know that."

Emily crumpled and pressed a hand against the wall to steady herself. "He moved out yesterday," she whispered. "That's why they took me to lunch, you know. To tell me the news in a public place so I wouldn't make a scene."

Ali stepped forward. "I'm so sorry."

Emily recoiled. "I don't need your pity." She took a shaky breath. "I went to see the seals again yesterday."

"You did?" It made Ali sad to imagine Emily at Tin Can Beach all by herself. "How many are still there? When I went last weekend, there were only five left."

"One."

"Only one?"

Emily nodded. "Dr. Reynolds was there. She thinks the seals came ashore because one of them was sick, but when they realized he wouldn't make it, they left."

Ali pictured the seal with the patchy fur and milky gray eyes and winced. "That's awful."

Emily stared off in the distance. "Dr. Reynolds said that it was sad, but that the herd had to leave the sick one behind so it didn't drag them all down. But I don't agree with her. I don't think you abandon your family. Or your friends."

Was Emily talking about her?

"I didn't abandon you," Ali whispered.

Emily seemed taken aback. "I didn't mean *you*. I barely know you. And I know you aren't what you seem. You say whatever you think the other person wants to hear. You act like whoever you're with. I don't need a shadow. I need a real friend. You're nothing but a copycat."

Emily's words hurt Ali, because she knew Emily was right. She was a Copycat, through and through, in every way a person could be one.

"I want to be your real friend," Ali whispered.

"Do you? A friend does their share. A friend invites friends to sit with them at lunch," said Emily.

"But you sit with Taylor and hate Cassie."

"You don't understand anything, Ali Sloane." Emily burst into tears and raced away. Stunned, Ali slid down the wall until her bottom touched the floor. This was the worst day ever. She was just like that seal. Everyone wanted to leave her behind.

THIRTY-EIGHT

Alfie was waiting at her locker after school. "Can we talk?"

Ali could barely see the street when they stepped outside, the fog was so thick. It reminded Ali of the spring she was five years old and had pneumonia. Feverish, she had stayed in bed for days, listening to the sound of kids playing outside. It was like they existed in a different world, a world she couldn't imagine being part of. The fog was the same. Somewhere in the world the sun was shining, but Ali didn't think she'd ever see the sun again.

"This isn't about Murray and Cassie, is it?" she asked.

Alfie stopped. "Has something happened?"

Ali shook her head, relieved Murray and Cassie hadn't complained about her to Alfie.

Alfie took a deep breath. "I need to talk to you about something."

"What?

"I'm in trouble."

"What kind of trouble?"

Alfie's hand shook as he rubbed his forehead. "Something's happened. I think you know what I'm talking about. . . ."

Confused, Ali stared at him. She'd never seen him so upset. Then it hit her: Digger's invitation. "Your grandfather's mad that Digger invited your family to Gigi's party."

"What? Oh yeah, I saw Digger out on the porch, putting it in the mailbox. For a second I thought it was my dad. They look so much alike."

"That must have freaked you out."

"It did. I knew Granddad would be furious if I talked to him, but I didn't care. I have so many questions, so I went outside."

Why hadn't Digger told her he'd talked to Alfie? "Did he answer them?"

Alfie took a ragged breath. When he finally spoke, his voice was flat. "As soon as I opened the door, he ran to his car and drove away. I waved for him to come back, but he didn't."

Ali's jaw clenched. She was so sick of the Sloane Family Feud she wanted to scream. It was ridiculous that Digger hadn't talked to Alfie!

"You didn't tell me he was bringing us a party invitation." It sounded like an accusation.

"I didn't know until just before he left."

Alfie's forehead puckered. "I didn't think we'd get one after last Sunday."

They stopped at an intersection and waited for the light to change. Ali scowled. Why was she even hanging out with Alfie? Before, when she was sure the Sloanes would be reunited, she'd loved walking home with him. Now it just made her sad and frustrated. She wouldn't do it anymore. Besides, she'd be moving soon and so would he. They'd never see each other again, so what was the point?

She didn't try to hide her annoyance. "Inviting your family was the right thing to do."

"Granddad was furious."

"Whatever. Your grandfather needs to get over himself."

The light changed, but Alfie didn't move. "He's not awful, you know. He's sad."

Ali's patience plummeted. "Well, that makes two of us."

"Why are you sad?"

"This stupid fog, the fact that I don't have any friends, the fact that Gigi's been sick. I'm sad all the time, and your big trouble is that my dad inconveniently left a party invitation at your house."

Alfie leaned back, as if she'd slapped him. "I didn't know Gigi was sick."

It figured Alfie wouldn't ask about *her* problems. He'd said he wanted to be her friend, but he sure didn't act like one. "She was really sick with a bad cold and sometimes she gets confused. I'm worried about her."

"But she seems okay. I mean, you're having a party for her."

Really, Alfie was too much. "How would you know? You don't even know her! Guess what? Gigi is going to die soon, that's why we're having the party. All you care about is your precious grandfather. I did the right thing and went to see him. If you care as much as you say you do, you'd visit Gigi before it's too late!"

> ALI'S RULES ABOUT NOT
> LOSING FRIENDS
> 1. Don't pick a fight.
> 2. Try to walk in their
>   shoes for a minute,
>   really understand them.
> 3. Listen to them.
> 4. Seriously, listen to them.

Alfie opened his mouth, then shut it. The light changed again, and he rushed to cross.

Ali stayed put. "That's right," she called after him. "Run away! That's what Sloanes do!"

Alfie disappeared into the fog. Ali wrapped her arms around herself and began to cry. Why had she been so mean? Things had started so well for her in Saint John, but she'd ruined everything. For someone who could be anyone, she realized there was one thing she couldn't be: happy.

* * *

Ali was relieved to find Digger the dog asleep in front of the fireplace when she slipped into the house. She wasn't ready to talk about her day. Since everyone always said "quiet as a mouse," Ali set her knapsack on a chair, morphed into a brown mouse, and snuck upstairs. She was scurrying past Gigi's room when her great-grandmother called out to her.

"Alison, is that you?"

How Gigi heard her was a mystery, but Ali switched back into herself and stepped into Gigi's bedroom. Gigi was in her chair, staring out the window.

"How are you?" Ali asked, leaning over to kiss Gigi's wrinkled cheek.

"Surviving. You, on the other hand, look terrible."

Ali didn't try to deny it. "Today was the worst day of my life. Everybody hates me."

"You must have done something horrible; there are lots of students at Princess Elizabeth School and you've been there only a couple of weeks."

Ali collapsed onto the floor and buried her face

against Gigi's knees. "Things were supposed to be better here, but it's the worst place ever. Except for living with you," she added, looking up at Gigi with tearstained cheeks.

"That goes without saying. Want to talk about it?"

"Do I have to?"

"I find talking things out helps. Why don't you start at the beginning?"

What was the beginning? Debate team? Meeting Alfie? Becoming friends with Emily? Turning into a Copycat? Disappointing Murray and Cassie? Arguing with Alfie?

"I never should have joined the debate team."

"Why did you?"

"To meet Alfie, and then I pretended to like it because he did. But I hate public speaking; I'm terrible at it."

"I was terrible at first too."

The idea that Gigi could be terrible at anything shocked Ali. "Every time I do it, my stomach hurts."

"Then don't do it."

"But they're counting on me."

"They'll get over it. That's one problem solved. What's next?"

"In my old school, I tried to act like everyone else to get along. But it's not working here. Emily says I don't have opinions of my own. Murray and Cassie only like me when I do what they want me to do. They got mad at me because I didn't look happy during their presentation. But I was upset because they didn't choose me to play their stupid Jeopardy game. And I've been so busy learning to be a Copycat that I haven't kept up with my schoolwork. I didn't help Emily with our project and I did a terrible job of presenting to the class. And today I lost my temper at Alfie because he won't come to your party—"

"My goodness! That is a litany of woes! What do your problems have in common?"

"I don't know."

"I think you do. They have YOU in common."

Ali was not liking this conversation at all.

"But it's hard to be a Copycat *and* a new kid!"

"It is. But it sounds like you haven't been honest with people about the real you."

"The real me? You and Digger don't tell people that you're Copycats."

Gigi held up a bony finger. "It's not the same thing. We choose not to tell most people something that is very personal about ourselves. Everybody is entitled to have a personal life, Ali, even Copycats. Do any of your friends know about your powers?"

"Just Murray and Cassie."

"Have they told anyone?"

"No . . ."

"So, you're telling me they have been loyal to you but you haven't returned the favor?"

Ali didn't like the way that sounded.

"When you change just to impress people, whether you're a Copycat or not, you're not being true to yourself."

Ali let that sink in. "I don't even know who I am," she whispered. "I've been the new kid so many times I've *had* to be like everybody else to fit in."

For the first time, Gigi sounded sympathetic when she responded. "What's happened to you isn't fair. You've paid a price for your father's pain."

Ali didn't know what that meant, but she decided it was time to come clean about everything. "I went to see Andrew Sloane."

Gigi nodded. "I knew you would. You're a sweet girl, trying to fix something that isn't your responsibility to fix."

"I should have told you and Digger before I went. I'm sorry. He's not coming."

"Andy is doing what he thinks is right. And he's right about me. I failed Teddy, and not just because I bought him that boat."

"I don't understand."

Gigi's hand trembled as she smoothed Ali's hair. "I should have forced Andy to train Teddy, but I didn't, because I wanted to get along with Andy. Remember what we told you the night we started your training?"

"That an untrained Copycat is a dangerous thing?"

Gigi nodded. "Teddy was dangerous. What little

he knew, he'd taught himself or learned from Digger, but Digger wasn't as serious as he is now. He trusted Teddy would figure things out. I loved Teddy, but he was a terrible show-off. He tried to change as they went over the rapids and ended up overturning the boat. Digger was fine; he changed into a fish and swam for shore. But Teddy didn't have Digger's abilities. . . . Later, when Andy blamed Digger for Teddy's death, I lost my temper and blamed Andy. I told him that his pigheadedness about Copycats had killed his son. That was unfair. He never spoke to me again."

"It was an accident, Gigi."

"It was. And instead of coming together as a family, we blamed ourselves and one another. Teddy would be so disappointed in us. Does Digger know you went to see Andy?"

"Yes."

"How did he take it?"

"Okay, I guess. And even though he knows they won't come, he invited the Other Sloanes."

"That's my Digger. Thank you for trying, Alison.

You did your best. That's all any of us can do."

"What am I going to do about everything else? Should I call everyone and apologize?"

"Take your time. The history of this planet is people rushing to say and do things, when a day's reflection would make all the difference. You don't live to be my age and not realize that time is the great healer. Though not always. Sometimes, we have to heal ourselves."

Gigi seemed to sense that Ali was confused. "Here's what you're going to do: don't go to school tomorrow. Your problems will still be there on Monday, and sometimes taking a day to be nice to yourself is the best medicine. Besides, the house needs to be decorated."

"What will people think if I quit debate team?"

"They'll survive without you, especially if you're as terrible as you say you are."

"Gigi! But what if my quitting disappoints them?"

"You've spent your whole life trying not to disappoint anybody. Why don't you try to not disappoint

yourself and think about what
you'd like to do? Once you do that,
I promise that the right people will

ALI'S RULES FOR BEING HAPPY
1. Tell the truth.
2. Play Scrabble with Gigi.

show up in your life and you'll make real friends. Now,
how about you go grab the Scrabble board? I feel like
playing a game."

Chapter Thirteen
FOG RECORDS

The longest period of fog ever reported in the Bay of Fundy occurred at Saint John in July of 1833. The fog lasted twenty-eight days and resulted in three buggy accidents, the accidental death of an unlucky Mr. Morris Ryder, who stepped off a dock by mistake, and the migration of fifty-six residents who packed up and moved upriver to Grand Bay and never returned.

—Percival T. Sloane,
   A History of Fog in the Bay of Fundy *(1932)*

THIRTY-NINE

It was easy to take Gigi's advice and stay home from school on Friday. Ali told her parents she had a stomachache. After her outburst earlier in the week, they were inclined to believe her. Best of all, Digger called the school and left a message for Ms. Ryder, letting her know Ali wouldn't be at the debate team event. Ali was surprised by her relief. If only a simple phone call from Digger could fix everything that was wrong with her life!

The funny thing was, Ali realized it bothered her more that Murray and Cassie were mad at her than it did that Emily was. This was a surprise, because she'd been so impressed by Emily, so excited to be her friend. But there was something sad about Emily, not just about her parents splitting up, but about how much she wanted to be the best. Ali also knew that neither Murray nor Cassie would tell anyone her secret, even if they were angry. But Emily? She'd like to think Emily wouldn't tell anyone, but she wasn't sure.

And then there was Alfie. She'd been mad yesterday, but that wasn't fair. He was trying to make everyone happy, just like she was. Worst of all, she hadn't shared the most important thing about herself. He was her cousin; he deserved to know, even if it did upset his grandfather. She vowed to apologize on Monday and tell him she was a Copycat.

She spent the morning finishing *The Golden Compass*. It was a hard book, but interesting. The idea that people in Lyra's world had souls that lived outside their bodies intrigued her. Maybe her ability to transform herself into other creatures was her way of expressing her soul.

Right after lunch, she got to work. She grabbed a handful of Post-it notes from Gigi's desk, and some colorful markers, and climbed back into bed. Today was the day to get to know herself. Unlike her rules, this wasn't about coping with the world around her. It was about learning about the world within her. It was strange at first, thinking about things she liked, but pretty soon it was fun. She started with food.

ALI'S FAVORITE FOODS
- Chocolate chip cookies
- Fried chicken
- Caesar salad
- Carrots
- Oranges
- Bananas
- Oatmeal
- Birthday cake
- Brown bread
- Just-picked apples
- Ketchup
- Hamburgers
- Tacos

She couldn't believe how satisfying it was to write down things she loved. Next was ALI'S FAVORITE BOOKS. So far, there were six.

- *Anne of Green Gables*
- *Charlotte's Web*
- *A Wrinkle in Time*
- The first two Harry Potter books
- *The Golden Compass*

It was a start. She tried to think of other favorites:

- Color: sapphire blue
- Music: Beyoncé
- Sound I love: laughter
- Sound I hate: the foghorn
- Favorite things to do: swim and read
- Least favorite thing to do: talk in public
- Subject: science

Everything she liked went on its own Post-it note. Soon there were so many colorful squares on the walls that it reminded her of a kaleidoscope that could be twisted and turned to reveal things that made her happy.

She stalled once, when she got to BEST FRIEND. Was Alfie her best friend? Not yet. Murray or Cassie or Emily? Nope. Truth be told, Ali had never had one. But what was the definition of a best friend, anyway? Someone who got you. Who liked you. Who was always there for you. Who wanted you to be happy. Once she realized that, it was easy.

- Best friends: Digger and Mom

This was a surprise. Ali had spent years being angry at her parents for dragging her from town to town. She'd thought they were unreliable. But that wasn't the whole story. They loved her. They were always nice to her. They worked hard in their own ways to care for her. And now that she knew the truth about Teddy, she understood why Digger had run away. Hadn't she run away from school when things got hard, too?

Ali pulled out her tattered notebook and reread her rules. She knew that rules and scientific laws were important because they were supposed to help people understand the world around them, but Ali's rules didn't do that. Now she could see that her rules were mostly about protecting herself from being hurt. But she'd gotten hurt anyway. It wasn't only her parents who'd made mistakes. She had too. It was time to forgive them and herself and move on. She tossed the notebook in the trash can.

Ali's mother popped in to see her after dinner. "How are you feeling?" she asked, nestling in beside Ali.

"Better."

Her mother studied the Post-it notes on the wall. "What's up?"

Ali took a deep breath. "I wasn't sick today."

"I figured. Want to talk about it?"

For the next hour, Ali told her mother everything that had happened since school started. Her mother kept her comments and questions to herself, though she did throw in the odd hug. When Ali finished, her mother sighed. "I'd say all that would be enough for three years, let alone three weeks. Why didn't you tell Digger or me before it got so out of hand?"

"I didn't want to make you worry," said Ali. She paused, then decided there was no more holding back. "Besides, you guys weren't getting along that well when we moved here. I didn't want to make things worse."

Her mother frowned. "I'm sorry we didn't keep that better hidden, but I don't want you to worry. Your father and I are fine."

"But he doesn't work and he spends half his day as a dog."

"I'm not going to lie to you: it's been hard for years, with your father feeling so guilty about Teddy's death and his ongoing struggle to find work he likes. I realize now that our choices have caused you anxiety. But that's going to change. Your father and I had a long talk. No matter what, we're not leaving Saint John. Digger and I agree that you deserve to live in one place for a few years."

"Really?" For a second, Ali was thrilled, then it hit her: she had no friends. "Maybe I wouldn't mind if we moved again."

Her mother shook her head. "You can't run from your problems, Ali. If you learn nothing else from your father, you should learn that."

"I need to ask you something," said Ali. "And you have to tell me the truth. Do you wish Digger and I weren't Copycats?"

"No! Never! The first time your father showed me he could change into other people and animals, I loved it. It was magical. I wish I could change too."

"Do you worry I won't be able to hold down a real job either?"

"Oh, sweetie. That's not why he can't hold down a job. Digger is one of those people who needs to do something different every day or else he gets antsy. And it's hard to hold down a regular job when you're a dog half the time, which is Digger's way to escape his grief about Teddy. But I actually think that coming back to Saint John and you becoming a Copycat has put him on a new path. You are *not* your dad, Ali; you'll have whatever kind of job you want and do well. I promise."

Ali snuggled into her mother's arms, relief washing over her. No matter what happened at school, at least things were okay at home again.

Her mother kissed her forehead. "Your father's washing the kitchen floor. Want to turn into a penguin and go sliding?"

Ali didn't have to be asked twice.

FORTY

It was party day. Ali got up early, anxious to begin decorating. Digger had bought a huge bag of balloons, which he and Ali blew up together and attached to a multitude of twirling silver and gold streamers that crisscrossed one another across the living room and hallway ceilings. The plastic Academy Award statues lined the fireplace mantelpiece, and Ali's mom hung golden paper stars that said GIGI and 100. Then Digger unrolled the red carpet. It ran from the bottom of the stairs, where Gigi would make her grand entrance, into the living room.

But there was one more surprise. Digger ran down

to the basement and returned with a life-size card-board cutout of Walter Pidgeon and placed it next to the fireplace. It was like Walter was just hanging out, waiting for a piece of birthday cake.

"Where did you find it?" asked Ali as she stood on her tiptoes to look into Walter's twinkly brown eyes.

"I had someone make it for her," said Digger, standing back to survey their decorating hand-iwork. He smiled at Ali's mother. "What do you think?"

"I think the house looks beautiful," she said, hold-ing out her hand so Ali could join them in a family hug. "Gigi is going to love this. I told her she had to stay upstairs today. No peeking!"

"How many people are coming?" asked Ali.

"Thirty-three. And no Other Sloanes, if that's what you're going to ask next. I did get a call from Teddy's sister, Karen. She asked me to wish Gigi a very happy birthday. Poor Karen."

Ali broke away from her parents and flung herself

on the couch. "I'll never understand why they all listen to Andrew Sloane."

Her mother joined her. "Honey, I know it's hard to understand, but they love Uncle Andrew. They're doing what they think is right, just like we're doing what we think is right."

Ali sighed. "I guess, but it would be a lot easier if we all agreed on what was right."

"Amen," said Digger, batting at a balloon that kept nudging the side of his head. "It's time to stop worrying about the Other Sloanes. You know what I'm giving Gigi as a gift?"

"What?" asked Ali.

"I'm forgiving myself for what happened to Teddy. It's time to move on."

Talking about gifts made Ali sad. "I don't have a gift for Gigi. I know we're not supposed to worry about the Other Sloanes anymore, but them coming to the party was supposed to be my gift to her."

"This party is your gift," corrected her mother. "And I'm with your father. As of right now, this family is going to have fun again. No. More. Wallowing." She glanced down at her watch. "My goodness—it's eleven thirty! We have to go pick up Gigi's cake, the hors d'oeuvres, and copies of the newspaper."

The previous day, Gigi's old law firm had called and asked Digger if they could supply a big cake for the party, as well as trays of finger food. They'd also told Digger that they were placing a birthday announcement in the city's local newspaper, the *Telegraph Journal*, to commemorate what the senior partner called "this auspicious occasion." The law firm planned to present a framed copy to her at the party. Ali knew Gigi would be thrilled.

"It should take us at least an hour to get everything," Digger told Ali as he put on his coat. "Can you make Gigi some oatmeal or something? The last time I checked on her, she was napping, conserving her strength for the party."

"No problem. Anything else?"

"That's it. We'll be back soon." After a quick hug, they rushed out the door.

Ali was lining up the tiny plastic Oscars when the doorbell rang. No doubt another flower arrangement; two had already arrived earlier that morning. Ali ran to the door and peeked out through the window. It was Murray and Cassie.

FORTY-ONE

The Christmas when Ali was six years old was the snowiest Christmas of her life. She was living in Miramichi, and the snow arrived early that year; by December 20 there was at least six feet on the ground and school had been canceled. They were renting an apartment in the basement of a house on Frances Street, and every morning Digger had to go outside and shovel out the area in front of the windows so the light could get in.

On December 23, Gigi called to say she didn't think she could make it for Christmas. The roads were terrible and the person who was supposed to drive her had backed out. It was hard not to feel glum. That night, Digger brought home a Christmas tree he'd found on the side of the road. They'd strung popcorn, hung paper snowflakes, and made sugar cookies, but it didn't feel like Christmas without Gigi.

Around six o'clock on Christmas Eve, there was a knock at the door. Digger opened it and there was Gigi, laden down with presents, groceries, and her suitcase. She'd managed to snag a place on the last train leaving Saint John that morning, but hadn't called due to rumors that the trains might stop running thanks to an incoming storm. But the train made it through, and so did Gigi, and Christmas was saved.

The same combination of surprise and happiness surged through her when she opened the door to Murray and Cassie.

"Hello?"

"Hey," said Murray, pointing to where the red carpet started at the bottom of the stairs. "Cool."

Cassie leaned forward so she could see into the living room. "We came to help you decorate for the party, but I guess you've got it under control. Cool piñata," she added, pointing at the piñata Digger had hung that morning. Shaped like a dinosaur, it was the only one he could find in Saint John. But Ali had sworn they needed a piñata, and he wouldn't disappoint her.

"You came to help me decorate?" Ali was afraid she might cry.

"I promised I would," said Cassie, who blushed.

"We owe you an apology," broke in Murray.

"What for?"

Murray smiled. "We talked after you left Thursday. It must be hard to find out you have special powers. We realized we've been treating you like a science experiment, not a friend."

"You still want to be my friend? Even after all the stupid stuff I've done?"

Cassie swallowed hard. "Murray reminded me last night that sometimes I can be a bit much. Ever since Emily—"

Murray jumped in. "What she's trying to say is: we want to be friends with you, Ali."

"I'd like that."

"Phew," said Cassie. "Glad that's out of the way. Want to know how today went?"

Ali had forgotten all about the Toastmasters event.

"She wants to tell you because she was great," said Murray, pretending to look disgusted.

"Really?"

Cassie turned her usual pink. "Even better than Ashok."

"How did Alfie do?"

"He couldn't come. Something came up."

"Murray and I were teammates." Cassie paused. "It's too bad. Alfie is really good."

Murray nodded. "And people can have more than one friend, can't they?"

Cassie's mouth twisted into an embarrassed smile. "Yes, Murray, people can have more than one friend. Would you consider coming back to debate team, Ali?"

Ali visualized the Post-it notes. If she was going to be real friends with Cassie and Murray, it was time they knew the real her. "Nope. I joined because of Alfie. I hate public speaking. Even if I practice and get better at it, I'm never going to love it."

Murray grinned. "You are *not* a good debater."

"Murray!" Cassie sounded scandalized.

Ali laughed. "No, he's right. I'm not. But I love to swim, so I've decided to try out for the swim team."

"You should do what makes you happy, but I'm glad you joined the debate team, even if it was only for a while and because of Alfie," said Cassie with a shy smile. "We might not be friends otherwise. Besides Murray, you're my first real friend since—"

"Emily." Ali didn't know what had happened between Emily and Cassie, but they'd talked about each other enough that she knew they regretted not being friends. "You know, I think Emily really misses you. I bet if you talked to her, you guys would be friends again."

"She's right. What do you have to lose, Cass?" Murray coaxed.

Cassie hesitated. "I'll think about it."

"Hey, would you guys like to come to the party?" asked Ali, changing the subject.

Murray pumped the air with his fist. Cassie beamed. "What time does it start?" she asked.

"Four o'clock. Gigi will be excited to meet you."

Murray eyed the currently empty dining room table. "There'll be food, right?"

"Tons."

He grinned. "See you at four, Sloane."

Cassie grabbed Murray's arm. "Let's go—we need to get permission! See you at four, Ali!"

Ali watched them bike away. As she closed the door, there was a thump upstairs. Gigi must be awake. This was going to be a great day.

FORTY-TWO

Ali decided to make Gigi lunch before going upstairs to check on her. She scrambled some eggs and made toast, whistling the happy birthday song as she did. The final meal wasn't perfect, but it was edible, and a liberal dose of pepper made everything tasty. She filled two plates and carried them upstairs on a tray. She paused when she opened the door. Gigi's bed was empty.

Gigi must have gone to the washroom. She set the tray on Gigi's dresser and went to check. No Gigi. Had she gone downstairs? There was no Gigi in the living room, the dining room, the study, or the kitchen. She ran back upstairs. No Gigi. She even checked the basement, though she didn't believe Gigi could have opened the squeaky basement door without her hearing. It was as if her great-grandmother had vanished.

Ali debated calling Digger, but decided to do one more search first, since she knew they were busy and Gigi had to be in the house somewhere. Ali decided to check her room one more time. She heard a noise outside the window. As she leaned out to take a look, her foot nudged against something. She looked down. A small brown sparrow lay on the floor. She picked it up to see if it was all right, then almost dropped it in fright when she realized that a diamond ring was tangled in one of its wings. Gigi's diamond ring. Then it hit her: she was holding Gigi!

Ali laid the bird on Gigi's bed and knelt down. She didn't know much about birds, but she recognized panic when she saw it. The sparrow was in a state. "It's okay, Gigi. Time to turn back."

The bird twittered. "I don't understand you, Gigi. Can you turn back?"

Another squawk, and there Gigi was, lying on her

left side, eyes closed. A lone feather poked through the back of her nightgown. At first Ali was afraid she was dead, but then Gigi reached out and clutched Ali's arm and whispered something indecipherable.

As Ali leaned over to hear better, there was a piercing cry. Ali ran to the window and stuck her head out. Topsy, the neighbor's cat, had cornered one of Gigi's squirrels. There was blood.

"Alfie!" Gigi yelled.

Ali glanced back at Gigi, confused. "It's not Alfie. Topsy's attacking a squirrel!"

The color drained from Gigi's face. "Save him, Ali! You have to save him!"

Ali knew Gigi was attached to her critters, but her terror was still a surprise. "I'll—"

"No! You don't understand!" cried Gigi. "The squirrel is Alfie!"

Alfie? Ali's head was a jumble. Alfie was a squirrel? He'd been visiting Gigi? For how long? And then a realization: Alfie was a Copycat too. Ali froze, trying to take it all in. The squirrel squealed again, and Ali

sprang into action. Alfie was being attacked. She had
to save him!

Ali pulled off her sneaker and threw it at Topsy's
head. The cat didn't budge. Supper was right there,
and she wouldn't give that up even if it meant a cuff
to the head. Alfie the squirrel tried to crawl away, his
chitter pitiful when Topsy batted him with a vicious
paw. Ali did a quick calculation: taking the stairs
and going out the front door would take too much
time; Topsy was about to pounce again. She took a
deep breath, closed her eyes, and jumped, trusting she
would change into a cat on the way down.

She did.

Ali landed on the grass beside Topsy and hurled
herself forward, claws and teeth bared. Startled, the
other cat hissed and tried to stand her ground, but
Ali's momentum was an advantage; she knocked
Topsy sideways like a bowling pin. Topsy righted
herself and yowled, but Ali was in warrior mode. Fur
straight up, back arched, she charged forward and
swiped a paw across the cat's face, drawing blood.

That was enough for Topsy. She fled home to lick her wounds.

Panting, Ali raced over to Alfie and nudged him with her nose. She expected him to panic and try to escape, but he'd rolled into a whimpering ball, his small heart racing so fast she could see it rise and fall in his tiny squirrel chest. Why didn't he change back? Was he too hurt?

There was no way she could help him as a cat, so she changed back and scooped Alfie up, cradling him in her arms. Her panic rose with his every chirpy sound of misery. Gigi would know what to do.

Chapter Fourteen
THE COMFORT OF FOG

On a foggy night, there is nothing so lonely and yet so comforting as the call of the foghorn, reaching out across the water to guide those at risk of peril to a safe harbor.

—Percival T. Sloane,
A History of Fog in the Bay of Fundy *(1932)*

FORTY-THREE

Ali rushed into the house. "Hang on, Alfie!" she implored, hoping he wouldn't wake up and decide to jump from her arms as she carried him up the steep staircase.

Gigi's face was the color of her snow-white nightgown. "How is he? I tried to change so I could save him, but my powers are too weak—I couldn't even fly."

Ali placed Alfie on Gigi's lap. "He's not changing back and he's bleeding and I can't tell if he has any other injuries. What do we do?"

Gigi bent forward and ran her hands along Alfie's squirrel spine. "Get a warm cloth," she directed.

Ali grabbed the softest cloth she could find, ran it

under the hot water faucet, and pulled a fluffy towel off the rack. Alfie was still unmoving when she returned. She handed Gigi the rag and waited, towel at the ready.

"Come on, Alfie," Gigi whispered. "You need to change back now." She began to clean his bloody paws.

Ali watched, fearful. Alfie wasn't even whimpering now. That was a bad sign, wasn't it? "How long has he been visiting you?" she asked.

Gigi, head down, continued to dab at Alfie's paws and fur. "He showed up two nights ago. He wanted to wish me a happy birthday. He's just started to change and he doesn't have very much control over his powers. He hoped one of us had powers too and could help him. Did he ever ask you for help?"

Ali recalled their last conversation, when he'd told her he was in trouble. She had been mean. This was her fault.

The front door opened. "We're home!" Digger's voice called out.

"Digger!" Ali hollered. "Alfie's up in Gigi's room and he's hurt!"

Digger flew up the stairs and through the door, Ali's mother right behind him. He paused, flustered, and pointed at the squirrel. "That's Alfie?" When Ali nodded, he leaned forward to take a closer look.

The story came out in one long run-on sentence. "He just got his powers and he came to see Gigi a couple of nights ago to wish her happy birthday and again today and then Topsy attacked him and Gigi tried to help but she couldn't, so I changed into a cat and drove Topsy away and now he's not changing back or waking up!"

Digger shook his head. "Oh Gigi—what have you done? You should have told me as soon as he came."

Gigi began to cry.

"I'm sorry, Digger. I just wanted to meet him. Can you help him?"

Digger patted Alfie gently on the head. "I don't know. But we have to call Colleen and Uncle Andrew and let them know." He pulled out his phone and punched in the number. "Colleen? It's Digger. Alfie's here and he's hurt. Apparently he's been changing. . . . Yes, I figured you didn't know. He's turned into a squirrel and was attacked by the neighbor's cat when he was leaving Gigi's room. . . . Yeah, I know. . . . Okay." Digger hung up. "They're on their way."

"I'll go down and wait for them," said Ali's mom. "What can I do to help?"

"Maybe a hot water bottle. I think he's in shock."

Ali's mother hurried away.

"Oh my," Gigi whispered. The look on her face reminded Ali of a small child caught doing something naughty. What would happen when Gigi and Uncle Andrew saw each other?

She didn't have to wait long to find out. Minutes later, Colleen and Andrew Sloane burst into the room and rushed toward Alfie, who lay on the towel, with the hot water bottle next to him. Ali backed against the wall and held her breath.

It wasn't the family reunion she'd dreamed about. Colleen wept as she knelt beside the bed. "My poor baby," she whispered, and kissed his head.

Andrew Sloane stood near the door, his arms crossed. "Did you know about this, Digger?" he demanded.

Digger shook his head. "I just found out, Uncle Andrew."

"It's my fault, Andy," said Gigi. Ali could hear the pain in her voice. "He showed up at my window out of the blue the other night. I was so happy to see him. I should have told you. Then you could have started to train him."

"If anyone should train him, it's Digger," said Colleen without looking up. "He told me he wants Digger's help, but he knew Digger wouldn't train him behind Andy's back."

The room got quiet. Everyone knew this was true.

Colleen held up a hand. "You Sloanes can fight later. Right now, we need to help Alfie. Why isn't he changing back, Digger?"

"Maybe because he's in shock? I think we need to let him rest."

"Should we take him to a vet?" Ali asked.

Everyone turned to look at her.

"I can't imagine a vet would want to help a squirrel, and what if he turned back into himself on the table?" said Colleen.

"Digger told me Uncle Percival was a rat for forty-two days," offered Ali.

"Forty-two days?" whispered Colleen. She closed her eyes and shuddered.

"I didn't know he was a Copycat," Andrew Sloane said, more to himself than to anyone in the room. "Did you know, Colleen?"

Colleen murmured in Alfie's ear and looked up. "I wondered. But I didn't think he'd keep it a secret from me."

"Or from me," said Andrew Sloane.

Digger turned to Ali. "There's a first-aid kit under the sink in the bathroom. Go get it."

It was awkward going past Andrew Sloane, but Ali ran for the kit.

"Can I wrap his paws?" Digger asked Colleen. She nodded and moved out of the way so Digger could get to work.

Colleen turned to Ali. "Do you change, Ali?"

"Yes, but I just got my powers too."

"Did you know he was visiting my mother?" Andrew Sloane asked her. It sounded like an accusation.

Ali shook her head. "He never told me."

Andrew Sloane began to pace. "He knew he wasn't supposed to visit her. He promised."

Colleen sighed. "Oh, Andrew. You made him make a promise he couldn't keep. We should have told him about Copycats a long time ago."

Digger finished wrapping Alfie's paws and stood up. "I'd like to move Alfie onto a bed in another room. Maybe with a little rest, he'll wake up and turn back into himself." He smiled at Gigi. "Besides, I think Gigi could use some rest too." He lifted Alfie and carried him out of the room.

Everyone followed, but at the door to Ali's parents' bedroom, Digger said, "Colleen wants you to wait downstairs, Uncle Andrew. She doesn't think Alfie will change back in front of you."

"Come sit downstairs in the living room with me,"

said Ali's mother, placing a gentle hand on Andrew Sloane's arm.

"But I'm his grandfather!" Andrew Sloane sounded like he on the verge of making a scene.

Something dark and angry bubbled up inside Ali, as if the stress of the last few weeks was a venomous ball that needed to be expelled.

"He needs to rest!" she shouted. "He needs to not have to sneak around anymore. He needs his family to get along."

Andrew Sloane opened his mouth, but Ali kept going, her words spilling out in one unstoppable wave. "You can be mad at everybody, but this wouldn't have happened if he could have just walked over and visited Gigi like a regular grandkid. If he could have been trained to use his powers. I never met Teddy, but everybody says he was wonderful and full of life. You want to suck every bit of happiness out of your family because you're so unhappy. I bet Teddy wouldn't like that at all. I bet he'd want Alfie to know Digger. Teddy and Digger were best friends. And Teddy loved Gigi.

It's cruel what you've done to our family. This is your fault!"

"Enough, Ali-Cat," said Digger. "Go to your room. I'll let you know when there's news."

Ali was glad to go if it meant not being in the same room as Andrew Sloane. She leaned over the banister and watched him follow her mother downstairs. But yelling at Andrew Sloane hadn't made things better. Her anger was replaced by shame and regret. Alfie wouldn't want her to be mean to his grandfather. Maybe she wasn't so different from Andrew Sloane after all.

FORTY-FOUR

Ali was five years old before she understood that not everyone's father could change into other things. She and Digger had gone to the park on a hot July day to cool off in the wading pool. When they'd arrived, no one was around, so Digger had changed into a short-haired terrier—it was too hot to be his usual collie/black Lab self—and romped with Ali in the shallow water. They splashed and chased each other for twenty minutes, until a mother and her little boy appeared and caught Digger unaware.

Digger couldn't change back into himself in front of them, so he scampered off behind a stand of pines. The mother was horrified to find Ali unattended;

when Digger emerged from the trees seconds later, she berated him for ten minutes, threatening to call the police and child protection, telling him what a horrible father he was. Digger didn't defend himself, just let her work through her righteous indignation.

"But Digger was here," protested Ali on his behalf. She didn't understand what all the fuss was about.

The mother patted Ali on the head. "A little girl can't be cared for by a dog," she said, which confused Ali, because she was cared for by a dog all the time.

Ali sat on the edge of the wading pool and drew figure eights in the cool water. "What does your mama turn into?" she'd asked the little boy, who'd taken a seat next to her. He was chubby cheeked and sprinkled all over with freckles.

"Nuthin'," the boy said, "'cept sometimes she changes from nice to mean."

"Not good," Ali had said, upset on his behalf.

The boy shrugged. "Nope."

Later, when Digger carried her home on his shoulders, Ali asked why the little boy's mother couldn't change into something fun, like a dog or a bird or a horse.

"Some people have special abilities and some people don't."

"She was mean."

Digger shook his head. "She was a good mother. She was worried about you. If everybody worried about other people's children like she worried about you, this would be a very different world."

Ali lay on her bed and stared up at the ceiling. She couldn't get the image of Topsy attacking Alfie out of her head. She reached for *The Golden Compass* to try to distract herself. Except someone had put the old book written by Gigi's uncle Percy in its place. There was a Post-it note stuck to the cover. *You haven't read this yet, but you must try again. Love, Gigi.* Ali wasn't in the mood to read about fog, but if it meant that much to Gigi, she'd try.

This time when she opened the book, she realized it wasn't what it had seemed before. The original chapter titles and opening paragraphs, along with Teddy and Digger's funny comments, dissolved and were replaced with information about Copycats. In fact, Uncle Percy's old book was actually a handbook for Copycats, and it included some of the stories Gigi and Digger had shared with her, along with other, stranger topics. For example, Chapter One, "How Fog Is Formed," became Chapter One, "How to Make Sure Your Family Recognizes You When You Show Up as a Ferocious Beast."

A History of Fog in the Bay of Fundy	*Copycats: A Primer*
CHAPTER ONE: How Fog Is Formed	CHAPTER ONE: How to Make Sure Your Family Recognizes You When You Show Up as a Ferocious Beast
CHAPTER TWO: The Bay of Fundy	CHAPTER TWO: How to Recognize Another Copycat
CHAPTER THREE: Deadly Whirlpools and Fog: A Disaster in the Making	CHAPTER THREE: Seven Ways to Be Your Best Copycat Self
CHAPTER FOUR: Fog and Marine Disasters	CHAPTER FOUR: What to Do If Your Child Doesn't Change

How had she missed this the first time she'd looked at the book? Then it hit her: she hadn't been a Copycat then. Thrilled, she skipped through the pages. It was like being inducted into a secret club, and it was the perfect diversion from what was happening in the rest of the house.

Twenty minutes later, when she was reading about how important it was not to panic when switching back and forth between lungs and gills, she remembered that Teddy had written one word on the original page: practice. It hadn't made sense when she thought the chapter was about fog technology. Had he and Digger practiced being fish? She shivered. It made her sad to think of eleven-year-old Teddy telling himself to practice breathing underwater and then drowning years later.

Digger stuck his head in the door. "Good news. Alfie is back, and he's fine. I was right; he was so shocked when Topsy attacked him that he couldn't calm down enough to change back. He's still pretty shook up."

Ali started to rise. "Can I see him?"

"Sorry, Ali-Cat. He just left with his mom and Uncle Andrew. I'm sure they have a lot to talk about, and Alfie needs to rest."

Ali slumped back against her pillow. "I'm glad he's okay."

Digger leaned down and kissed her forehead. "You were very brave, saving him like that. I'm proud of you."

"I don't feel brave. I'm pretty sure he tried to tell me the other day."

"Well, he tried to talk to me and I ran away. We've both made mistakes."

"I'm sorry I was rude to Andrew Sloane."

Digger chuckled. "You shouldn't have said those things, but maybe you gave him something to think about. We've all made choices. And some of them were mistakes. But I hope we can learn from them."

He pointed to the book in Ali's hands. "I see you're reading Uncle Percy's magnum opus."

"I can't believe all the stuff in here!"

"Pretty amazing, huh? Teddy used to pore over

that book when we were kids. I'm sure you saw that we wrote in it here and there. Teddy wanted to write a sequel. Chapter One was going to be 'How to Recognize Copycats on the Internet.'"

Ali smiled, but it quickly dissolved into a frown. "I suppose we have to cancel Gigi's party."

"Absolutely not! In fact, your mother's helping her change right now. A party is exactly what we need after what just happened, so get dressed; we're putting you in charge of greeting the guests. And wait until you see Gigi's cake. It's covered in flowers and butterflies and hummingbirds!"

As she changed into her party dress, Ali considered Digger's comment about choices. Why was making the right choice so hard? Digger marrying her mother was the right choice. Digger and Teddy going over the Reversing Falls was the wrong choice. But if Teddy had survived, would that have made their adventure the right choice? Probably not. Gigi had decided to help Alfie out of love, and you could argue all day about whether that was the right or wrong thing to do. It made her head ache, trying to make sense of it all.

In the end, she supposed the best thing a person could do when making a choice was to base it on kindness and be true to herself. She grabbed a Post-it note, scribbled that down, and stuck it to the wall next to her bed. This might be the most important note of all.

FORTY-FIVE

The first guests arrived promptly at four o'clock: Mr. and Mrs. Rudolph, Topsy's owners.

"Happy birthday!" they called to Gigi, who sat like a queen on her throne in the wingback chair next to Walter Pidgeon. She wore a tiara and her satin gloves and hadn't taken her eyes off Walter since she'd come downstairs.

"How's that mangy Topsy?" demanded Gigi.

"It's funny you should ask," said a perplexed Mrs. Rudolph. "I think he got into some kind of catfight. He has quite a scratch on his face."

"Serves him right," muttered Gigi.

The law firm arrived next: six lawyers in smart

suits. They made a big deal of presenting Gigi with her framed birthday announcement, and she pretended to swoon when the senior partner kissed her on the cheek.

"Don't be jealous, Walter!" she warned her movie-star boyfriend.

The doorbell rang again. Ali was surprised to see Emily and her father.

Mr. Arai stuck out his hand. "You must be Ali. Emily's told me all about you! Now where's the birthday girl? I haven't seen Gertrude in years." Ali pointed him toward the living room and he rushed away, leaving her and Emily in awkward silence.

"Can I take your coat?" Ali finally asked.

Emily took off her coat and gave it to Ali. "You look pretty."

Ali glanced down at the blue velvet dress her mother had found at the Salvation Army thrift store. "Really? Thanks."

Emily followed her to the den, where the coats were heaped on a couch. "Can we talk?"

Ali placed Emily's coat on the top of the pile and waited.

"I'm sorry," Emily said. "I'd like to be friends again."

"Really?"

"I was stupid. And bossy. I've been messed up since my parents told me they're getting a divorce. But I like hanging out with you. It reminded me of when—"

"You hung out with Cassie."

"How did you know?"

"You talk about her a lot."

Emily sagged. "I know. I still miss her. I kind of hoped she and I would be friends again when you and I became friends. Not that that's the only reason I wanted to hang out with you," she hurried to add.

"Why aren't you friends anymore?"

"It's my fault. My mom put me in a bunch of activities in third grade. I met a lot of new girls and wanted to hang out with them. They were so popular."

"But you're popular!"

"I know you think that, but that's not how it feels

to me. Anyway, Cassie's feelings were hurt, and they didn't want to hang around with her, so I did the wrong thing."

Ali knew what that was like.

"The day you went to sit with Cassie at lunch, I was so jealous. Not just because you were friends with her, but because you did the right thing. You didn't abandon your friend."

They were interrupted by the sound of a throat clearing. Ali and Emily spun around. Murray and Cassie were in the doorway, looking embarrassed.

"I'm sorry," Cassie whispered. "We didn't mean to eavesdrop."

Emily started to back away, but Ali grabbed her arm. "No. You guys both want to be friends again, so be friends again!"

"Way to take control, Sloane," said Murray, pushing Cassie forward.

Neither Cassie nor Emily spoke for a minute, and then, as if they'd choreographed the moment, they stepped forward at the same time and hugged.

"Folks, the war is officially over," said Murray in a news-anchor voice.

Everyone laughed. Cassie and Emily stepped apart, grinning.

But there was one more thing that had to be done. Ali turned to Emily. "I'm glad we're friends again, but there's something you need to know. I can change into other things, like people and animals."

Emily smiled. "Thank you for telling me, but I already know."

Ali's jaw dropped. "How?"

Emily's cheeks flushed scarlet. "I followed you guys to Tin Can Beach last weekend. I saw you turn into a seal. And I knew you were the cat in the bathroom that day. I'm sorry I talked about you behind your back. I shouldn't have."

Ali was pretty sure that Gigi's birthday was going down in history as the day every single one of her beliefs turned out to be wrong. "You don't mind?"

"Please. Half the kids at Princess Elizabeth School are trying to be someone else. You're just a little extra, that's all." And then the room exploded into laughter, because everyone knew that being a Copycat was *extra* extra.

They were interrupted by Ali's mother bursting into the room carrying a stack of coats. "There you are! I need you at the front door, Ali. The party's hopping." She dropped the coats on the couch and rushed out.

"I can help," Emily said.

"Us too," said Cassie.

"Actually, I was going to check out the food," joked Murray.

They arrived at the front door just as the doorbell rang. When Ali opened the door, she stepped back, bumping into Cassie. The porch was filled with the Other Sloanes.

FORTY-SIX

It wasn't just Alfie and Colleen and Andrew Sloane, but Aunt Karen and her family, too. They all wore the same half-nervous, half-excited expression, especially Andrew Sloane, who held a massive bouquet of flowers. Ali swallowed hard, afraid she might burst into tears. "You came."

Colleen, who held a stack of pizzas, stepped forward. "Can we join the party?"

Ali's parents stepped into the hallway and froze, unable to hide their dazed expressions. Her mother found her voice first. "Come in!"

Digger rushed forward, said a shy hello, and began to collect coats, which he passed to Ali's friends.

The arrival of the Other Sloanes filled an already-crammed living room and dining room to bursting, but no one seemed to care. Everybody cried when Karen introduced her daughters to Gigi, and they stared with disbelief when Andrew Sloane took a seat next to his mother and took her hand.

"We did it," Alfie mouthed to Ali, then hurried away to find Digger. Ali smiled; they would have so much to talk about later. Then Ali's mom and Digger presented both birthday cakes, and everyone sang happy birthday to Gigi, who managed to blow out every single candle without any help at all.

The party was like a happy dream. Digger and Alfie and Karen kept hugging. Andrew Sloane smiled at everyone, even at Ali when she took his empty plate. Across the room, her friends, along with her cousins Jennie and Jordan, passed a broomstick back and forth in an attempt to break the piñata. Everything was perfect, except one person was missing: Teddy. Overwhelmed with emotion, Ali escaped to the kitchen. She was rinsing dishes in the sink when she sensed someone behind her. She turned to find Andrew Sloane.

"You were right," he said.

Ali stared down at the plate in her hand, unsure of what to say.

Andrew Sloane kept going. "I'm sorry to say that I'm a weak man. I always wanted to be like everybody else. Since they didn't have powers, I didn't want mine, either."

"I used to want to be like everybody too," Ali offered. She wouldn't be mean this time.

"You're too kind, Ali, but it gets worse. I punished Teddy and Karen when they used their powers, and I was often petty with my mother and brother because I was sure they were doing things humans beings weren't meant to do. I thought I knew best. Now I see how wrong I was. We've been given these powers for a reason. They don't make us good or bad, but they do make us different. You saved Alfie's life, and mine too."

This was a shock. "I did?"

"Yes. You made me remember that there are only two important things in life: loving your family and others, and loving yourself. Want to know a secret?" He sounded giddy.

"What?"

"I'm going to sign this house over to your parents, if they'll let me live here for a while and help take care of Gigi. Would you mind having an old codger like me around?"

Ali flung herself into his arms. They hugged for a full minute before Ali broke away. "Thank you, Uncle Andrew."

"Thank *you*. Now, I think I'd better go check on Gigi and Walter Pidgeon."

Ali watched him leave. You never really knew what was going to happen in life. She used to think that was a bad thing, but now it was kind of exciting.

Ten minutes later, Alfie found her on the back deck, bundled up in Digger's plaid coat and staring up at the sky. She smiled when he sat down beside her.

"Look—the fog is gone! I forgot how much I missed the stars."

"You know, there used to be a squirrel constellation. Sciurus Volans, the Flying Squirrel, named by William Croswell in 1810," said Alfie. "Sadly, it got sucked into Camelopardalids, the giraffe constellation, which totally bites."

They gazed upward, neither speaking. For the first time in weeks, the foghorn was silent.

Alfie exhaled. "Saying thanks doesn't seem like enough, but it's the best I can do."

"You would have saved me if the situation was reversed," Ali pointed out.

"Yup. And Gigi got her birthday party and Granddad has forgiven everyone, including himself. He told me he's always regretted not training my dad." He took a breath, and there was a catch in his throat. "You know, when I found out that they never found his body after the accident, I used to pretend he was just lost somewhere, even though I knew it wasn't true."

A strange jolt reverberated through Ali. "They never found his body?"

"Nope. Granddad says that's not unusual when someone drowns in the ocean."

Ali closed her eyes. Uncle Percival's chapter about not drowning when you were a fish or a whale popped into her head. Teddy had written "Practice" at the beginning of that chapter. But if Teddy had practiced, what had happened?

She hopped up. "I need to go the bathroom."

Instead, she ran to her room and began to thumb through the book. Why was Alfie's comment nagging at her so much? Since she hadn't had time to read it all yet, Ali began to flip through the book to see what she'd missed. She stopped at Chapter Two, "How to Recognize Another Copycat." Why hadn't she bothered to read this chapter earlier? "Copycats have one thing in common," wrote Uncle Percival, "every one of them has pale gray eyes."

Ali took a deep breath. She scanned the table of contents and went to Chapter Fourteen, "What to

Do If You Can't Change Back." It was a recounting of Uncle Percival's forty-two days as a rat. Several lines jumped out at her:

I blame my inability to change back on my shock at nearly being a tomcat's dinner. Nothing I did seemed to return me to my natural form. By day seven, I realized I must try and learn the rat language if I was to do more than simply survive. Given the simplicity of a rat's linguistic abilities, I managed to achieve fluency by day seventeen. I secured a rat guide named Stinky, who agreed to guide me home, for the narrow streets were like boulevards to me. From days twenty to thirty-six, I hung about my house, doing my best not to be trapped or attacked, for my dear wife is no fan of vermin. Still, I could not change back. It was not until day forty-one, when I met a fellow Copycat named Arthur Smart, that I was saved. Arthur was patrolling the neighborhood in the form of a raccoon and recognized that I was a Copycat straightaway. Given the fact that he could not speak rat, and I was not proficient in any other language but human and yet could not speak it due to my unfortunate circumstances, we could not communicate. Finally, out of desperation, he led me to an alley and transformed back into his human form. For whatever reason, seeing him change made me suddenly understand what I must do, and within one hour I was reunited with my family and in a hot bathtub scrubbing off a month's worth of grime.

Trembling, Ali went to find Cassie, Emily, and Murray.

"Are you okay?" Cassie asked when they were all in Ali's bedroom with the door closed.

"I know this is going to sound bizarre, but Emily told me that there's only one seal left at Tin Can Beach. The sick one. I think it's Alfie's dad."

Nobody spoke, just exchanged wary expressions. "No—listen! I found out this afternoon that Alfie is a Copycat too. He got hurt and had trouble changing back into himself because he was so scared. Everyone believed Alfie's dad drowned going over the Reversing Falls, but what if he changed into a seal and then couldn't change back?" She held up Uncle Percival's book. "This is a book about Copycats, and there's a whole chapter about what to do if you can't change back, which means it must happen a lot. My dad says Alfie's dad's powers weren't very strong."

Cassie took the book and began to thumb through it. "Ali, this book is about fog," she said, looking at Ali like she'd lost it.

Ali grabbed the book back. "I know that's what it looks like to you. It's what it looked like to me before I became a Copycat too. But once I changed, I realized that it was really a handbook for Copycats." She ignored the doubt on Cassie's face and kept going. "A couple of minutes ago, Alfie told me that they never found his dad's body. What if the reason the last seal hasn't left isn't because it's sick, but because it's Teddy? Remember last week, when I changed into a seal—the sick seal was the only one that reacted? But that doesn't make any sense, because it's supposed to be blind."

Emily's voice was gentle when she spoke. "Ali, I know you want this to be true, but it doesn't make any sense."

"You know that the simplest explanation is always the most likely explanation," added Cassie.

"And he's been gone for over a decade," Murray reminded her. "How could he possibly survive?"

Frantic, Ali tried to think of a rebuttal to their arguments. She needed to persuade them; if it was Teddy on that beach, she'd need their help. She took a deep breath and began, refuting their points one by one.

"Emily, I know you think this doesn't make any sense, but does it make any sense that there are a whole bunch of people on this planet who can copy other creatures?"

"Nooo," said Emily,

She turned to Cassie. "I agree, the simplest explanation is always the most likely explanation. But you're forgetting that Alfie's father is a Copycat, not a regular person. He goes over the Reversing Fall and drowns? Yes, he wasn't as talented a Copycat as my dad, but he'd read all about not drowning in this book. For a Copycat, I think the simplest explanation is that he changed into a seal when the boat turned over, got carried away by the current, and then couldn't change. Maybe it's taken him all this time to find his way back."

"Maybe . . . ," conceded Cassie.

Murray was her last rebuttal. "How did he survive over a decade? He lived like a seal. Eventually he must have joined a pod of seals. In this book, Uncle Percival talks about learning to speak rat." When the others raised their eyebrows, she shook her head. "Listen. I know it sounds bizarre, but stick with me. Uncle Percival was stuck as a rat for forty-two days. He had to learn to speak rat so he could get the other rats to lead him home. What if it took Teddy years to figure out how to speak seal? And when he finally did, he told them his story, and they brought him back to Saint John. But for whatever reason, he still can't change, maybe because he's sick. I thought the sick seal's eyes were gray because it was blind. But apparently all Copycats have pale gray eyes. I didn't know that until today. I need to go to Tin Can Beach to see if it's him, and I can't tell Alfie or my family in case I'm wrong. I can't go without you guys. I may need help."

There was a long silence. Ali was sure her counter-arguments hadn't been enough to convince them. But then Murray smiled. "Cassie and I have our bikes. We'll double you and Emily. It sounds wacky, but then your whole family is kind of wacky, Sloane. Let's do it!"

Emily grabbed a throw blanket off Ali's bed and wrapped it around her shoulders. "I'm bringing this, in case."

Ali, on the verge of tears, pulled them into a group hug. She scribbled a note to Digger—*Back soon*—and then the four of them snuck down the stairs and slipped out the front door.

The bike ride to Tin Can Beach was the longest half hour of Ali's life. It was slow going along the dark trail, and when they had to bike on the street again, they discovered that the few cars on the road were still crawling, like they weren't used to driving without fog. Despite the starry sky, the night was dark, with only streetlights and their bicycle lights to guide them.

"Well, this is super creepy," a cheerful Murray called over his shoulder when they reached Tin Can Beach. "It's like every scary movie ever."

"Assuming your theory about this seal is right, how exactly are you going to change him back?" asked Cassie.

Ali thought of Uncle Percival and the raccoon. Instead of saying anything, she morphed into a copy of Alfie and then turned back to herself.

"I don't get it," said Cassie.

Emily did. "Ali's going to change into people Alfie's dad knows to see if she can get him to remember."

"That's brilliant!" Murray cried.

"It's only brilliant if it works," said Ali.

The beach was eerily quiet, with only the odd slosh as a wave crested against the rocky shore. Far away, Ali could see the flickering lights of the freighters anchored offshore. Murray, Cassie, and Emily pulled out their cell phones and cast light into the endless darkness. Ali stumbled behind them, straining to try and find the seal. Was Teddy still here? He had to be.

"I think it's gone," Emily moaned.

"Keep looking," begged Ali. It wouldn't be fair if she'd finally figured out that the seal was Teddy, only to discover it had gone back to the bay.

They trudged on. Minutes passed, and Ali became increasingly despondent. She'd failed.

And then: "Look up toward the grass!" shouted Cassie.

The other two lights turned in the direction where Cassie pointed.

They'd found the seal.

FORTY-SEVEN

When Ali was little, the game she hated most in the world was hide-and-seek. It didn't matter if she was the hider or the seeker; they were equally terror inducing. If you were the hider, you were forced to huddle in tight, dark spaces, holding your breath until someone pounced on you. If you were the seeker, you had to look in nooks and crannies that a person had no business looking in. Either way, you were going to be scared. Now, as they picked their way across the slippery rocks toward the sick seal who might or might not be Teddy, she had the uncomfortable sensation that she was about to get a nasty scare.

"It looks worse than it did a couple of days ago,"

said Emily when they reached the seal.

Emily was right. It lay on its side, panting, each breath a strangled rattle. Its patchy coat was now mostly bald and covered in nasty red welts. Emily pulled the blanket from around her shoulders and draped it over the seal.

"Do we really think this is Alfie's dad?" Murray asked, leaning over to look at the seal.

"I think we're too late," Ali said in despair.

Cassie squatted down and reached out to pet the seal's head.

"The marine biologist told us not to touch them," warned Emily.

Cassie looked down at the sick seal. "I'll take my chances," she said, and began to stroke its head. The seal didn't react. "You don't know that it's too late, Ali. You have to try."

Murray moved aside, and Ali crouched down and looked into the seal's eyes. "Shine the light on just me and the seal, okay, Murray?"

Murray adjusted the phone so that only Ali and the

seal were in the small circle of light.

"You have to come back, Teddy," she implored. The seal blinked. It was a quick blink, but Ali was sure she saw pale gray eyes, and not just any gray eyes. They were Ali's eyes, Alfie's eyes, Digger's eyes, Gigi's eyes. Ali's heart leapt. "Come back," she whispered again. The seal grunted.

"You should change now, Ali," suggested Emily.

Ali became her father. "It's me, Teddy!" cried Digger's voice. "Come back!"

Nothing.

She switched to Gigi. "Come home, Teddy," she said.

"Okay, this is like the freakiest thing ever," said Cassie.

Ali ignored her. The seal wasn't reacting; it was time to try someone else. She became Alfie's mother. "Teddy," she called.

Ali thought she saw a flicker of recognition, but the seal's eyes glazed over again. She was running out of time.

"Try Alfie," suggested Cassie.

"He doesn't know Alfie," Ali argued. "He died—I mean, he left—before Alfie was born."

The Sloane family Christmas photograph popped into her head, and she became Andrew Sloane, his wife, and Teddy's sister, Karen. Nothing. Frantic, she cycled through everyone Teddy loved twice more, until her body began to protest and she began to shake.

"You've got to stop, Ali," said Emily, laying a gentle hand on her back. "You're going to hurt yourself. You've tried everything. Either it isn't him or he can't change back. Maybe he's trapped for good."

Ali collapsed against the seal and began to cry. "I was sure if he saw all the people he loved, he'd remember how to come back."

"Maybe it's not him," said Cassie.

Murray shook his head. "You saw its eyes, Cass. Someone *is* in there. I think he's too sick to change back."

"Should we go get your dad? Or Alfie?" Cassie asked.

Ali watched the seal with anguish. "I don't know. What if he doesn't make it? It'll break everyone's heart if Teddy made it home and then . . ." She couldn't finish the sentence.

The seal moaned.

"Why doesn't he remember who he is?" said Emily. "This is horrible."

Emily's question triggered a memory in Ali of all the first days of school when Digger had changed into Ali to get her to pay attention to him. She laughed out loud. She'd forgotten to change into the one person who could help Teddy remember. She morphed again and leaned over so the seal was looking at her face.

"Um, who are you?" Cassie asked.

"I'm Teddy," said Ali. "Remember who you are, Teddy." She said it like an order. "Look at yourself."

The seal groaned.

"Something's happening!" Murray shouted.

"Come back, Teddy," Ali begged. "Remember."

The fur on the seal's head began to lighten and disappear. Ali as Teddy turned to Emily. "I'm glad you covered him with a blanket. I don't know what his clothes are going to be like when he changes. He's been a seal for a long time."

"Whoa," said Murray. "This all just got real."

Ali leaned down again. "Come back, Teddy. You can do it," she pleaded.

And then he was there, curled up on the stony beach under the blanket, his clothes in tatters. Ali shook him. "He's not breathing!"

"Thump him on the back!" Cassie yelled.

Ali's Teddy hands thumped hard six times on the real Teddy's back, but nothing happened.

"Sit him up and try again!" Murray cried.

Ali pulled Teddy forward and thumped again.

"He needs the Heimlich maneuver!" cried Emily. She pushed Murray aside, wrapped her around Teddy's chest, and squeezed hard.

All of a sudden, Teddy gasped. Then everything went quiet as they watched him cough and hack and shiver. Another minute more, and his breathing was regular. He glanced up at Ali, stunned.

"Who are you?" he gasped.

"Whoops," Ali said, and changed back into herself. When Teddy continued to look bewildered, she said, "I'm Ali, Digger's daughter."

Teddy shook his head. "You can't be Ali. Ginger hasn't had her baby yet."

"Uh-oh," said Murray.

"You've been gone a long time, Teddy," said Ali. "Twelve years."

Teddy swayed a little, like he might faint. Murray wrapped the blanket around him and put an arm around him so he'd stay sitting up. "It's okay, Mr. Sloane; you're home now."

"He's going to get hypothermia if we don't get him something to wear," said Emily. "My house is just up the hill. I'll run home and get him some of my dad's clothes."

"I'll go with you," Cassie said. They hopped on the bikes and raced off.

Murray tried to help Teddy to his feet, but years of being a seal had left him wobbly. Ali changed into

Digger, and the two of them managed to get him onto the grass that bordered the beach so he was away from the frigid water. Murray took off his jacket and put it on the ground for Teddy to sit on.

Ali held out her hand. "Can I borrow your phone? I need to call my dad."

Should she tell him what was going on? No—it would be easier if he saw for himself. She dialed the number, never taking her eyes off Teddy. "Digger, I'm down at Tin Can Beach. Can you come get me? I'll explain everything when you get here." She passed the phone back to Murray. "He's super annoyed."

"He'll get over it," said Murray. He sounded choked up when he spoke next. "Alfie is going to be so happy."

Ali began to cry. "Everyone is going to be so happy."

Beside them, Teddy huddled under the blanket. Ali wasn't sure if he was too cold to talk or was still confused, but she decided that the best thing was to leave things to Digger now. Five minutes later, Cassie and Emily arrived with clothing: shirts, pants, socks, her father's heaviest parka and winter boots. They turned their backs as Murray helped Teddy dress. He was just zipping Teddy's coat closed when Digger's headlights raced down the hill and the car pulled up at the side of the road.

Digger jumped out and raced over to Ali. "You are in such big trouble. We're having a party! Everybody's been frantic, and—" He stopped abruptly.

"Hey, Digger," said Teddy.

Digger put his hand over his mouth and staggered backward. After a few deep breaths, he was able to speak again. "Teddy? Is it really you? Where have you been? I thought you were dead. . . ."

Teddy shrugged. "I kind of got lost for a while."

Digger's laugh was half bark, half laugh, and pure delight. Tears streaming down his face, he hurried to Teddy and pulled him into a hug. "I've missed you so much. I can't believe you're back."

"Me neither," answered Teddy.

The car door opened. Alfie stumbled forward. When he reached Teddy, he stared at his father. Neither of them seemed to know what to say or do.

Luckily, Murray was never at a loss for words. "Alfie, meet your dad. Dad, meet Alfie. Boy, are you two going to need a lot of therapy."

And then everybody laughed, and Alfie and his father hugged for a long time, like they were trying to get twelve years' worth of hugs into that first one.

"We need to get Teddy warm," said Digger.

Alfie and Digger helped Teddy to the car. Once Teddy and Alfie were settled in the back seat, they began to whisper. Ali was dying to know what they were saying, but she knew the moment belonged to them and no one else.

"I'm sorry; I don't have enough room to take all of you," Digger said to Cassie, Murray, and Emily.

"No big deal," said Cassie. "We'll bike Emily back to your house so she can meet her dad." She smiled. "I guess we're part of the Copycat world now too."

Digger shook their hands. "You absolutely are. Thank you for everything."

Murray grinned. "No problem. Call us anytime you need someone saved."

* * *

"How did you know the seal was Teddy?" Digger asked Ali on the car ride home. He kept peeking in the rearview mirror to make sure Teddy was still there. Ali supposed it would be a long time before the Sloanes let Teddy out of their sight.

Ali laughed. "I finally looked at Uncle Percival's book. I saw where Teddy had written 'Practice' in the chapter about not drowning, so when Alfie told me tonight that they'd never found Teddy's body, I started to put two and two together."

"But how?" marveled Teddy.

"You don't know this, but Alfie got attacked by a cat today when he was a squirrel, and he couldn't change back for a long time. Uncle Percival has a whole chapter about what to do when you can't change back. It made me think of Alfie, but also of you. I wondered if maybe you went into shock in the water and got confused and then weren't able to change."

"That's exactly what happened," said a dazed

Teddy. "It's amazing that you thought of that."

Ali twisted around to look at Teddy. "Honestly? The thing that finally convinced me was learning that all Copycats have pale gray eyes. When we saw you for the first time down at Tin Can Beach, the scientists told us your eyes were a different color because you were blind. But really, it was because you were you. Plus, during another visit, you reacted when I transformed. Do you remember?"

"I was pretty sick by then. I thought it was a dream," said Teddy.

Ali turned to Digger. "If you'd told me about the Copycat eye thing, I might have solved this a long time ago."

"I thought I had told you," said Digger.

Teddy leaned forward and patted her shoulder. "I can never thank you for what you did."

"Ali's been a superhero today," Alfie added. "First she saved me, now you."

Ali shook her head, but then, just because she could, she turned into the Incredible Hulk.

Digger groaned. "Gigi told you." He peered into the rearview mirror again. "You showing up is going to be a big shock, Teddy."

"A happy shock," corrected Ali.

And it was.

Chapter Fifteen
ANIMAL VICTIMS OF FOG

There are many records of seals and whales washing ashore during a thick fog. On the morning of May 8, 1847, six dolphins were found stranded on the beach at Haggerty's Cove. The locals managed to pull three back into the water, but the animals refused to leave until it was clear to them that the other three had truly expired.

"It was dreadful sad," Walter Powning told a local newspaperman. "You could tell they was heartbroken. You should have heard the sounds they made. Chillin', it was."

—Percival T. Sloane,
A History of Fog in the Bay of Fundy *(1932)*

Alligator Balm

Mix 1/4 cup olive oil with two cups mashed blackberries, 1 teaspoon thyme, 1/4 cup chopped sorrel. Whisk until reasonably smooth, adding additional oil as required. Apply twice daily until symptoms subside. Note: It is recommended that the patient NOT turn into an alligator again until skin has returned to normal. If symptoms worsen, call your local Copycat apothecary (see directory at the back of this book).

It doesn't work, Digger! (scratch, scratch . . .)

I know! ☹ (scratch, scratch . . .)

The Following Summer

No one knew who had donated the picnic tables to Tin Can Beach or paid to have it cleaned up, but everyone who lived in Saint John agreed it was a good thing. It was an early afternoon in July, and the cool breeze riding the incoming tide was a welcome relief to the picnickers—two girls and a boy—who'd claimed the table closest to the water. They unpacked a lunch of fettucine alfredo and pink cupcakes. For some inexplicable reason, they thought it was a good idea to bring a cat to a public beach. The cat was curled up on the bench next to the tall freckled girl, but woke up when they called to it, insisting on a bite of cupcake. Now and then the group was joined by a fuzzy gray squirrel, which not only didn't mind the cat, but seemed to engage it in a strange, chittering conversation. Uproarious laughter filled the air. Later, you'd swear your mind was playing tricks on you, for five kids left the beach, not three, and the animals had disappeared.